THE
POTUSGEISTS

WILL WORSLEY

HEDGELAND PRESS

THE POTUSGEISTS

Copyright © 2025 by Will Worsley

This book is a work of fiction. All of the characters, organizations, and events portrayed in this novel are either products of the author's imagination or are used fictitiously. Any similarity to real persons living or dead is coincidental and is not intended by the author.

Illustration: Ed Steckley
Cover Design: Gareth Southwell
Interior Design: Alt 19 Creative
Author photo credit: Aaron Clamage Photography

ISBN 978-1-7356652-4-5 (tradepaper)
ISBN 978-1-7356652-5-2 (e-book)

Published by:
Hedgeland Press
4314 35th Street South
Arlington, Virginia 22206
www.willworsley.com

*For my great niece Victoria Pope,
whose gift of stem cells saved my life
and made this book possible.*

CHAPTER 1

The Inauguration

NO ONE AMONG the living noticed the television remote rising from the credenza and floating away in midair. The only Secret Service agent on duty in the West Wing's basement had fallen sound asleep, his body sprawled across a red leather chair.

Two semi-transparent ghosts, outlined by a shimmering light, took shape. One was tall and gangly with unruly gray hair, the other short, portly, and balding, with a round face. Both ghosts wore frock coats and knee breeches.

Now is our chance, thought the tall one, clutching the remote. Eyeing the snoring agent, he motioned toward the other side of the room, where colorful images flashed across a big screen. They crept toward it.

The problem was that the screen was silent, despite never having been silent before. One of the living had inopportunely made its sound go away.

The tall ghost folded his brow. Puzzling over the remote, he whispered to his comrade, "This object controls the sound as well as the screen, if I remember rightly." He flipped it over.

Observing that there were no buttons on the back, he held it up to the light and shook it, as if that might yield some clue about how it worked.

The short ghost cupped his palsied hand to his ear and said with a toothless lisp, "I can't hear them, Jefferson. Make the talking box talk louder, if you please."

Jefferson chuckled. "It's a television, not a talking box, Mr. Adams. They've been using them for decades. You should at least try to keep up."

Adams scowled at it. "I know very well what it is, sir—a contraption that promotes sloth and witlessness in equal measure. And I have seen, to my horror and deep regret, how thoughtlessly they stare at it, for hours at a time! It is misnamed. They should have termed it a stupidifier. Television—bah!"

Jefferson enjoyed watching television no more than Adams but sometimes found it useful. The ghosts were stuck at the White House and couldn't slip down to the Capitol to see the new president for themselves. Television would summon the Capitol to them.

The two beheld America's president-elect: a thin, flat-chested woman in her fifties with short-cropped brown hair. Wisely, she wore no hat, as it would have been carried off at once by the stiff breeze. Her pink woolen overcoat, fluorescent in the midday sunlight, dazzled the crowd. She stepped cautiously toward the podium on pink platform shoes, nearly tipping over like a bowling pin.

The ghosts looked quizzically at each other. This was the new president?

"Hurry, she's getting ready to speak," said Adams. "Make them talk louder!"

Jefferson's fingers fumbled over the remote's buttons. There were so many. What did they all do? Power ON/OFF? No, that one couldn't be right—the image was already there on the wall. What did CH plus or CH minus mean? Or REC, or LAST, or VOL plus or VOL minus?

"Be quick about it, or we'll miss her address," Adams urged. "Or worse, that stout young fellow there may awake and see us. Just try one of them. Any of them."

Jefferson tensed up. VOL? Could it signify volition, perhaps? No, that made little sense. Voluminous? Voluble? Volume?

That had to be it: not volume as in three-dimensional Euclidean space, but as in sound.

"Oh, isn't this device fascinating, Mr. Adams?" asked Jefferson with glee. "Why, discovering its secrets would afford me untold hours of amusement."

"We haven't got hours, nor even minutes. Hurry!"

Jefferson pressed the VOL plus button and heard a faint noise. "Ah, success!" He pushed the button again until the sound was loud enough to overcome Adams's deafness, but not so loud as to wake the guard.

"Well done, Thomas." Adams patted Jefferson on the shoulder. "Your tinker's knack for gadgetry has won the day. You would have made a fine clockmaker."

The president-elect turned her brown puppy-dog eyes to the smiling crowd standing on the Capitol steps. Women wearing pink hats, presumably her most fervent supporters, dotted the river of people spilling down the Mall. To suffer the bitter January cold so patiently, they must harbor high hopes for this unprepossessing woman. But why?

The new president's critics complained she had little knowledge of the workings of government or anything else of utility. She was even considered by some to be quite stupid.

Jefferson sensed that the charge of stupidity was unfair, that it carried the odor of naked partisanship. The woman must possess some skill or virtue that had gone unrecognized. Hadn't she once been governor of the great state of California? Was it possible to become president with absolutely no qualifications whatsoever? Could a complete fool be elected to the White House these days?

The corners of her mouth turned up in an odd, self-satisfied way. Jefferson took this to be a sign of smugness, excessive self-regard, or conceit. He had witnessed that same odious look many times before—on the proud faces of kings and princes, their flatterers at court, and even the lowliest politicians of backwoods America. Conceit, he observed, was a most empty and unsatisfying trait, requiring neither talent nor pedigree to strut its stuff.

And conceit in a woman, it was universally agreed, was worse, being more repellent than in a man, a vice unbefitting the sublime humility expected of the fairer sex. Men could be more readily forgiven for being blowhards, as it was ingrained in their nature, even making them attractive to certain kinds of women, notably the foolish ones.

A haughty president, with the highest station in the land within her grasp? Jefferson could imagine nothing worse. What did she intend to do with her newly acquired powers?

"Repeat after me, please," said the black-robed chief justice. A gust of wind hoisted his thinning mane of white hair as if it were unfurling a sail.

The woman's words echoed slowly after his, with a delivery stiff and practiced. "I, Patricia Ingratelli Pitypander," the woman enunciated with a queenly air, following the justice's cue.

She repeated the oath of office without misspeaking a single syllable. As the tension drained from her face, she shook the old man's hand and grinned. The second female President of the United States, Patty Pitypander, had sworn on a Bible to protect the Constitution and faithfully execute the laws of the country. But would she?

Just then, the Marine band struck up "Hail to the Chief."

"I don't like the looks of this...this Pitypander woman," Adams announced with a snort.

Jefferson hung his head. "Nor do I, sadly. From what little I have heard about her, she has nothing to recommend her for the presidency, or any high office."

Despite the ghosts' reservations about the new president, a twenty-one-gun salute boomed across the Capitol grounds in her honor.

"Is that the new vice president behind her to the left, that young man with the wolf-like eyes?" Adams asked.

"I suppose he must be."

Adams stroked his chin. "Yon Cassius has a lean and hungry look, does he not?"

"I hadn't noticed the vice president," Jefferson replied. "I was too busy thinking she might imagine herself to be Julius Caesar to worry that he might play the part of Cassius. With all due respect to Shakespeare, Mr. Adams, we can only hope Mrs. Pitypander's drama will prove more a comedy than a tragedy."

Adams sniffed at the screen. "Hard experience has taught me to always keep a watchful eye on the vice president, and I'm quite sure there's something amiss with this one. He's a mountebank if ever I saw one."

The caption at the bottom of the screen identified the incoming vice president as Tony Sartini. He was a good-looking man overall, most likely in his late thirties, with hooded eyes that suggested a certain seductive sleaziness common to some grasping politicians. His most distinguishing feature was a large Roman nose, which curved like a vulture's beak.

"Ah, I see we are getting yet another Italian in the bargain," said Adams, continuing to rant. "No doubt a double-dealing agent of the Pope, descended from the murderous Machiavelli himself!"

Jefferson smiled. "Machiavelli is he now, and no longer Cassius? Has Mr. Sartini improved so quickly in your estimation? I think you risk being unfair to the fellow, Mr. Adams. In fact, we know practically nothing about either of them. The election was so close that some have described her victory as an accident."

"Hmm, yes, in that immodest pink garb, she looks every inch an accident," Adams said. "And, Heaven knows, accidents happen in the electoral college." He looked accusingly at Jefferson. "Don't they?"

Jefferson held his tongue, hard as it was to do. He would not be baited into yet another pointless quarrel about whether he or Adams should have won the vitriolic presidential election of 1800. In the end, Jefferson and his Republicans had triumphed, and that was that. Would the old curmudgeon ever get over the Federalists' stinging defeat?

Not in this afterlife, Jefferson knew. Adams nursed ancient grudges like newborn babies.

"Ah, she's about to speak," Adams said. "Let's listen."

Pitypander tiptoed up to the podium, glanced at the teleprompter, and yanked on the microphone. She set forth her sweeping plan to remake America.

"My fellow Americans, as I promised you in my campaign, as part of my Better America plan, we will immediately institute my policy of guaranteeing not just the pursuit of happiness but happiness itself, to one and all. To accomplish that, we must streamline all levels of government, including the states, which I fully expect to be our biggest obstacle."

Her coat billowed as another powerful gust blew through.

"Some governors have already announced their intention to block my proposals. Well, I have news for them: I've always thought fifty states are way too many. Who can remember the names of so many places? Iowa, Idaho, Illinois, Indiana—so many I's, and they all sound alike. And don't get me started on the state capitals. Heck, memorizing them all drove me nuts when I was in school. So, as our first order of business, we'll abolish the states and replace them with six new regional administrative units, each to be led by an appointee of my choosing. This will give us a modern, united, efficient government, like the ones they have in Europe."

Jefferson dropped the remote, his mouth agape. He turned to Adams. "Abolish the states, did she say, in the name of efficiency, to guarantee happiness and bring us a European-style government? Is this woman mad or profoundly ignorant?"

Adams pulled his waistcoat tight around his chest. "Mad or ignorant? Why not both? The two infirmities are frequent bedfellows."

Jefferson's brow knotted up. "So, her remedy for slow government is fast government. Sir, the most efficient government is a dictatorship!" He pointed an accusing finger at Adams. "Is this where your notions about Federalism and monarchy have led us—back to dictatorship and tyranny?"

"Pffft! Stuff and nonsense," Adams roared. "I accept no blame for her views. No Federalist would advocate eliminating the states. Without states, how can federalism exist? Abolish Massachusetts? I think not! Not while I have a breath left in my...well, I mean..." He stopped, looked down in dismay at his translucent torso, and pursed his lips. "I mean, not while I can do anything to stop it."

"On that point, at least, we are wholly agreed," said Jefferson. "Abolish my beloved Virginia? God forbid it. Centralizing power cannot unite a vast nation such as ours. It can only foster the country's dismemberment by drawing power away from the people. Does she know nothing about our founding principles?"

"It would seem not. If she knows them, she has no respect for them—or us."

"That, most likely, is because she knows us not, nor the smallest particle of our famous history," said Jefferson.

The living understood so little about the past. History had fallen on hard times, abused and misunderstood like a ragged beggar who, though once a figure of some importance, had lost his place in the world.

The new president droned on for several minutes more and seemed poised to rattle on for a full hour despite the cold, but the two ghosts had been chilled enough by Mrs. Pitypander herself and could bear no more.

"It is well that we witnessed this travesty," Adams said in a low tone, with the gravity of an undertaker. "No wonder the country is in such deplorable condition. Every president they elect is worse than the last. Incredibly, this woman exceeds even Diebold. True, he was a shameless, self-dealing swindler, but he knew himself to be so. Mrs. Pitypander, in contrast, adamantly believes that she possesses a high-minded and unyielding virtue. What she calls reforms will wreck the country in a trice. We are duty-bound to report this calamitous development to the Council."

Jefferson thought about how that would be received. Convening the Council of White House Ghosts to challenge a president's fitness for office was an almost unprecedented step. It could lead to nearly anything. "What do you suppose they might do about her?"

Before Adams could answer, a rustle came from the other side of the room. They froze.

The Secret Service agent had awoken. Yawning, the man looked up and stared back at them in wonder and alarm.

The agent rubbed his eyes. "Potusgeists? Nah, can't be." He observed them for a few more seconds and then grabbed for his phone and pointed its camera at them.

At once, the two shadowy figures exited through the wall.

CHAPTER 2

THE OVAL OFFICE

THE WHITE HOUSE would do just fine, even for a woman with several mega-mansions.

Flanked by Secret Service agents, the newly inaugurated president ascended the steps and passed triumphantly through the front door into the Entrance Hall. She took in the twenty-foot ceiling, the checkerboard marble floor, the interior columns, and the Grand Staircase to the upper floor. It was all just as thrilling as Patty remembered from her earlier visits as governor.

Except now, at last, it was hers—the whole place and everything that came with it.

"Welcome to the White House, Madam President," said a dignified gray-haired man standing nearby. He identified himself as Chief Usher Leo Twiggs, the general manager of the White House's domestic staff. His one hundred employees, including the seven other ushers and the housekeepers, doormen, and cooks who worked under them, would be on call for Patty around the clock. Twiggs and his staff would attend to her every need, from the Residence to the Oval Office.

The White House, though smaller than her Durango Beach mansion and lacking its breathtaking view of the Pacific Ocean, boasted one hundred thirty-two rooms, thirty-five bathrooms, twenty-eight fireplaces, a bomb shelter, a staffed kitchen capable of serving one hundred forty guests, and a crew of Navy Seal snipers on its roof.

Snipers! None of the other five Pitypander mansions, though they also had large domestic staffs to wait on Patty hand and foot, came with snipers. At last, she had one-upped her billionaire husband, Benny.

The White House had something else, even better. Its walls and floors, having earned the rich patina of more than two centuries, conveyed the aura of dignity and importance she had long striven to acquire.

Respectability came with the place as part of a package deal, including Air Force One, Marine One, the bombproof limousine called "The Beast," the domestic staff, and the ever-watchful Secret Service. The ancient walls and floors cloaked their occupant with the majesty of the nation's highest office, however humble her birth or reprehensible her path to the presidency. Already Patty could feel the executive mansion redeeming her, cleansing her, forgiving her. Soon, the scandals, the lies, the dirty political tricks, and all the other unpleasant things she had done to get there would be forgotten. The power that emanated from this singular house ensured it.

She peered down a hallway. There was just enough time to give Olympia, her elderly mother, a brief tour of the Oval Office. Soon, the four of them, including Benny and top adviser Nigel Windborne, were due at the inaugural parade. Patty asked Twiggs to escort them to the West Wing. As they approached the famous chamber, Patty laid her hand gently on Olympia's stooped shoulder and motioned to her to lead the way inside.

The old woman's face lit up. "The Oval Office! Oh, my!" She turned around, wide-eyed. "Your father would be so proud of you, Patty girl. He said you would get here someday. You always had that bee in your bonnet. You had to be president. And here you are."

Papa would be proud. The late mayor's headstrong daughter had followed him into politics and outdone him, fulfilling his prophecy that she was destined for the White House. Nothing could stop his little Patricia from reaching a goal once she set her mind to it.

Olympia toddled into the room. An old wooden desk with intricate carvings on the front anchored the floor at one end, while at the other, a fire crackled in a hearth. A grandfather clock stood at attention against the curved wainscoting. A band of dentil crown molding, thirty inches wide and backlit by a white glow, ringed the overarching oval ceiling. Behind the massive desk, long golden curtains hung down over a set of tall windows. At Olympia's feet lay the famous carpet bearing the presidential seal, eliciting from her yet another "Oh, my!"

The old woman's eyes fastened on a portrait hanging beside a built-in bookcase. The man inside the gilded frame stood erect, his black uniform topped by gold epaulets. His face was long, intense, and rutted with deep tracks, the kind left by a life of worry. His ample, untamed hair was swept back from his sideburns and forehead like a lion's mane.

"Who is that guy?" Olympia asked.

Patty admitted she wasn't sure. Benny shrugged his shoulders.

"Andrew Jackson," Nigel answered without hesitation.

"Is that so?" Benny whipped out his wallet, pulled out a twenty-dollar bill, and frowned upon seeing that the hairstyle was a perfect match. "Okay, I'll admit he does look something like Jackson. Younger, though."

Nigel smiled. "The one on the wall is obviously an earlier portrait than the one on the money. It was done several years before Jackson became president, to celebrate his victory at the Battle of New Orleans. As I recall, the battle was in 1815, the year after the White House burned down."

"Oh yeah, the British did that!" Benny perked up, his eyes filling with glee. "I remember that from high school. The War of 1812. You guys torched this place, Windborne!"

Nigel tossed his head back. "I beg your pardon. I did nothing of the sort. I am a naturalized American citizen, and proudly so. As for burning Washington, the enemy's capital was fair game. If it makes you feel any better, the British paid dearly for their actions in New Orleans, where Jackson's ragtag troops decimated them."

Benny smirked. "Yeah, I gotta admit, the thought of you being decimated does make me feel better." He raised his right hand and saluted the painting. "Way to go, Andy! You decimate Windborne all you like."

Nigel sighed. "This portrait commemorates Old Hickory's astonishing victory over an army that had recently defeated none other than Napoleon. It catapulted Jackson into the national spotlight and helped restore America's fragile pride back then and...hmm...apparently still does to this very day."

Nigel was a walking encyclopedia and knew just about everything, which Patty attributed to his reading books—serious ones, not like her romance novels, but weighty nonfiction tomes that took days to plow through. Plus, the Englishman had a nearly perfect photographic memory. If Nigel were ever a guest on the quiz show *Jeopardy*, Patty was sure he would win a gazillion dollars.

He was worth every penny. It was Nigel Windborne, after all, who had persuaded her to run for president over Benny's selfish objections and assertion that she wasn't fit for the job. Nigel had skillfully guided her campaign to victory over President Diebold.

Her political enemies jealously called him Pitypander's brain, but Patty resented the implication, as she was proud of her own mind. Nigel was a mere extension of her. His job was to fill the gaps in her knowledge, render advice, and allow her to focus on more important things than silly facts.

Nigel chattered on like a museum docent. The Oval Office, he said, was originally built in the West Wing at the order of William Howard Taft and later renovated by Franklin Roosevelt. He described the history of the Resolute Desk, a gift from Queen Victoria to President Hayes that was fashioned from the oak timbers of an old British ship called the HMS *Resolute*.

Patty bent over to inspect the intricate carving on the desk's front. It was the presidential seal—her personal seal now—marking this desk as the world's most important, where the buck stopped. A talisman of Patty's power, the massive antique was as close as any U.S. president could come to having a throne. It would, like a queen's scepter, command the respect of one and all.

John F. Kennedy's small children had played underneath the mighty desk. Bill Clinton had done unspeakable things on top of it.

Here, in wood, was history itself, the good, the bad, and the naughty. The desk, with layer upon layer of history written on it, possessed magical, transformative powers that could make even the most unworthy leader seem legitimate.

She went around the other side of it, sat down, and pulled out a drawer, absorbing the musty smell left by her many predecessors. "Do I look resolute?"

"You do indeed, Madam President!" Nigel pumped his fist. "Ready to take on the world."

Benny put his head in his hands. "Lord, what a load of bull-shit. I think I'm going to hurl. You're going to take on the world? God save America."

"And I will save it, too. You just watch me," Patty shot back.

Just then, Olympia cried out, "Oh, dear."

"What's that, Mama?" Patty put her hand on her mother's shoulder. "Is something wrong?"

Olympia had turned her attention back to the painting of Andrew Jackson. "Dear me, I think that man on the wall is staring at me."

"Staring at you? Mama, that's silly. It's nothing but a painting. Why would Andrew Jackson want to stare at you?"

Olympia backed away from the painting and shuffled to one side. "I don't know, but I'm sure his eyes are following me. Everywhere I stand, there they are."

Patty got up from the desk and confronted the painting. Jackson's eyes seemed to stare at her as well. Moving to the other end of the room made no difference. "Yes, he's definitely staring at us. He's kind of spooky, isn't he?"

Benny waddled about the room, looking over his shoulder at Jackson. "I don't see anything."

"It's just an optical illusion," Nigel said with an air of certainty, folding his long arms. "Lots of old portraits have that effect. It's a trick of the imagination. Wherever you are, the eyes seem to follow you." He arched an eyebrow. "And yet, there are stories..." He paused. "No, never mind. I shouldn't tell you."

"What stories?" Patty asked. "About what? Tell me."

"Oh, I don't want to put disturbing thoughts in your head," Nigel said. "They're just old legends. No one takes them seriously."

"She might," Benny said with a sneer. "She has lots of nutty ideas. Like the one that she's qualified to be president, for start-ers. You didn't think twice about putting that crazy idea in her head, did you, Windborne? But then she did get you out of that boring L.A. law firm and into the White House, didn't she?"

Nigel clenched his fists. His face flushing red, he blinked at the casino magnate three times, a sure sign he was about to issue one of his withering Oxford-educated invectives. "Why should she need your permission to run for president? I say—"

Patty stepped between them. It was a good thing Benny was going back to Las Vegas after today to run his vast empire of garish casinos. Boorish Benny and her prim chief of staff would never get along here in the White House.

"Don't mind him, Nigel, he's just jealous," she said. "Let's not start that again. Go on, tell us about the legends. I want to know."

Nigel exhaled and paced around the room for a few seconds to cool off. "Very well then, I will. You'll hear about it anyway, so it's best that you get it from me. You see, rumor has it that this place is haunted by former presidents and first ladies. They've been nicknamed the Potusgeists—a poltergeist who inhabits the White House. POTUS and *geist*, get it?"

"Potusgeists?" Patty began to laugh but stopped right away, as there was no trace of amusement on Nigel's face. "Has anyone actually seen one of them rattling around in here?"

"Well, not in the West Wing itself. But Winston Churchill did see something over in the Residence. He was staying here as a guest of Franklin Roosevelt, in the Lincoln bedroom, and claimed he saw Abraham Lincoln, stovepipe hat and all."

"Churchill saw Lincoln's ghost?" said Olympia. "He must have been terrified."

Nigel chuckled. "Yes, and Lincoln even more so. You see, madam, as the story goes, Churchill had just returned to his room from taking a hot bath, naked but for his cigar, when he looked over and saw Honest Abe, big as life. Whereupon old Winnie, though startled and amazed, nonchalantly tipped the ashes off his cigar and said to the fully attired apparition, 'Good evening, Mr. President. You seem to have me at a disadvantage.'"

They all laughed heartily, except for Benny, who had wrung his mouth into a spiteful twist. "Oh, come on, Windborne. Do you believe that really happened?"

Nigel gave the billionaire a disdainful look. "No, of course not. The story has clearly been embellished. There's a simpler and more likely explanation."

"Like what?"

"Alcohol," the aide replied. "Sir Winston was an avid drinker, some would even say an alcoholic. He very much enjoyed a glass of scotch, which the White House staff would have dutifully provided. It must have been a long, exhausting day, what with the horrid business of World War II hanging over him like a cloud. There on his night table was all that wonderful scotch, calling him to escape his troubles for a while. So, he succumbed to temptation and drank his cares away. That's my theory, at any rate."

"You mean Churchill got so drunk he started imagining things, like Lincoln's ghost?" Benny asked. "That would be pretty drunk, all right."

"Yes, I believe so," Nigel replied. "The idea that he actually saw Abraham Lincoln is too silly to believe. Inebriation explains many so-called ghostly encounters. Imagination accounts for the rest. So many historical people have lived here that it's easy to conjure up their spirits in our minds, thinking a few agonized souls from the mists of history might still be hanging about this place, literally waiting in the woodwork, ready to pop out at any time. Of course, that's irrational and superstitious, as I'm sure we all agree."

It didn't sound so irrational to Patty. She had never reached a firm conclusion one way or the other about the existence of ghosts, although it didn't seem like a very wise idea to be one. Dead people ought to stay dead and not bother the living, for everyone's sake. Then again, if ghosts did exist, it was only logical that they would inhabit the White House, where so much history had occurred. With all these antiques and relics of the past around to encourage an infestation of ghosts, her new digs might be Ghost Central. What a frightening thought!

She took another gander at Jackson. His gaze was piercing and relentless, growing more so the longer she looked at him. Nigel was probably correct that the portrait was just a portrait and nothing more. On the other hand, she was going to be spending a lot of time in this famous room, and she couldn't afford to be constantly distracted by those eyes, those fierce, devilish eyes.

How could she roust Andrew Jackson out of her Oval Office without revealing that she might be superstitious about ghosts?

Patty quickly hit on the answer. She didn't need to admit she was superstitious. She would deflect the issue by pinning the blame on someone else. The portrait made her guests uncomfortable.

"If that painting is bothering Mama, then it will bother others, and it's simply got to go. Please have it removed immediately, Mr. Twiggs."

The chief usher smiled at her knowingly. "As you wish, Madam President. We'll have Old Hickory boxed up, staring eyes and all, and put safely in storage, where the old boy won't be able to disturb anyone."

CHAPTER 3
SAVING CAMEMBERT

THE DENSE PROSE of the State Department briefing book ran to a hundred pages, overwhelming Patty with facts about French cheese.

France had been famous for the stuff, the document declared, ever since Gallic tribes started exporting it to Rome two millennia ago. Ninety-five percent of the French consumed cheese. The average citizen ate fifty-seven pounds a year. To satisfy demand, the French cheese industry proudly churned out over twelve hundred varieties.

But being cheesy wasn't easy. Cheese could kill, the briefing book warned ominously.

U.S. food inspectors had discovered that some of France's most prestigious cheeses were tainted with deadly *E. coli* bacteria. The finding was angrily denounced by France as a smear concocted by powerful American cheese interests to gain market share.

To protect American consumers, the Food and Drug Administration leaped into action, outlawing four popular French cheeses: Vieux-Boulogne, Époisses de Bourgogne, Munster, and Camembert. Indignant French producers retaliated by dumping truckloads of stinky cheese outside the American embassy in Paris. The stench was so overwhelming that rats were poking their heads out of nearby sewer grates and fleeing for their lives.

Milton Borders, the bald new Secretary of State, insisted that something be done to defuse the *crise du fromage*.

"I'm appalled," said Patty. "The FDA can't be serious. We're banning Camembert?"

"Yes."

She stole an admiring glance at the young Marine standing guard outside the Oval Office door, his muscular build bulging through his black coat. It was a pity the guards weren't supposed to speak to the president. She wouldn't mind at all if that one came over and joined them. Marines always had been a weakness of hers.

"Ahem," said Nigel, his eyes signaling disapproval.

Patty forced her mind to return to the problem at hand. "Well, I don't care if the FDA bans Vieux-Boulogne. Let them have it. It smells like old gym socks to me. But I'm very fond of Camembert. I've served it at my own dinner parties. Can't we save Camembert?"

"The problem is the way the French make it," said Borders. "They age it in caves so the cheese will get moldy with a bacterium called, um ... I can't remember the name."

"*Brevibacterium linens,*" Nigel offered helpfully. "According to page three, line seven, of your briefing book."

Borders found the reference in that exact place and looked at Nigel in amazement. "Yes, that's it. The good bacteria give the cheese its taste and distinctive smell. Unfortunately, *E. coli* bacteria is also getting on their cheese and slipping past the food inspectors. The FDA has to clamp down."

"And if they do?" Patty asked.

Borders's face grew pale. "Then the French trade minister says France will retaliate by outlawing American wheat. The whole thing might escalate. A full-blown trade war could erupt with the European Union. Things could quickly get out of hand."

The buck did stop at the Resolute Desk. So did the cheese.

It sounded like things had already gotten out of hand. "A trade war? Over cheese and wheat?" said Patty in disbelief. "This is the thanks we get for saving them in two world wars? What's wrong with our wheat?"

"Nothing," Borders responded. "The French, as usual, are being difficult, playing tit-for-tat. We say their cheese is rotten, so they pretend that our wheat is unhealthy because it's genetically modified. They know that will cost us millions in exports and rile our Midwestern farmers. It's a shot across our bow."

Nigel pointed out that Patty's polls in the Midwest had barely cracked thirty percent. If she didn't stand with the farmers, she could face defeat in the midterms and lose her thin majority in the House of Representatives, dooming her agenda.

"But we're in charge of the FDA, aren't we? Can't we stop the cheese ban?" Patty asked.

Borders didn't see any way to do that. A federal law required that any food with significant *E. coli* risk had to be banned. No exceptions or presidential discretion were allowed. The FDA's hands were tied.

"Then let's abolish the FDA," Patty proposed.

Nigel grimaced. "No, Congress won't let you close down the FDA to placate the French cheese industry. Americans would sicken and die from a thousand other causes and blame you for that."

"Oh, dear. That wouldn't do."

Maybe the French could be reasoned with, although that seemed unlikely, as it had been tried in vain many times before on less weighty matters than cheese.

Going to war with France was also off the table. Too easy, said Borders. The French would just surrender, and they would be back where they started.

That left socializing, which suited Patty just fine. From what little she knew about French President Bertrand Dubois by watching him on the nightly news, he seemed like a nice young man. Only thirty-seven, he looked even younger, thanks to his boyish smile and cute curly hair. Best of all, he was single and had a reputation for being a playboy who loved to gallivant around Paris dinner parties. Lively young Frenchmen always had been a weakness of hers.

"That's it! Dubois is supposed to be a fun guy. Let's throw a dinner party for him!"

"A dinner party?" asked the secretary of state, rubbing his bald spot. "What good would that do?"

"A really big one, big enough to impress upon Bertie that we have the best of intentions for his cheese. We can set up a band to play music and have a little parade of soldiers march around in a straight line on the South Lawn."

"I believe you are referring to a state dinner," said Nigel.

Patty grew excited as the event unfolded in her mind. It would be glorious, with all the pomp and circumstance the nation could muster. "Yes, that's it, a state dinner. We can call it the cheese summit. We'll put on the dog for Bertie. Make him feel special. And we'll have lots of Camembert at the table as a peace offering. We'll all eat his poisoned cheese right in front of him. That will show our goodwill and get him to chill out about our wheat, don't you see?"

"But a state dinner would be serious overkill," Borders objected. "It's not protocol for a mere trade dispute. It's a high diplomatic honor. It's a big deal."

Patty raised her chin in defiance of diplomatic protocol. Her stuffy Secretary of State was not impressing her with his grasp of global politics. Who needed diplomats, she wondered, when the answer to a problem was so obvious? They just got in the way and made things complicated.

"Protocol, shmotocol," Patty replied. "A food problem needs a food solution. We've ruffled Bertie's feathers, so we must be as hospitable to him as possible. He can stay here at the White House during his visit."

"We have the Blair House for that purpose, don't we, Milton?" Nigel asked.

"Yes," said Borders. "But sometimes foreign dignitaries stay here too, if they're specially invited."

Nigel glared at him.

"What's wrong with you two?" said Patty. "You just finished telling me that France is America's oldest ally. Nothing is too good for our old friend Bertie. Invite him already! We must save Camembert!"

CHAPTER 4

THE COUNCIL OF GHOSTS

IN A FORGOTTEN storage room in the White House sub-basement, behind a tall stack of wooden crates left by the Harding administration, there was just enough space for a meeting of up to fifty people.

Or fifty ghosts.

The members of the August and Prudential Council of White House Ghosts (for so they called themselves) had been milling around inside the space for twenty minutes when Thomas Jefferson and John Adams appeared.

The meeting, though billed as urgent, was lightly attended. The presidents and first ladies who made a habit of sitting in on all Council meetings were there—the Roosevelts, Hayeses, and Coolidges—but many other regulars were absent due to the short notice they had received. Presumably, Adams surmised, they were off haunting their other former residences or simply lounging quietly in their coffins, as they often preferred to do, particularly the first ladies, some of whom were sensible and despised Washington.

Adams pulled his gold watch out of his vest pocket and scowled at the timepiece. "Late again. The damn thing keeps losing time. At this rate, it will lose the entire future. If only I could find someone to fix it. I don't suppose they make parts for pocket watches nowadays."

"Make parts for watches? These days, they don't even make watchmakers," said Jefferson. "But no matter. Whatever the time, it is time for us to get the meeting started, is it not?"

"Quite so." Adams grasped his cane in his left hand and stepped up onto a small wooden box set in the front of the room for a podium. "Ladies and gentlemen, if I could have your attention. Your attention, please." He banged on a nearby water pipe with his cane's handle, producing a tinny sound that rose above the conversations of the assembled ghosts. The furnace fans stopped for a moment, making it easier to hear. "There, that's better."

Adams slipped his right hand inside his waistcoat, as he used to do before addressing a jury, out of nervous habit. "Ladies and gentlemen, Mr. Jefferson and I have convened this meeting of the Council to report on our most recent findings in the matter of the new president, Mrs. Patty Pitypander. You will recall that Mr. Jefferson had performed for us the laudable service of researching Mrs. Pitypander's dubious background, following her unexpected victory this past November. He and I witnessed her inauguration ceremonies, enlisting the aid of a talking box—er, television. We have since then endeavored to follow her activities in her first days in office, taking the utmost care—I repeat, the *utmost* care—not to expose ourselves to the living."

Adams's eyes zeroed in on a short phantom in a dark coat sitting in the corner. The specter had stacked two crates and perched himself on them so he could see over the other ghosts.

"You do approve of our caution, I assume, Mr. Madison?" asked Adams with an air of genuine solicitude.

James Madison smiled down at him, as if thankful to be asked his opinion. "I do approve, so far, Mr. Adams. And I commend you for it. You well know my strict views on that troublesome subject. They are enumerated in the Rules." Madison tapped his finger on a small booklet resting on his lap. It was entitled "The Rules of Proper Conduct for the August and Prudential Council of White House Ghosts, by J. Madison."

"Very well," said Adams. "Then Mr. Jefferson and I will deliver our report on the troubling case of Mrs. Pitypander, the new president. I yield the floor to Mr. Jefferson."

Jefferson took Adams's place on the podium box. He cleared his throat, looking awkward and self-conscious about his squeaky, high-pitched voice, which was so hard to hear across a room the ghosts had to strain their ears.

"Ladies and gentlemen, I will waste no time in getting to the point. Mr. Adams and I have come to inform you in the plainest terms that, as a result of Mrs. Pitypander's unexpected ascension to the presidency, our sacred republic is in the greatest danger."

A hush fell over the group.

Adams chimed in. "As far as we can tell, this Pitypander woman was narrowly elected through fraud to keep her party in power."

The ghosts traded glances, looks of concern filling the room. The recent election was hardly the first chaotic or questionable one in American history. One had been so divisive that it led to civil war.

"Mr. Adams, if I may," said Andrew Jackson, shaking his head. "A fraudulent election to keep her party in power? I hope that is not the entirety of your complaint about the new president. If so, it is hypocritical indeed, coming from you. The same accusation could be leveled at your own son."

Jackson directed a scowl at John Quincy Adams, who had named Henry Clay as his Secretary of State to beat Jackson in the hotly contested election of 1824. "I don't recall anyone ever bringing such a matter to us. What has Mrs. Pitypander done that is so bad as to warrant calling us here for an emergency meeting?"

Jefferson was undeterred. "If you will permit me, Mr. Jackson, I shall lay before you a brief list of her many shortcomings."

"Such as what?"

"First, Mrs. Pitypander possesses none of the qualifications or virtues necessary to hold any high office, and far less the presidency."

"None? How is that possible?" Jackson asked. "She was elected by the people, after all. Are the people not by themselves sufficient arbiters of her qualifications that we, the deceased, must rush in to fill the gap? Do we no longer vest our trust in the people's wisdom, as expressed by their votes?"

Jefferson remained serene. "Of course we do. But Mrs. Pitypander is woefully uneducated and incurious, and her highest intellectual achievement is her addiction to reading tawdry romance novels. Further, she speaks neither Latin nor Greek, is wholly uncultured, cares nothing for our revered American democratic traditions, knows nothing of the law, and yet aspires to redesign the fundamental institutions of government to suit her arrogant belief that her election, although fraudulent, entitles her to overthrow centuries of established practice.

"As for her character, she lacks all the graces expected of a lady of high station and is notorious for her questionable morals, in particular a scandalous attraction to young men, which she can barely conceal. She possesses none of the accomplishments expected of a well-bred lady and cannot spin cloth, sew, play the pianoforte, or sing. So devoid of womanly skills is she that you would not hire her to empty your chamberpot, and yet the American people have somehow been hoodwinked into hiring her to be their leader. And, to top it off, Mr. Jackson, she has had the effrontery to remove your hallowed portrait from the Oval Office."

"She removed my portrait?"

"Yes, she had it boxed up and sent to storage in Bladensburg."

"Boxed up in Bladensburg? Incredible!" cried Jackson. "But why would she do such a damnable thing?"

"I believe she described your eyes as 'very creepy,'" Jefferson answered.

"Very creepy, am I? Oh, well then. Have your way with her!"

A burly man with a heavy brown mustache and thick pince-nez glasses stepped forward. "But how is she worse than President Diebold?" asked Theodore Roosevelt. "Her predecessor was an empty-headed ninny too, as fit for the gallows as the grubbiest New York politicians I ever knew. Several of us were appalled by his swindling and self-dealing, but we convened no meeting of the Council in his case."

"Diebold, to his credit, was only a swindler, and no worse," replied Jefferson. "Mrs. Pitypander, by contrast, is out to demolish the very underpinnings of the republic, without even the understanding that she is doing it. She wishes, for example, to abolish the states, thinking that doing so will render her goal to vastly enlarge the federal government easier to attain. All in the name of guaranteeing happiness to one and all, a goal so preposterous that no previous president has proposed it before."

The room was abuzz with whispers. No one had heard of such a ludicrous thing as the government actually guaranteeing happiness, not even Herbert Hoover, who had promised a chicken in every pot just before driving the nation into the Great Depression. President Pitypander was clearly not well. Someone in the meeting murmured the word "madwoman."

Roosevelt flashed his famous toothy smile. "Then her crime is not her intent, which may be virtuously inspired or even saintly, but her misguided ignorance of reality. Is that it?"

Jefferson bobbed his head in agreement. "Yes, that is the gist of it. Ignorance is the wellspring of most of her frailties. All her delusions, which are legion, flow from it and are compounded by her feminine foibles, to which all members of her sex are subject by nature."

A jowly woman with a pearl necklace and buckteeth perked up. One of the Council's regulars, Mrs. Eleanor Roosevelt always became roused to speak her mind when the men brought up the nature of women and their limitations. "But Mr. Jefferson," she asked in a piercing voice, "if ignorance is Mrs. Pitypander's problem, is not reforming her ignorance through education the obvious solution?"

"Why, of course, it would be, if she were a mere child, Mrs. Roosevelt," replied Adams curtly before Jefferson could answer. "But Mrs. Pitypander is well into her fifties and sitting in the Oval Office as we speak, at the head of our nation, making this a most urgent matter. There's no telling what her ignorance may lead her to do with her newfound powers, and we fear to contemplate what terrible consequences for the nation may ensue."

Mrs. Roosevelt nodded. "Yes, I fully agree. Fearing such consequences, as we should, we must remedy her ignorance at once. President Pitypander clearly needs a mentor."

"A mentor?" said Adams. "You mean to suggest that one of us should be her mentor?"

"Well, of course, it must be one of us," replied Mrs. Roosevelt. "Who else could we prevail upon to do it? Surely, no one among the living. As you yourself are fond of saying, these days, the living are all blockheads."

"Indeed they are," replied Adams. "You have me there."

"Excellent. Then, for the role of mentor, I nominate Mr. Jefferson," said Mrs. Roosevelt. "Who among us, after all, could be better suited to raise poor Mrs. Pitypander up from the pits of ignorance than our own Mr. Jefferson? He is the founder of a great university, a patron of higher education, and the most knowledgeable and talented of us all. Might you coach and instruct her, despite the weighty encumbrance of her feminine foibles, Mr. Jefferson?"

Jefferson's face fell. "Me?"

"You do have the time for the project, do you not?" she asked, looking around the room. "I believe we are all here for eternity, as far as we know. You cannot help but have more free time than President Pitypander does."

Jefferson's eyes darted about, searching desperately for an escape. "Well, yes, but I wouldn't know how—"

"Then I hereby nominate Mr. Jefferson to educate Mrs. Pitypander, foibles and all, and to improve her weak feminine mind as well as he is able, for the safety and welfare of the nation," said Mrs. Roosevelt. "Who will second the motion? Ladies?" She looked beside her.

A woman wearing a bonnet raised her hand.

"No, Abigail, please don't," said Adams to his wife.

Undeterred, Abigail Adams kept her arm in the air and looked expectantly at the woman beside her. Dolley Madison giggled and raised her hand as well. The motion carried.

John Adams and James Madison glared at their wives.

"Sorry, Jefferson, I would fain spare you from this trial if I could," said Adams. "But I must agree with Mrs. Roosevelt that you are the one most fit for this mission, impossible as its object may be. I would volunteer to attempt it myself, you understand, but I have neither the personality nor the patience to teach anyone, much less a recalcitrant dullard like Mrs. Pitypander."

"Wait!" James Madison waved his pamphlet. "If Mr. Jefferson is to undertake this daunting task, for everyone's sake, we must lay down some helpful guidelines for him to follow, in conformity with our Rules."

"Isn't there already some provision about a ghost appearing before a living president?" asked Adams. "Don't we place certain limits on appearances, even those sanctioned by the Council?"

"It has been so many years since we expressly authorized an appearance, I cannot recall the precise language," Madison replied. He thumbed through his dog-eared rulebook. "Ah, here it is. Article Six, Section One, Paragraph Three. *Exposure of Visible Image to Living Persons.* No ghost may expose his visible image before any living person in the White House, or upon the grounds thereof, except in the most rare and dire circumstance, as necessary to protect the welfare, safety, or security of the United States of America.'"

"The most rare and dire circumstance? That's rather vague," said Adams, "as well as very limiting and inconvenient."

"In my humble interpretation of this rule, Mr. Jefferson, you must not show yourself to Mrs. Pitypander unless absolutely necessary," said Madison. "Appearing before her must be a last resort."

"But if I cannot speak to the woman, how am I to instruct her?" asked Jefferson, his voice quivering.

"I leave that up to your famous ingenuity, my good friend," Madison replied. "I'm sure you, of all people, will find a way."

CHAPTER 5

THE JUMPING BOOK

MOST OF THE staff had gone home for the night. Patty rested her chin on her hand and noticed the two uneaten slices of pepperoni pizza she'd left in the cardboard box. The clock on the fireplace mantle showed nine-thirty.

Who knew the presidency could be so frustrating? The day had been an endless parade of people bringing her one vexing issue after another, and she hadn't solved any of them. The answer to one problem only gave rise to a worse one. She was spending all her time weighing the cost of doing this or that in favor of one selfish interest group at the expense of another, as if they were the big boss instead of her.

Thirteen hours of nonstop aggravations—it was all too much to bear.

Cain and Abel, her two corgis, lay curled up on the floor, sound asleep. The White House staff had pampered her beloved pooches for her and brought them back to the Oval Office. Patty had scarcely had time to notice them.

She had neglected her reading as well. It was time to remedy that. She reached into a side drawer in the Resolute Desk, pulled out her paperback novel, *A Bed Too Far*, and read from where she had left off the night before:

> Jenessa Fuller, whose deepest desire had been to meet with Dirk that evening, had made the critical mistake of overestimating his interest in her. Dirk was a busy man, after all. When he wasn't on the practice field or lifting weights to keep his taut, muscular body in a state of absolute perfection, he was at the stadium with the Marlins or out of town at a road game. Being madly in love with a professional baseball player—the world's most handsome relief pitcher at that—had its downside, Jenessa realized. Dirk was just too perfect, too good to be true, and getting his attention for very long seemed well-nigh impossible.

Jenessa was so lucky. The heroine of Marjorie Mickle's romance novels was, as always, consumed solely with how to conquer a single, elusive man with her beauty and feminine wiles. She knew nothing of the burdens of the presidency. Unlike Patty, she didn't have to deal with recalcitrant Cabinet members, corrupt congressmen, or a fickle press. People didn't lay the world's most intractable problems at her feet all day long. No one demanded that Jenessa be anything but sly, slinky, and beautiful or dream up a solution for France's smelly cheese. In every way that Patty could think of, in every way that mattered, Jenessa had a more glamorous job than she did. It probably paid better, too.

A rattling sound came from Patty's left, awakening the corgis. Cain trotted over to the built-in bookcase with the big clamshell molding on top, Abel following close behind. They jumped up on their hind legs, pawed at the wainscoting below the shelves, and barked as if there was an intruder inside it.

But there was no intruder. Patty was all alone. Or was she?

The White House staff had tastefully decorated the bookcase with sets of old hardcover books, interspersed with some black statuettes about eight inches high.

Patty patted Cain on the head. "It's nothing, boy. Just a bunch of old books. Nothing to get upset about."

Then she heard what sounded like a low, agonized groan.

As she scrutinized the bookcase, one of the dark blue books fell over, flat on its side. Patty walked over and stood it up properly and then turned around and went back to her desk.

No sooner had Patty sat down than another sickening groan emanated from the bookcase, followed by a clunk. The same book had fallen over again.

Once more, Patty went to the bookcase, but this time she slid one of the heavy statuettes over to hold the book in place. Again, she returned to her desk.

Within seconds, something crashed. All by itself, the book had jumped off its shelf and fallen to the floor!

Patty drew back.

What on earth? What is going on with this old book?

She crept toward the bookcase, extended her arm slowly, snatched the book off the floor, and quickly retreated, eyeing the bookcase warily.

The book cover's gold lettering marked it as the first volume of John Marston's *Governing a Constitutional Republic.*

Patty opened the book, noted its 1850 publication date, and began to page through it. The first chapter was titled "A Brief History of Self-Ruling Republics, From Ancient Greece to the Present Day."

It was some sort of ancient primer on civics, the kind of academic book one would find gathering dust in the stacks of a university library. She turned to the first section and read it:

> The foundations of the modern self-ruling republic were laid in sixth-century Greece in the city-state of Athens, where in 594 B.C., chief magistrate Solon issued reforms with the aim of reducing some of the inequities of Athenian society and the aristocracy's monopoly on political power. He gave free male adult Athenians the right to participate in assembly meetings and created four property classes based on annual income instead of aristocratic birth. Solon's nascent democracy was overthrown by the tyrant Peisistratos but later reinstated and extended to lower property classes, in fits and starts, by subsequent rulers.

Marston proceeded to describe the repeated cycles of collapse and rebirth of democracy in Athens. In the end, the famous city-state was defeated by Sparta in the bloody Peloponnesian War, a catastrophic event that terminated Greece's golden age and any hope for rule by the people during that ancient era.

Patty struggled through the dense prose to page five, then yawned, closed the book, and put it back on the shelf. The problem with history books was that they had no plot, no romance, and no entertainment value. For sheer drama, John Marston's tomes couldn't hold a candle to Marjorie Mickle's exciting page-turners.

Patty was just about to leave the room when she heard another weird groan and another crash.

She glanced back at the bookcase. Again, Marston's thick book lay flat on the floor, but this time open to the very page where she had stopped reading.

What were the odds of that happening by accident? Zero.

There could only be one explanation: There were ghosts in the Oval Office.

She shrieked and ran to the door. The Secret Service agent stationed outside rushed toward her, followed by her secretary.

"What's the matter, Madam President?" asked the agent, sweeping the room with his eyes.

"We have...!" Her voice trailed off. They wouldn't believe her. Nobody would. They would think she was crazy. She looked at her frightened secretary. "Never mind. Please call the chief of staff!"

CLINT CRANBERRY WAS the youngest FBI agent Patty had ever seen. He sat down on one of the sofas across the coffee table from her and gazed around the room, taking in the crown molding and the portraits on the wall. His eyes finally settled on the Resolute Desk. "Wow, I can't believe I'm really here. I'm actually in the White House."

The Oval Office got that reaction a lot. Patty never got tired of it. It was an affirmation of her success.

It was so sweet, that soft drawl of his. Southern boys always had been a weakness of hers. She smiled coquettishly and offered him some coffee.

Nigel gave her a disapproving look. "Ahem, let's get down to business, shall we?"

He explained that Clint had been rushed to the White House from the FBI's specialized investigations division.

"The FBI director sent over some brief notes about you." Nigel reached into his briefcase, grabbed a folder, and re-read the two pages inside. "I'm afraid we've been in a bit of a mad rush since all the excitement Patty had last night with the ghost, and your dossier is a bit...uh, skimpy on details. I'll have to ask you to fill in the holes if you don't mind."

"Not at all, sir."

"Now, it says here you're twenty-three and got your degree in electrical engineering from North Carolina State University."

"That is correct, sir."

"Hmm. Twenty-three. So, you must have recently joined the FBI."

"A few months ago. Just got out of basic training at Quantico, sir."

"Ah, yes, and I see you're in the FBI's paranormal unit. Very interesting. Until last night, I had no idea there was such a thing. What exactly is it that you people do?"

"Ghost investigations."

"Really? Is there a need for that at the Bureau?"

"The FBI gets some pretty weird cases, sir," said Clint. "Eighteen percent of American adults say they have seen a ghost. Whether they have or not, somebody in the FBI has to know how to investigate their claims because sometimes the cases involve federal crimes. That's where we come in. Usually, somebody has experienced something that seems supernatural."

"Eighteen percent have seen ghosts? That's amazing. How many paranormal investigators does the FBI have?"

"Just four, sir," Clint replied. "We have enough work to keep a lot more investigators busy, but it's hard to get funding for ghost hunters, even when we can find them. We're a rare breed."

"I would think so," said Nigel. "Where are you located?"

"In the basement of the Hoover building. Except this week, I'm by myself. One of us is out sick. The other two are on vacation."

Nigel's lips curled into a restrained smile. "You're the only paranormal specialist working this week—in the whole FBI?"

"Yes, sir. I'm all there is."

"Well, that wasn't very considerate of them, was it? Leaving you alone to defend the nation against the dark forces of the paranormal."

Clint's back stiffened. "I can take care of myself, sir. I'm not afraid of ghosts."

"Tell me, how does one get into the ghost-investigating business?"

The young man rubbed his knee nervously. "Well, for me, it all started when I was a kid. That's when I saw my first ghost."

"Did you? A real one? Could you tell whose ghost it was?"

"Sure. It was my grandfather."

"Oh, my goodness," said Patty. "How did that happen?"

Clint's face grew somber. "It was shortly after his funeral. The family was still all sad and depressed about his death, especially my father. One night, Grandpa just showed up in my bedroom, sitting on a chair, looking as real as you do. I was only thirteen. I was scared half to death."

"Quite rightly, I should think," said Nigel. "Especially at such a tender age. What did the ghost do when you saw him?"

Clint shrugged. "He just sat there quietly, like he did when he was alive, and said he had come to tell me something. He kind of glowed, and you could see through him, but his voice sounded normal, and he didn't act weird or spooky or anything like you see in the movies. He told me everything would be okay and that I shouldn't worry so much about my father. See, Pop had taken Grandpa's death pretty hard, so we were all worried about him. The ghost told me to help Pop any way I could. So, I promised I would."

"What else?"

"That was it," said Clint. "Grandpa just up and disappeared. I blinked, and he was gone. He had delivered his message. I didn't sleep well for several nights, thinking he might come back anytime and sit in that chair, but he never did."

"Not even once, in all the years since?" asked Patty.

"No, and after I got over the shock of that first time, I wanted him to come back. I had a lot of questions for him, like what it was like being a ghost. I even did séances, hoping to speak to him. I guess you could say I've been trying to get him back ever since. But I haven't had any luck so far."

"Okay, that experience got you into ghosts," said Patty. "But how did you get involved with the FBI?"

"It happened out of the blue," Clint replied. "One of their recruiters contacted me. He had heard that somebody at N.C. State was into ghost hunting and was trying to invent an electronic ghost sensor. The Bureau was having trouble finding a paranormal specialist and wanted to hire me straight out of school. I hesitated at first. The paranormal unit is not exactly a career builder at the FBI, you know. But the job would give me a chance to do my ghost research and get paid for it, too. I decided to take it."

"You say you started this, uh, hobby when you were thirteen?" Patty asked.

"Yes, ma'am."

"Then you have ten years' more experience with ghosts than we do. We're total novices here. We don't know the first thing about them."

Patty told Clint about the mysterious jumping book, which had prompted her frantic late-night call to the FBI director to send someone over to investigate. "That book kept falling down on its side on that shelf over there, so I kept propping it up, and then it jumped right off the shelf onto the floor. And just like that, it opened itself to where I had been reading it, like it wanted me to read some more."

Clint got up and examined the bookcase, running his hand over the books and peering behind them. "Well, I don't see anything physical that would make a book act like that. These shelves look level enough. They're not tilted or anything, so it's not gravity. An earthquake could make a book fall off a shelf, but there haven't been any earthquakes around here lately. From the looks of it, I'd say you experienced a UKE."

"A what?" Patty asked.

"An unexplained kinetic event," Clint replied. "Ghosts can make things move. They can easily knock a book off a shelf. I'll bet your ghost did want you to read something. And whatever it was, I'm sure it was pretty important, at least to him or her."

Nigel scoffed. "This is ridiculous. Books don't jump off shelves, Patty. The White House is not actually haunted, and there are no such things as ghosts. It was your imagination, I tell you."

"It seemed real enough to me," she insisted. "And another thing happened last night, too. I saw writing on my bathroom mirror. It was steamed up from the shower, and there were words on it, like someone had written them there with their finger."

"Oh, yeah? That's cool. What did it say?" Clint asked.

"It was in French. I wrote it down so I wouldn't forget." Patty walked over to the Resolute Desk and reached into her purse for a slip of paper. "Here it is: *Méfiez-vous du fromage puant.* Something about cheese. Sorry, my high school French is shot. Nigel, what does this mean?"

The chief of staff took a look at the slip of paper and laughed. "It says, 'Beware of stinky cheese.' Your mirror is haunted by a French ghost who just happens to work at the FDA. Don't you see, Patty, it's not a ghost at all. It's your subconscious mind, giving you a daydream, that's all."

"It could be your subconscious. That does happen," Clint said. "Or it could be you have a ghost here who knows French."

"But I barely know any French anymore. Why wouldn't it write to me in English?" Patty asked.

"If it is a ghost, he's trying to send you a personal message," Clint replied. "Ma'am, have you been dealing with something French? Or something to do with cheese?"

"Yes! French cheese! That's amazing! How could you possibly know that?"

Nigel rolled his eyes.

Clint smiled knowingly. "I thought so. That's what we in the ghost business call a DPC, ma'am. A directed paranormal communication."

"Heavens to Betsy, what's that?"

"A directed paranormal communication is a message tailored to a specific recipient instead of just anybody," Clint replied. "Sometimes the spirits want to let you know they're watching you—just you—so they use something only you know about. That's so you'll pay close attention to their messages and what's going on around you. Your ghost is giving you a heads up, telling you to expect more messages."

"Oh, no, you mean it's going to happen again? Will the messages be on my mirror?"

"Not necessarily. They could be anywhere. Ghosts have lots of ways of communicating with us, although they do have a weird fondness for mirrors. They like to write on them and appear in them too."

"Is there anything that will keep them out of my bedroom, some kind of ghost repellent or something?" Patty asked.

"No, ma'am, unless you want to try folk remedies. Some say sprinkling salt around a room will ward off ghosts. Personally, I doubt it. There's no science behind salt."

Patty crossed her arms. "Salt? Well, it couldn't hurt to sprinkle a little salt here and there, could it? I'll have Mr. Twiggs get the housekeepers to spread some salt around the room."

"You must be kidding," said Nigel. "That's superstition."

"I don't care what it is. If it keeps ghosts away, it's all right with me," Patty replied. "And another thing—Clint here is clearly an expert on ghosts. We need him on our team. Maybe he can use his expertise to figure out what's going on in this nut house."

Nigel shook his head. "It's nothing but your vivid imagination. But if it will ease your mind, I'll call the director and arrange for Clint to be transferred to us temporarily from the FBI. We'll put him over in the Eisenhower Building."

"No, the ghost problem isn't over there. Get him an office right here—in the West Wing—and give him all the support he needs. I want him to get to the bottom of this ghost business, and fast."

Nigel closed his eyes for a moment and let out a groan. "All right, have it your way. My God, I can't believe we're hiring a ghost hunter."

CHAPTER 6

A Letter of Instruction

JEFFERSON WATCHED NERVOUSLY from a window as a crew of six men entered the Rose Garden, equipped with heavy gloves and pruning clippers. One of them caught his left foot on a tree root and stumbled headfirst onto a boxwood shrub, breaking off two of its branches.

The ghost's hand flew to his chest as if he'd been stabbed in the heart. "Oh, the clumsy oaf," he muttered. "He'll trample the poor plants to death if he carries on stomping around like that." He jotted down an entry in his gardening notebook: "February 25. Winter pruning of roses commences. Workmen most unsatisfactory, as usual."

"Ahem. What are you doing there, Jefferson?" said a lispy voice behind him.

It was Adams.

Jefferson shut his notebook and slipped it into his coat pocket. "Observing the annual damage to the garden, to my horror. Those butchers down there are getting a late start on the winter pruning, and they're already wrecking the shrubbery. The musk and damask roses have barely recovered from last year's trimming. Do you recall how Mrs. Madison reacted when she saw what they had done?"

Adams laughed. "Yes, I hope she doesn't do that again."

Mrs. Madison had shown up the next day when the workers were mulching the flower beds, raised a blood-curdling howl, and sent them running for their lives. The gardening contractor had to hire a new crew to finish the job.

The first lady regarded the roses as her personal property, inspected them daily during the growing season, and stood ready to haunt any bungler who dared abuse them.

Jefferson, an avid gardener himself, was sympathetic. "A well-kept garden is so rewarding, so ethereal and stimulating. Every spring gladdens my heart with the great progress that has been made in the development of new and better varieties. The perfection of them bodes well for our species, I believe, Mr. Adams, for if even a rose can be improved upon, there must be hope for us humans too."

"Why, it is on that very point of improving humans that I have some business in coming to see you, Thomas," said Adams.

"About what?"

"I was curious to know what progress you have made with Mrs. Pitypander."

Jefferson rubbed his forehead. "Alas, I have nothing good to report to you. I'm quite at a loss to know what to do about her."

"How so? Has she not responded to your efforts at all?"

He looked vacantly out the window at the water fountain bubbling on the South Lawn. "Not in the least. I've strewn her path with worthwhile books to read, but she spurns them in favor of romantic novels. I've scrawled messages on her bathroom mirror, but she doesn't comprehend them. Honestly, women are hard enough to communicate with when one can approach them forthrightly. I haven't any idea how to instruct a woman on the sly."

"I was afraid of this," said Adams. "Madison's insistence that you not appear before Mrs. Pitypander unless necessary seems an unfair encumbrance to your efforts. But I've been thinking about how you might get around the problem."

"How?"

The old man clattered across the floor with his cane, holding his finger to his cheek the way he always did while making a subtle legal distinction. "I noticed that Madison did not say you should not communicate with Mrs. Pitypander. He merely opined that you should not appear before her. That leaves you a bit of room to wiggle, doesn't it?" He smiled knowingly at Jefferson.

The old lawyer was looking to find a loophole in the Rules so he could get his way. It was just like him.

"Surely you aren't proposing that I speak to her while I am invisible," said Jefferson. "A disembodied voice coming out of the walls would send the lady into a panic."

"Yes, I am sure it would," Adams replied. "But it seems you have already done that—so much so that she has employed a young man to investigate us."

So that was it. Adams was worried about the young FBI agent who had been brought in to search for ghosts. He wanted to make sure Jefferson didn't do anything unnecessarily risky.

"All right, what is your suggestion?"

Adams had come armed with a plan. "Given the difficulty of speaking to Mrs. Pitypander under the Rules, you might try writing her an anonymous letter instead. Or, better yet, a series of letters, each containing a pertinent lesson to improve her mind. If she finds them acceptable, she can read them at her leisure. That approach sounds more likely to succeed than throwing books at her. It should be less frightening for her and healthier for the books, don't you agree?"

Jefferson slapped the side of his head. Why hadn't he thought of that? There was no need to confront Mrs. Pitypander. He could educate the new president simply by writing her some helpful letters. "Yes, I think you're on to something there, Mr. Adams. I'll give it a shot."

THE ROLL OF white paper on the Resolute Desk was tied with a red bow. Patty studied it for a few seconds, wondering who had put it there and why. The Oval Office was a high-security area, guarded around the clock by the Secret Service, and only the housekeeping staff were allowed to enter the room overnight. Things didn't just show up on the president's desk out of nowhere.

Nonetheless, there it was, waiting for her. She thought of calling in her secretary for an explanation but decided not to bother. It didn't look dangerous. Patty picked up the roll and untied the bow. Ten unruled white sheets, covered with handwriting, unfurled.

"It's a letter," she said to herself, flipping through the pages. "But who writes a letter like this?"

The letter was dated the previous day and written in a small, neat hand in thick black ink. Patty began to read it:

My Dearest Madam President,

Please forgive this strange mode of introduction. It is with the greatest reluctance that I find myself compelled to greet you in this roundabout way, but I know no other permissible means of obtaining your attention. With this epistle, I mean to begin a course of helpful instruction for you which will, I hope, acquaint your mind with the fundamental precepts of republicanism that have formed the basis of government in the United States of America from its felicitous founding in 1776 to the present day.

A free people can remain free only through education in the art of government, which must start with a deeply rooted understanding of history. Good government never did happen by accident, but has always been the fruit of learning about the many mistakes made in the past, including the ancient past, dating back to Greek civilization. As the Greek tragedian Aeschylus instructs us, "Πάθει μάθος," or in English, "There is learning in suffering." Thus, we learn most painlessly when we heed the painful errors of our forebears, rather than repeating them. In this simple truth consists much of the value of history.

The writer wanted to acquaint her mind with the principles of republicanism? "What the hell?" said Patty, mystified.

The letter went on for ten pages, tracing the development of democracy over twenty-five centuries, from ancient Greece to the upheavals of the Roman Republic, to the Magna Carta and the English Revolution. It ended with the theory of natural law expounded by John Locke in his landmark work, *Two Treatises of Government*. The author of the letter concluded:

Our brief journey through the history of democracy has brought us to the revolutionary ideas of Locke, who showed how the right of men to govern themselves derives not from any king, potentate, dictator, or government but solely from God by virtue of the divine law of nature. It is this inalienable birthright which gives rise to any people's right to reclaim the management of their government and reorganize it entirely for their own benefit at any time.

Madam President, I do hope you have found this initial missive edifying, and I look forward with fond hope that you may eagerly await the next.

Respectfully,
Anonymous

Patty stared at the letter for a moment, picked up the phone, and summoned Nigel.

The chief of staff paced the floor as he perused the letter. "I must say, this is an interesting mystery indeed."

Patty could almost see the gears turning inside Nigel's head as he analyzed the writing. "Who do you think wrote it?"

Nigel held the letter up to the sunlight coming in from the window, examining the paper itself for any identifying marks. "This looks like ordinary copy paper, and I see nothing unusual about it. However, the text contains some clues, particularly the archaic sentence structure and writing style."

He reread the letter's opening paragraphs. "Anonymous purports to be classically educated, as he quotes Aeschylus in ancient Greek. The views expressed suggest a man of the Enlightenment and an advocate of the tenets in the Declaration of Independence. He has a strong fondness for the philosophy of John Locke. Offhand, I would say our culprit is some kind of prankster pretending to be someone from the eighteenth century."

"Why would someone pretend that?"

"This person is clearly unhinged."

"You don't think it's a ghost?"

"Of course not," Nigel replied. "That's silly. Ghosts don't exist. And if they did, why would a ghost go to the trouble of writing you a letter when he could simply walk through the wall and tell you what he wants you to know?"

"I have no idea. Why would a ghost write in French on my bathroom mirror and make a book jump off my shelf?"

"I'm not convinced that happened," said Nigel.

"Well, I am." Patty reached into the Resolute Desk, pulled out a salt shaker, and proceeded to shake salt on the floor.

"What in the blazes are you doing?"

"Warding off ghosts," she said, sprinkling salt all around the desk. "Some people say salt gets rid of ghosts. Maybe if I do enough of this, they won't bother me anymore." She gave a few extra shakes to the area near the windows, in case any ghosts tried to sneak up behind her.

"Have you gone daft?" Nigel hovered over her, looking at her sideways. "There are no such things as ghosts, I tell you. A conman of some sort is engaging in some devilry here, trying to fool you into believing in him. Forget the letter—I'm much more concerned about the security breach it represents. An intruder has entered this room. Instead of a letter, he could have left a bomb. Think about that."

"Believe what you want, Nigel. I want Clint's opinion."

"This is a matter for the Secret Service, not some wacko ghost hunter."

"Fine, get them in here, too. But first, I want to talk to Clint. Please call him."

Clint arrived within minutes and read the letter.

"I have a hunch who it might be," said the young FBI agent. "The handwriting is the most obvious clue. Let's start there. I'll Google it."

Clint pulled out his phone and typed something onto the screen with his finger. He looked at his phone and then at the letter.

After making a few entries, he found a match. He held out his phone for Patty to see.

She squinted at the screen. It was a photograph of an old letter.

"Compare the handwriting. They're the same," he said. "It's Thomas Jefferson. He's the one who wrote this."

Nigel made a face. "Oh, please. That proves nothing. It's a clever forgery, made to look like Jefferson's writing. Whoever wrote this letter simply copied Jefferson's style. Anyone can find one of his letters online as easily as you did. It's a hoax."

Clint stood his ground. "Maybe, but it could also have been written by a ghost. We could send the letter to the FBI lab to have a handwriting expert verify it's Jefferson's. In the meantime, I could go looking for his ghost, if you'll let me."

"Of course, I want you to," said Patty insistently. "That's why we brought you in. Nigel doesn't mind, do you, Nigel?"

The chief of staff bit his tongue.

Clint's eyes zeroed in on the corgis curled up near the fireplace. "Can I borrow your dogs?"

"Borrow them?"

"I'm not done perfecting my ghost sensors, and dogs can sometimes feel the presence of ghosts. Your corgis barked at the bookcase when the book jumped off the shelf, so they might make good ghost hunters. Could I borrow them for a couple of hours?"

"By all means." Patty reached into the Resolute Desk, pulled out a pair of dog leashes, and handed them to him.

"Canine ghost hunters, in the White House no less," Nigel grumbled. "Now I've seen everything."

CHAPTER 7

HUNTING FOR GHOSTS

CLINT CLIPPED THE president's leashes onto Cain and Abel's collars and walked the corgis to the Oval Office bookcase. Cain looked up at the clamshell molding above it and stuck his nose in the air but gave no sign that anything was wrong. Abel was disinterested in the bookcase and started wandering away from it.

Clint led the dogs around the room twice. They sniffed at the furniture but didn't bark or growl or seem to notice anything out of the ordinary.

No ghosts in the Oval Office.

The young FBI agent steered the dogs out the door and turned right, past the office of the president's secretary, checking his map of the West Wing.

Starting at the Cabinet Room, Clint walked the dogs through every office and meeting room, making a circuit around the West Wing's second floor. At every door, he was greeted by puzzled looks from White House staff.

Secret Service agents stopped him along the way to ask what he was doing. He flashed his badge, told them he was giving the president's dogs some exercise, and they waved him on.

Tugging at the dogs' leashes, Clint exited the West Wing lobby and strolled along the West Colonnade to the mansion. There had to be ghosts somewhere in there.

At the Entrance Hall, he climbed the stairs to the Residence's second floor and strolled down the Center Hall, making his way through the Treaty Room, the dining room, the kitchen, and the president's bedroom suite.

When he reached the Lincoln Bedroom at the east end of the building, the dogs suddenly reacted. Both refused to take another step, stopping cold outside the doorway.

Abel struck a fighting pose, pawed at the air, and barked furiously. Cain crouched down and growled at the bed.

"What is it? What do you see, boys?" Clint pulled on their leashes. "C'mon, let's go inside."

The dogs would not budge. Clint yanked harder, but it was no use. He would have to look the room over by himself. He tied the leashes to the doorknob so the dogs couldn't run away and stepped inside the mysterious chamber.

The Lincoln Bedroom was like a one-room museum, decorated to look as it must have at the time of the president's assassination in 1865. A massive mahogany bed featuring an elaborately carved headboard over eight feet tall dominated the space, backed by light yellow wallpaper with a brown diamond pattern. Against a side wall stood a mirrored dresser. Above it hung a portrait of Lincoln, his glum visage gazing down as if to ward off intruders. Golden curtains with fancy gilded cornices framed the windows. A gold camelback sofa, paired with a circular marble-topped table, offered seating.

It was as if the martyred sixteenth president had just gotten up to get a cup of coffee, ambled out of the room, and might return at any moment.

An eerie presence pervaded the place. The curtains shifted slightly, as if wind was blowing through the windows, yet the windows were closed tight. A shiver ran down Clint's back. For all he knew, Lincoln might still inhabit the room at that very moment, watching his every move.

So many years and presidents had come and gone, and yet Lincoln's ghostly existence was still palpable. Unseen and hiding, his past lingered, ready to resurface from behind the Victorian wallpaper.

It was as if 1865, the year of Lincoln's assassination, wasn't dead but only sleeping and might reawaken anytime. History had been recreated and resuscitated in this room. Its indelible marks on the present waited patiently to be rediscovered, unperturbed that it had been temporarily forgotten or misinterpreted.

A ghost hunter had to be attuned to history, to feel it in his bones. The past was what he was really looking for.

The past itself was a ghost. It disappeared, reappeared, but never really went away. It lurked everywhere, watching the present unfold in an infinite parade, constantly adding to itself with every irreversible tick of the clock.

A high-pitched sound suddenly pierced the walls. Clint turned his ear toward it and determined that it must be coming from somewhere down the hall. He listened for a moment and realized it was classical violin music. Who would play the violin on the White House's second floor at this time of day?

He unfastened the leashes from the door and led the dogs back down the Center Hall, following the sound. It grew louder with every step he took. He looked left into a large room with curved yellow walls.

The music ceased. The space appeared to be empty.

Clint checked his map. It was the Yellow Oval Room, in the middle of the mansion. He grabbed his phone and scrolled through his notes, looking for his list of past White House ghost sightings.

He found the reference: Jefferson had been seen playing his violin here. It was his favorite hangout.

If Jefferson were in the White House, he might be sitting somewhere in this very place. Yet Clint saw nothing.

The corgis yanked on their leashes, pulling the junior agent inside. Their eyes were fixed on a golden settee in front of the center window. He stepped slowly toward it.

"What is it, boys? Do you see him?"

The corgis growled in unison at the settee but kept their distance.

Through the windows, Clint saw the curved Truman Balcony, which looked out over the South Lawn, with its water fountain. Beyond was the Ellipse, the Washington Monument, and, in the distance, the Jefferson Memorial. What a thrill, to think what history had happened on the very spot where he stood, made by all the famous people who had lived here once.

And what if they were still here, waiting?

Jefferson was in this room. Clint could feel his presence. He looked down at the dogs. "What do you think, boys? I'll bet he's just waiting for us to leave so he can get back to playing his fiddle."

CHAPTER 8
Peddling Influence

THERE WAS A knock at the door of the Oval Office. Patty put down the report she was reading and wilted at the sight of Benny standing in the doorway, wearing a rust-colored suit, a yellow shirt, and a glowing green tie.

"Hi, Doll," he said with a grin.

Patty watched in dismay as he waddled inside and plopped himself down in a chair like he owned the place. "How did you get past my secretary?"

Benny lifted his shoulders in a half-shrug. "Doll, they don't stop the First Gentleman from dropping in to see his wife. It's not like I need a badge or an appointment or something. I'm family. They know who I am, and they let me in, that's all."

A gentleman? Hardly. Benito Pitypander from Jersey City was a low-class, self-worshiping vulgarian—Las Vegas personified. Flashy, pretentious, and vacuous, the so-called Casino King erected fifteen-foot statues of himself at his lavish resorts. His greasy black hair and owly brown eyes sent shivers down her spine.

She had trouble deciding whether it was Benny's absence or his presence that irritated her more. While she had been running for the presidency, instead of being at her side, he had been gallivanting around the globe, endangering her campaign by doing shady business deals with America's foreign enemies.

He had bothered to attend her inauguration only because he wanted to bask in the glow of her victory. Being First Gentleman would add to his own mystique. She had wanted him there for the sake of appearances.

The supposed power couple of Patty and Benny Pitypander was a sham, the shriveled husk of a former relationship. Over the years, their marriage had degenerated into a cynical bargain: He made her rich, and she connected him to the ruling elite. Divorce, they both tacitly understood, would benefit neither of them. They both had their own public image to consider.

Patty thanked her lucky stars that they never had children. Any child of theirs would be just another sham, an insecure mess torn asunder by the opposing centrifugal forces of greed and power that Benny and Patty embodied.

Now that Patty was living in the White House goldfish bowl, with the merciless eyes of the world trained on both of them, Benny was no longer just a minor irritation. His crooked business practices made him a direct and growing threat to her political future.

To protect herself, she would have to give Benny some boundaries. For starters, no more barging into the Oval Office. From now on, the mogul would have to make appointments to see her like anybody else.

Benny ran his pudgy fingers over the arm of the sofa. "By the way, who was that kid I just saw walking out of here? Your latest boy toy? How old is this one? Old enough to shave, I hope."

"Just an employee, bringing my dogs back after a walk," Patty replied.

Benny smirked. "Yeah, I'll bet."

She glowered at him. "I still don't know what you're doing here, but I have a sick feeling I'm about to find out."

He reclined in his chair, his hands cradling his head. "I'm just back from the Middle East, and I thought we could discuss a little problem I'm having over there."

A little problem—she had heard that before. As governor, Patty had spent half her time solving Benny's little problems and the other half covering her tracks so she wouldn't be indicted for them.

"It's my new casino in Qatar," he said. "The place is almost finished, but the government bureaucrats there are holding up the approval. They want more money—fifty million more. They think their approval should be worth more just because you're president. Since it's all your fault, I came to see you to get it fixed."

Her political career was once again interfering with his sprawling business operations, and he thought that was her responsibility. "I'm sorry to have messed up your business deal by becoming president," she said without the least regret.

"Apology accepted." Benny put his feet up on the coffee table. "But there's a way you can make it up to me, Doll."

"Oh, how is that? I'm just dying to know."

"Meet with the emir, Sheikh Abdullah. Put the squeeze on him for me."

It was so typical of Benny. Somebody was standing in his way and needed to be pressured. Patty had lost count of how many officials in California she had strong-armed for him.

"You know I can't do that."

He dismissed her with a flick of his hand. "Sure you can. You have a million ways to do it. Just move an aircraft carrier off their coast. Or threaten to close down our Air Force base there, or ask to renegotiate a mutual defense pact. You don't even have to call the emir yourself. Have somebody like the Secretary of Defense do it. The emir will get the message."

To hell with the emir. Benny hadn't gotten *her* message. Everything was different now. There could be no more influence peddling. She had barely gotten away with doing him favors when she was in Sacramento.

"I'm not risking my presidency for your damn casinos."

"But Doll—"

"Forget it. Not gonna happen. I'm going straight. This is gonna be a clean administration. Washington is not Sacramento on the Potomac. I won't let it be."

Benny puckered his lips into a pout. "A clean administration. You're going to reform Washington. Well, isn't that nice? Hey, I'm your husband. Aren't I entitled to something for all I've been putting up with? I told you not to run, but you wouldn't listen. Now look what's happening. You become president, and suddenly, everybody wants a piece of me. The IRS is crawling all over me. The press is following me everywhere. Your political enemies are setting traps for me. I can't take a crap without some paparazzi snapping my picture. This presidency thing may be peaches and cream for you, but it's all downside for me."

"Tough. Suck it up. Be a real gentleman for once."

"Just a little squeeze on the emir is all I'm asking for. A teeny weeny squeeze."

"No. Forget it. I'm not getting involved."

"Ah, crap, you're useless." Benny waved his hand at her. "Why do I bother with you? Forget I ever came here." He got up to leave.

As he walked to the door, Patty thought she heard something in the distance. It was music. "Do you hear that?"

"Hear what?"

"That music. I wonder where it's coming from."

"I don't hear a thing. It's your imagination again. You live in a fantasy world, I tell you. The doctor told you to stop reading all those stupid romance novels. They've made you crazier than ever."

Benny stalked out of the room.

Good riddance.

There was the music again. It sounded like someone was playing a violin in the Rose Garden. She got up from the desk and looked through the window, but there was no one down there.

Maybe I am going crazy.

She looked outside again, and still nobody was there. Yet she could hear the music anyway, loud and clear.

VICE PRESIDENT SARTINI'S eyes wandered across his desk to the framed photo of his wife Julia and his three small boys. The vice presidency, she reminded him every morning over coffee, was a perfect stepping stone to the Oval Office, and to fatten his political resume, he should be content to tolerate the ennui of being vice president. Only thirty-eight, he could afford to bide his time.

If only he had the patience. The idea of wasting four to eight years in the prime of his life playing second fiddle to a light-weight like Patty Pitypander was becoming more intolerable by the day. Was the vice presidency truly "not worth a bucket of warm spit," as the saying went?

Sartini had gambled that the position was much more valuable than that. It had better be. He wasn't born to play a merely ceremonial role. He was a doer, not a bench sitter.

He bristled at suggestions by political pundits that it was not his merit but his obscurity that had motivated Patty to pick him for her running mate. A harmless nonentity, a walking blank slate, he was the only candidate in the primaries with no national constituency. Labeled by the press as "Tony Who," the glad-handing congressman from the third district of Ohio wouldn't overshadow her.

Tony Who?—Sartini would fix that.

The vice presidency, Patty had promised, would raise his visibility. He would be her junior partner, she assured him. The problem was, the payoff was too many years in the future. If only he could fast-forward the tape and hasten the process.

The president, to her credit, had at least invited him to attend many of her meetings. That was almost enough to make him feel important and satisfied, temporarily. In time, she might get around to giving him something meaningful to do, something bigger than attending state funerals.

Drowsy with boredom, Sartini looked up from his desk and noticed Benny Pitypander walking past the doorway of his office. Sartini waved at him.

Seconds later, Benny had done a U-turn, appearing in the doorway with a gleam in his eye.

"Hey, Tony, you got a minute?" Benny asked.

"For the First Gentleman, anytime," Sartini replied with an accommodating grin.

Benny shut the door and pulled up a chair. "Do you know Sheikh Abdullah of Qatar?" he asked in a voice just above a whisper.

Sartini had never heard of him. "No, what about him?"

Benny explained the problem he was having with Qatar's corrupt government officials and their demand for a bigger bribe.

Sartini leaned back in his chair and looked lazily out the window, fixing his eyes on the Washington Monument. "You're asking me to call him for you? Sorry, I don't think I can do that. The State Department would have a conniption. If that kind of high-level communication doesn't go through the proper channels, the bureaucrats around here will get their knickers in a twist. They'd feel like I had cut them out of the loop."

"Oh, no, of course, you couldn't call the sheikh himself," said Benny hastily. "Nothing like that. I was thinking of something a little more, um...indirect, like maybe you could schmooze with the Qatari ambassador and put in a good word for me. I think that would carry some weight, coming from the vice president."

"That's not as bad, I'll admit," Sartini replied. "Not as blatant."

"So, you'll do it?"

Sartini squirmed. "Gosh, Benny, I don't know. I could get in trouble with a certain lady down the hall. I assume you tried her first."

Benny's mouth tightened. "Yeah, I did. The problem is, Patty's got the nutty idea that she was elected to be a saint, and Saint Patty wants to run a 'clean' administration, whatever that is." He made air quotes with his fingers.

"Sure. We all do."

"What she hasn't realized yet is that Washington runs on favors even more than Sacramento does. Or she has realized it, but she can't bring herself to do a teeny little favor for her own husband because it would look like a conflict of interest and might get blown up by the press into an enormous scandal. Oh, she's so crazy, that woman."

"Crazy? How so?"

Benny looked down at the floor. "Ah, I shouldn't say. It's private stuff."

"Sure, I understand."

Benny paused for a moment. "No, doggone it. Why shouldn't I tell you? You're gonna find out eventually."

"If it's private stuff, don't tell me, Benny. I don't want to know what I shouldn't know. Worrying about other people's secrets is too much of a burden."

Benny drummed his fingers on the armrest of his chair. "No, on second thought, I want to tell you. Come to think of it, I *have* to tell you. It's a matter of national security. As vice president, you need to know."

"Wow, national security? Is it that bad?"

"Isn't the president being crazy a national security risk?"

"I would sure think so," Sartini replied. "Depending on how crazy she is, of course."

"Okay, then. I'll let you decide. Did you know she has wild fantasies? Do you know she even went to see a shrink about them?"

Sartini's eyelids stretched wide. "No. You don't say."

Benny leaned forward and lowered his voice. "Yeah, during the campaign, Patty was wigging out under the stress, and she started having conversations with a character in one of her romance novels. Her name was Jenessa, as I recall. Patty would see this Jenessa character appear in front of her out of the blue, and Jenessa would start talking to her, giving her advice. And Patty would actually follow the advice, like Jenessa was a real person!"

"No kidding."

The Casino King's eyes narrowed into slits. "Her doctor said she suffers from 'fantasy-reality confusion.' He advised me to take her novels away from her, but you know Patty—she simply refused to give them up and told me to mind my own business. She's addicted to them, like a chain smoker, only with paperback books. She says they help settle her nerves. Most people in her situation would just take Xanax, but she doesn't want to get hooked on drugs."

"Can't blame her for that. Reading novels is less toxic than taking mind-altering drugs, I guess. So, what did you do about this?"

Benny flung his hands into the air. "I did what any red-blooded patriotic American would do—I tried to talk her out of running for president. But she wouldn't listen to me. The woman is way too stubborn for that. Being her husband, I couldn't speak out against her publicly. I had to just hope Diebold would beat her so the problem would go away by itself. But somehow, she beat him, with the help of that Windborne wiseass, and now we have a lunatic in the White House who talks to people who aren't there. How do you like them apples?"

"Fantasy-reality confusion—I've never heard of that," said Sartini. "It sounds like paranoia. I guess that would be a national security issue—for instance, if she thought the country was being attacked, but it wasn't, she could start a nuclear war over nothing, couldn't she?"

"Yeah, something like that. As president, there's no telling what she could do. Her delusions could get us all killed."

"Gosh, I had no idea Patty had a potentially disabling mental disorder," said Sartini, rubbing his cheek. "I sure hope it doesn't affect her behavior here."

"But enough about her problem. Let's get back to mine. Do you think you can help me in Qatar?"

Sartini's expression eased, forming a smile for his new friend. "Sure, Benny, I'll see what I can do."

CHAPTER 9

THE SPEAKER

SPEAKER OF THE House of Representatives Iris Underdown, a mountain of a woman with short brown hair and bangs, pounded into the Oval Office, all smiles.

Nigel had warned Patty about Underdown. As speaker, she controlled which bills reached the House floor for a vote, picked who was on key committees, and oversaw the rules of order. She could turn a president's budget into confetti. Nothing got through Congress without her help. Freshman congressmen groveled at her feet.

"We absolutely must have this woman on our side," Nigel insisted. "Whatever you do, don't piss Iris off."

Vice President Sartini agreed. "I had a few nasty run-ins with her when I was in Congress and learned my lesson. She's a female Jabba the Hutt. To earn her respect, you'll have to take command right off the bat and let her know who's boss. If Iris thinks you're a weakling, she'll eat you for breakfast in one gulp."

Eat me for breakfast? Not likely.

That didn't make sense. Underdown was a fellow feminist and should be a natural ally.

The speaker lowered her plump body into a stuffed chair across the coffee table. She poured herself a cup of coffee and gave Patty a big grin. "What can I do for you, dearie?"

"Well, Iris, we have a long list of things we'd like to get done in this Congress, and I'd like to get started on them," said Patty.

Underdown inspected her fingernails. "Oh, yeah? Such as?"

Patty recited her campaign pledges to reform America, beginning with her most controversial one: She had proposed that Americans shouldn't have to pursue happiness all by themselves. The federal government would guarantee happiness by setting up a vast new department. Although Diebold had ridiculed the idea, it polled so well that Patty had made it the centerpiece of her campaign. Fifty-four percent of registered voters wanted government to make them happy. Among voters who didn't pay taxes—half the electorate—the figure was eighty-five percent.

"So, my first order of business," said Patty, taking a sip of coffee, "is to make everybody happy." She ticked off a list of items her new Department of Happiness would need: an eight million square foot headquarters building, twenty-five regional offices around the country to handle citizens' complaints about their unhappiness, one hundred eighty thousand happiness agents, and a couple of trillion dollars to fund the department's happiness outreach and enforcement activities. "Once we've made everyone happy, we can move on to other things, like abolishing the states. Or, if you prefer, we could do the states first."

"Whoa, whoa, time out." The speaker made a T with her hands and leaned toward Patty, gasping for breath. "Are you completely nuts? Eight million square feet? Two trillion dollars? That's more than twice the Pentagon's budget! Where's the money coming from for all this happiness? Don't you know inflation will soar with all that spending? You didn't actually mean all that B.S. you said in the campaign, did you?"

Patty drew back, startled at the surprise on the speaker's face. Didn't Underdown understand the Better America agenda? "Why, yes, of course I meant it, Iris. That's the platform I got elected on. And now, with your help, we're going to implement my plans. So, here's what I want you to—"

Underdown sank into her chair, slapped her ample thighs, and guffawed. "Honey, I hate to be the one to burst your bubble, but there is zero chance you're going to get any of that through Congress. A Department of Happiness? Are you kidding? And you think you can abolish the states just like that, by snapping your fingers? Oh, my, please tell me you know that's nuts."

Patty regarded the speaker with thinly veiled contempt. "What do you mean? I don't think it's nuts. The people who elected me didn't think so either. It's my job to get these things passed. And that's where you come in. Now—"

"No way!" Underdown's eyes flared. "First, my dear, slow down a minute. Let me set you straight about the election. You beat President Diebold by a few thousand votes because the party did some last-minute ballot finagling in Florida and Pennsylvania. You don't have a national mandate to do squat. In fact, if Harry Clement hadn't dropped out of the primaries because of his blackface scandal, the party wouldn't have nominated you to begin with, no matter how much money your rich husband gave you to run for president."

Patty's face grew crimson. Nothing made her angrier than the false charge that she had bought the White House with Benny's money. "Listen here, Iris. Benny didn't give me a thing, not one red cent, and I not only made it through the primaries without his help, I won the presidency all by myself!"

Underdown wagged her head. "No, honey, you didn't do it by yourself. The party just barely succeeded in pulling you over the finish line. Besides, it doesn't matter anymore how you won the presidency. That was last year. Check your calendar. The election is over. The inauguration is over. The parade is over. Now it's reality time. Nobody in this town gives a tinker's damn what pie-in-the-sky crap you promised on the campaign trail last year. Get real."

Patty's eyes bored into Underdown. "That's not true. The people care. They sent me here. I've come to Washington to do the people's business."

Underdown looked like she was ready to spit on the floor. "The people's business! Good God, how arrogant can you get? Listen, the people sent me here too, but unlike you, honey, I'm a shoo-in to be re-elected. Look, I'm gonna be brutally honest with you. To the party, you're nothing but a seat warmer to keep us in power and stave off the Republicans for another four years until we can swap you out for a qualified nominee in the next election. In the meantime, we're gonna work on *my* agenda, not yours, or else nothing will get through Congress and your legacy will be toast, got that?"

Patty and Nigel stared at each other, dumbfounded. The Pitypander agenda had smashed into a brick wall—a fellow Democrat, no less!

"But Iris, if you felt this way about Patty's agenda, why didn't you warn us during the election?" Nigel asked. "Why did you wait until now to raise your objections?"

"For Christ's sake, I didn't think you'd be sitting here!" Underdown thundered. "Nobody in Washington did. It still blows my mind that you jokers beat Diebold with such lame proposals. Department of Happiness—what a crock."

The four of them looked at each other in silence for a few seconds, trying to think of a way around the impasse.

Sartini, unfazed, offered a conciliatory grin. "So, Iris, what would you like us to do for you? How can we work together?"

Underdown folded her hands. "Ah, now there's a sensible attitude. Tony here understands how Congress operates."

She rattled off various federal grants she wanted steered to her congressional district. "And let's talk about the new Housing and Urban Development building they're putting up in downtown Chicago. The plan was to name it after Clement, but now that he's gone, I think it would be nice if it were named after me. Can you call HUD and make that happen, dearie?"

"Sure, we can try to arrange that," said Sartini. "But what are you going to do for us?"

"For appearance's sake, I'll keep some parts of your agenda in play—the few things I think have a prayer of getting passed—and I'll pretend all your silly Better America proposals are still under consideration so you can save face with your supporters long enough for them to forget all the nonsense you promised. I'm sure we'll find some common ground when budget time rolls around this fall."

"Thanks, Iris," said Sartini. "I think we can make this relationship work."

"No, thank you, Tony. I'm glad to see somebody in this building understands how bills actually get passed in this town."

CHAPTER 10

OUT OF THE BOOKCASE

WHAT WOULD HAPPEN to her grand agenda to transform America now, Patty wondered as she watched the sun set behind the clouds.

The day had been another long one, with one interminable meeting following another, forming a single blur of difficult people and intractable problems in her mind.

How unfair it was that a single obstinate woman like Iris Underdown could stand in the way of what millions of voters had sent her to Washington to accomplish for them. The speaker's demand to share power wasn't reasonable either. No one had elected Underdown to be president.

What was the point of being president if she could be so easily blocked by a single intransigent legislator? The power she had fought so hard for was being wrested out of her hands. Yet she could do nothing about the speaker except try to cooperate with her.

Every day furnished Patty with more proof that the presidency wasn't even close to what she had expected. It wasn't a throne, or anything like that, but a game of give and take, bluffing, pretending, persuading, bargaining, and commanding—an ever-changing game she didn't know how to play and didn't want to learn.

She looked at her watch: seven o'clock. Feeling close to collapsing, she opened the box of pizza left by the housekeepers, nibbled at a slice, and pulled out a wine glass and bottle of chardonnay from the Resolute Desk. A few sips later, her shoulders slumped comfortably, her muscles relaxed, and she felt at peace, as if her encounter with the speaker were all just a horrible dream.

She opened a drawer, grabbed her paperback novel, *A Bed Too Far*, and propped her feet on the desk. Turning to page one hundred, she began to read:

> Jenessa exhaled. Dirk had scolded her for interrupting his workout, but it was worth it, if only to remind him that she existed. She also got to see his sweaty torso, with his muscles rippling across his chest, as he thrust the barbell up and down, up and down, until he could do no more. He laid the barbell on the gym floor in a state of satisfied exhaustion.
>
> Was it strange of her to envy an inanimate object like a barbell, Jenessa wondered? The inescapable truth was that she did envy it. And why shouldn't she? After all, Dirk's barbell was getting action, and she wasn't.

"Oh, my," said Patty with a delighted grin. "That is so steamy."

She heard a long groan, like someone was in agony, and then a rattling noise. The corgis cocked their heads, ran to the bookcase, and barked and growled at it.

"Down, boys," she ordered. "Get back. Sit still and be quiet."

The dogs whimpered but complied.

Patty walked to the bookcase. There was nothing on the shelves that could rattle—just the usual bunch of boring old books.

Suddenly, a man's voice rose up from the wall behind the shelves. "I must do it, Adams. I've tried everything else with her. We have no choice. I'm going out there."

Patty jumped back. "Oh, my God. What is this?"

It all happened in less than a second.

Right before her, a human form stepped out of the bookcase, bathed in shimmering light. It was a man, a tall figure in a frock coat, wearing knee breeches and slippers. A full head of gray hair covered his ears and spilled down to his collar. His cheeks were ruddy, his nose was long and straight, and his eyes sparkled with intelligence.

Patty's jaw fell. A cold shudder shot down her back. "What the...who are you?"

The apparition stood erect, floated slightly above the floor, and bowed his head. "My name is Thomas Jefferson, madam. At your service."

Patty gasped. "*The* Thomas Jefferson? As in President Jefferson?"

"The very same, madam."

It had to be a dream. She touched her hands to her face to confirm that she was awake.

The bottle of wine lay on the desk where she had left it. The small amount she had imbibed couldn't give her a hallucination. She was sure she wasn't drunk. In fact, she was barely buzzed.

Yet there it was, standing before her—a presence, a figure, or...a ghost. She swallowed hard and struggled to speak but could barely get the words out. "That's impossible. You can't be Thomas Jefferson."

"I can't be? I assure you that I am, madam," replied the specter, "and for better or worse have been since 1743, though at present I am much diminished in substance, as you see."

"I...I..." Patty stammered.

The thing stepped closer. "I'm sure this is a great shock to you, Mrs. Pitypander, and I regret having to disturb your peace. Please understand that I mean you no harm."

Patty retreated to her desk and sat down. "But what...what do you want with me?"

The specter's face stiffened. "Only to assist you, madam, in the execution of your presidential duties. Nothing more than that."

"Assist me? But I don't need any help."

Staring at her, the ghost answered in a most gentlemanly tone of voice: "Ah, but you do. You require a great deal of assistance. Your evident unfitness for the presidency has been duly noted by my peers on the Council of White House Ghosts, and they have sent me to help you."

"The Council of what?"

"White House Ghosts, madam."

"There's a council of ghosts here?"

"Yes. All around here."

"What do you...I mean...how—?"

The apparition raised his hand slowly, as if trying to soothe her jangled nerves. "Do not be alarmed, madam. We are entirely peaceful and benevolent. As a demonstration of our good intentions, the Council has specifically requested that I instruct you on how to conduct affairs of state in this country."

Patty looked at him indignantly. "But that's crazy. Who are you to instruct me? I'm the president. I'm the one who decides who my advisers are."

Jefferson lowered his chin, his hands fumbling in his pockets. "Yes, of course you are. I assure you, madam, lest you think me presumptuous, it was not my idea to intrude on your prerogatives. Far from it. I am not the sort who enjoys meddling in the affairs of others, particularly when it comes to the fairer sex. I am merely doing my civic duty as a humble public servant, at the bidding of the Council."

There was that council again. Who in the dickens were they? Whoever they were, they had a lot of gall, disturbing her like this. "How did this so-called council of yours get here? Who put you here? How did you get past the Secret Service?"

Jefferson laughed. "So many questions! Our presence here is a complicated matter, madam. We do not understand how we got here ourselves. As for the Council, you might call it a sort of...what's the modern term? Alumni association, I believe. I am not at liberty to reveal more than that. You see, there are certain rules that we must follow regarding disclosing information to the living. That would be you."

Ghosts had rules? Patty looked around the Oval Office. "This is a joke, isn't it? That's it, somebody is playing a sick joke on me. You must be some kind of high-tech image."

Jefferson denied it. "No, madam, I am quite in earnest. The Council is of the opinion that you need instruction, as your proposed Better America reforms pose an unacceptable danger to the republic and our cherished American freedoms. There seemed to be no other option than to reform your thinking, which is the formidable task they have set before me."

Patty waved him off. "But there are no such things as ghosts. You're a figment of my imagination. I'm just exhausted. If I blink, you'll disappear."

She did blink—once, twice, three times, in fact—but the phantasm was still there, standing in front of her, as before.

"No, madam, blinking will do you no good. I am as real as that little mole on your neck. I will prove it to you." Jefferson turned and picked a book off the shelf. It was Marston's *Governing a Constitutional Republic*, exactly the same volume that had jumped onto the floor. "I am the one who caused this book to fall off your shelf. Here, on page five, is where you stopped reading."

It was page five. There was no denying it.

"You made it fall off my shelf? In heaven's name, why?"

Jefferson put the book back on the shelf. "In the fond hope that you would read it thoroughly and thereby become informed. But sadly, you did not. You prefer instead to fritter away your time reading vapid novels about lonely women hungering desperately for romance. If I may say so, madam, you ought to treat your time with more regard and waste no more of it on such idle pleasures. Did you at least read my recent missive on the historical development of democracy?"

"You're the one who wrote that?"

Jefferson grasped the lapels of his frock coat and looked at her proudly. "Yes, madam. It was a nice summation of the history of democracy, was it not?"

A ghost was writing letters to her! Patty put her hand to her forehead. "Sorry, mister ghost, I don't believe you exist, or your council either. I'm just seeing things, terrible things. It's the stress getting to me again, like my doctor warned. I've had such a hard day. I think I'm getting a headache."

Jefferson hung his head. "Oh, the frailty and illogic of women! I feared this would happen. I see I will need more proof to convince you. Fortunately, I came prepared for this." He snapped his fingers at the bookcase. "Mr. Adams and Mr. Jackson, could you come out from there, please? She doesn't believe we exist."

The ghost of another old man, this one short, rotund, and balding, floated out of the bookcase, dressed much like Jefferson. "Good evening, madam, I am John Adams," he announced with a lisp, bowing graciously. "How do you do?"

Patty recognized the next ghost who emerged from the shelves by his wild hair and sad-looking eyes. "Why, it's you—the man in the painting. You're Andrew Jackson, aren't you?"

Jackson scowled. "I am, lady, and I won't pretend I like what you've done with my portrait, either. Put me in a warehouse, will you? I don't think so. I'll box you up in a coffin and see how you like it." He raised his fist and shook it at her.

Patty screamed for the Secret Service, but before anyone could respond, the images of all three ghosts flickered and vanished into thin air.

CHAPTER 11
THE MOTION TO HAUNT

WHEN JEFFERSON WALKED into the ghost den, Adams was already there, sliding the speaker's podium box into place.

Knowing how the Potusgeists delighted in gossip, Jefferson was not surprised that this meeting was better attended than the last. The whole spectral community was eager to hear first-hand how miserably his attempts to educate the new president had backfired, and what he proposed to do about it.

Adams looked up and caught his eye. "You have your work cut out for you, Thomas. A number of them are saying our cause with Mrs. Pitypander is hopeless. I hope you can persuade them otherwise."

That wouldn't be easy. Many of the ghosts, having heard how stubborn the president was, were already growing skeptical of the reform effort and expecting it to come to grief. Jefferson assured Adams he would do his best to allay their concerns.

Adams tapped on a water pipe with his cane to start the meeting. The White House furnace shut off right on cue, making it easier to hear. "Order, order. Ladies and gentlemen, please give us your undivided attention. Mr. Jefferson has arrived and will now report on his meeting with Mrs. Pitypander."

Jefferson stepped onto the podium box and told them about his frustrating encounter with the new president. "Mrs. Pitypander not only rejected my help but even denied our existence, claiming she was seeing things because of overwork."

Madison lowered his brow. "Then the rumor is true? You did appear before her?"

Jefferson looked squarely into his friend's eyes. "I was forced to, sir. My attempts to educate her by stealth having failed, I concluded that if I was to have any hope of success, that I must speak directly to her and plainly explain my mission. What else could I do?"

The room was alive with murmurs. A ghostly confrontation with the living was always a serious matter.

Madison put his hand on his cheek. "Well, I hope you have something to show for the great risk you took. She is open to being instructed, then?"

Jefferson looked down glumly. "Not at all, sir. She is as obdurate as we feared. She thought I was an illusion resulting from her state of extreme exhaustion. And when I called forth Mr. Adams and Mr. Jackson to appear beside me to provide her with additional evidence of our existence, she became quite overwrought—so much so that she cried out in alarm for the guards to come to her aid. We thought it prudent to disappear before witnesses could arrive and lend credence to her story."

Madison's shoulders slumped. "Well, thank God for that. At least only one living person saw you. It is bad enough that she has seen three of us. What if you had been photographed?"

The ghosts traded looks of horror and stood frozen in silence. A photograph would be proof of an encounter. They would be exposed!

Madison laid his hand on his forehead, his face growing dark with worry. "This is a most grievous situation, fraught with danger. If we aren't careful, we may all be discovered to exist by the general public, and if we are—if it is proven beyond any doubt that the White House is actually haunted—we all know what mischief that would lead to. No longer would the living view us as the subject of fanciful ghost stories but as an immediate physical threat to the president and, therefore, to the whole country. It would be their duty to eradicate us."

Eradicate them! Could ghosts be eradicated? Not as far as anyone knew, but there was no telling what the living could do these days with their fantastic modern technologies.

"It's too bad George Washington can't be here," said someone in the crowd. "He'd have some sensible ideas about what we should do."

Washington couldn't be there because he had never lived at the White House, which wasn't finished until 1800, after he had not only left office but died. Alas, his spirit was assumed to be stuck roaming around his Mount Vernon estate, doing no one any good. Though Jefferson hadn't always agreed with Washington, he was the first to concede that at troubled times like these, the general's prudent leadership was sorely missed.

"You speak of mischief, do you?" cried out a small lady in a black mourning dress. "And well you should."

It was Mary Todd Lincoln. Everyone groaned.

"As far as I can tell," said Mrs. Lincoln, "this Pitypander woman is nothing but mischief from head to toe. They say she's very rich and spoiled and is no better than she should be. We should consider what mischief will ensue if we allow her to stay."

Madison gave the woman a contemptuous stare. "Yes, that is true enough, but I don't see your point, Mrs. Lincoln. What does that have to do with—"

"My point is, why do we tolerate her at all? Why can't we just drive her out of here now and be done with her?"

A tall, bearded man with a stovepipe hat and a craggy face rushed to her side. "Mary, you must know that is quite impossible. Mrs. Pitypander is the duly elected president, whether we like it or not. We've never yet forced a president to flee the White House. We've spooked a few, but never have we been so shamelessly brazen as to drive one out."

Mrs. Lincoln laid her hands on her hips. "Then I say it's high time we did. Anyone can plainly see this Pitypander woman is a born troublemaker. She'll only get worse if we allow her to remain. Why does she, of all women, deserve to be president? She thinks this place belongs to her. She's very high-handed and needs to be cut down to size. I'd cut her down to size, all right—with this." She drew out a knife and brandished it for all to see.

There was an audible gasp. "My goodness! Someone restrain her!" a voice cried out. "This is insupportable," said another.

Mr. Lincoln turned to the assembled ghosts with an embarrassed look on his face. "Mrs. Lincoln has not been well of late. My deepest apologies to all of you. Please forgive her outburst. We'll be going now, Mary. Come, dear." He held out his arm and led his wife through a stack of crates.

The ghosts heaved a sigh of relief at her departure.

Eleanor Roosevelt raised her hand. "See here, I think we ought to be kinder to poor Mrs. Pitypander, especially we ladies. I find this talk of driving her out not only inexcusably arrogant but entirely premature. I believe she can be reasoned with. You men have barely tried."

A woman in a white bonnet stood up. "I agree with Mrs. Roosevelt. We must be fair to her. Lady presidents are such a great rarity around here that we mustn't think of condemning her without overwhelming evidence. Let her prove herself or not. We'll have plenty of time to judge her worthiness for office later."

"My dearest Abigail," said John Adams. "We have every intention of being fair to Mrs. Pitypander. But we can't very well reform her if she doesn't believe we exist."

"And how, pray tell, shall we make her believe that, my dear husband?"

Adams leaned forward on his cane and smiled at her. "Why, that should be an easy task, my dear. We will simply haunt her until she acknowledges us. Once she is persuaded that we are who we claim to be, she is bound to be more receptive to listening to us."

Madison frowned. "If her mind is as fragile and unbalanced as you claim, haunting may do more harm than good. You might drive the president to distraction, and then where would we be? We could end up with another mad Mrs. Lincoln on our hands, except this one would be in office."

"No, we'll be right where we already are," Adams replied. "Mrs. Pitypander arrived here in a state of madness—madness for power. That is what we aim to correct. I propose that we perform some modest haunting exercises to gain her cooperation. If she continues to resist, we can escalate our haunting, at our discretion."

"At *whose* discretion?" Madison raised his booklet high above his head. "The Rules, remember the Rules, gentlemen. We all took an oath to abide by them, and it was for just such feverish moments as this that we adopted these restrictions on our passions. Remember our vow: We are not to harass the living except in a time of great peril for the country, and an overwhelming vote by the Council is required to do so."

He flipped to the appropriate page. "Here, I read from the

text: 'Article Seven, Section One, Paragraph Two. *Intentional Haunting of Wayward Presidents.* No ghost may intentionally haunt, hound, bedevil, beset, terrorize, or seriously annoy a living president or his family to influence his official actions without a three-fourths majority vote of the Council.'" He slammed his rulebook shut. "Those are the Rules we agreed to abide by, gentlemen."

Eleanor Roosevelt tilted her chin down and frowned. "Mr. Madison, has the Council ever actually invoked this article and authorized a haunting? What male president was ever subjected to such callous and frightening treatment as you men propose to inflict on poor Mrs. Pitypander? Tell me that."

"There is some precedent for a haunting, rare as it has been," Madison replied. "We haunted Lincoln pretty hard during the Civil War. It was a period of terrible upheaval for those of us on the Council. We were as divided as the country was. A group of us broke off from the rest, rose up, and didn't let Lincoln get much sleep for months."

"Yet he is no worse for wear despite the dark bags under his eyes," Adams pointed out. "Lincoln has turned out to be a model ghost and enjoys the most majestic monument on the Mall. I should be pleased to have been haunted if I were later remembered with a monument half as grand as his—alas, I have none to show for all my tireless work in founding this ungrateful country." He looked sternly at Jefferson, as if it were his fault that he hadn't gotten a nice monument.

Monument envy—oh, not that again. Let it go, Adams.

The old grump had been known to rant for an hour in Council meetings about the gross unfairness of not having his own monument or even a prominent Washington street named after him. But what did he expect? It served him right for being so cantankerous.

"Please, let us stick to the business at hand," Jefferson said quickly. "To address the problem of Mrs. Pitypander's willfulness, I make a motion that we vote to haunt her until she agrees to be educated."

"I second the motion," said Jackson. "And as soon as we have brought that woman to heel, I want my portrait put back on that damn wall in the Oval Office!"

As there seemed to be no other way to make Mrs. Pitypander pay proper attention to them, the motion to haunt carried easily.

CHAPTER 12

FIRST HAUNTINGS

THE OLD PAINTING on Patty's bedroom wall was not one of the many historical portraits that graced the Residence. It was just a landscape of the craggy coast of Maine, with a red and white lighthouse and a tall clipper ship sailing on the horizon.

She rarely noticed the painting and wouldn't have this night either, except for the fact that it had been hanging to the left of the door, but now it was on the right. Patty couldn't recall asking anyone to move it. The nail hole where the painting had been confirmed that she wasn't imagining things. The painting's location had changed.

She scanned the room, thinking that paintings didn't just move by themselves, when the lamps on her bedside tables flickered.

Cain and Abel jumped up from the fireplace and barked.

She walked over to quiet them. "Sit, boys. Be still."

The dogs paid no attention. Cain scampered to the window and growled. Abel ran to the door, raised himself on his hind legs, and pawed at it.

"That's strange. I wonder what that is." A disquieting feeling came over her. The room grew chilly.

The curtains in the bedroom billowed, as if blown inward by a gust of wind. Patty shuffled to the window to close it, but when she pressed down on the frame, she found it locked.

That was odd. The White House windows were bombproof and airtight. Wind couldn't pass through them.

She took in the peaceful scene outside on the South Lawn. There wasn't any weather to speak of, and the branches on the trees were still. The March storms had come and gone. All was peaceful outside.

Yet something had disturbed her curtains. If it wasn't the wind, what could it be?

"There are no such things as ghosts," Patty said to herself, a feeling of dread welling up within her. Just let the stress go, her therapist would tell her, and the terrifying fantasies would go with it.

There were three knocks at the door, each separated by a full second: "Knock...knock...knock." A woman's voice called out, "Madam President. Oh, Madam President. Let me in, won't you?"

"Who is it?"

It had to be a housekeeper. The staff knew her routine and often came just before her bedtime to ask if she needed any-thing. Patty cracked open the door a few inches, but nobody was outside.

"Hello, anyone there?" She waited a moment and called out again. There was no response.

She stuck her head through the doorway and peered into the West Sitting Hall. No one was there. Whoever had knocked must have left immediately.

"That's strange." She closed the door.

The staff wouldn't knock and run away. It couldn't be a prankster, not in the heavily guarded presidential suite.

Seconds later, three more knocks came, and again, Patty opened the door, but once again, no one appeared.

She noticed a Chippendale armchair with a red seat in the hall. A minute earlier, it had been positioned against the wall, but somehow it had moved. She kept her eyes trained on it. Ever so slowly, it glided across the oriental carpet, as if being dragged by an invisible force. Then, all of a sudden, it stopped cold right in the middle of the floor.

A moving chair! With a mind of its own!

Astonished, Patty watched the chair rise two feet into the air. It lingered there a few seconds, descended to the floor, and slid across the carpet again. It was inching directly toward her.

It's after me!

Patty slammed the bedroom door shut, locked it, and leaned her back against it, gulping three deep breaths.

It had to be her imagination. Chairs didn't move by themselves.

Just let the stress go, Patty. You can do it.

She decided to take a nice, warm bath to calm herself.

As she entered the bathroom, she felt a chill. It sent an uneasy shiver down her spine. The hairs on her forearms stood on end.

Relax. It's nothing. There's nothing in here.

She prepared the bath, filling the tub with warm water and adding a few drops of lavender oil.

A strange noise emerged from the bathtub—not a plumbing noise, but a low, guttural groan like a person in distress would make. The sound echoed ominously across the tiled room. Patty froze in place, her heart pounding with fear as she listened.

She watched with horror as the bathwater rippled, bubbled, and churned, as if agitated by some unseen force stirring beneath its surface. A human figure slowly formed, rising up from the water, complete with head, torso, and legs.

Her hands flew to her face. There, lying in her bathtub, was a man—an immense, obese naked man with a handle-bar mustache! He looked like he weighed well over three hundred pounds.

His spectral outline wavered in the dim light of the bathroom. His eyes glowed with an otherworldly intensity, and his moans filled the room with a weird resonance.

"Oh, help me," he called out to her. His thick hands gripped the sides of the tub as he struggled to raise his gigantic, blubbery body and get free of it.

Patty's breath caught in her throat as she stumbled backward. Her mind reeled with disbelief. She tried to scream, but no sound escaped her lips.

The apparition continued to thrash about in the water and holler for help.

"Oh, my God! Who the hell are you, and what are you doing in here?" Patty yelled.

"Thank goodness you've come to my rescue, ma'am," said the ghost in a deep, booming voice, his face contorted as if he were in pain. "My name is Taft—William Howard Taft. Say, would you mind calling a couple of men out there to help get me out of this damn thing? I'm stuck."

"You're stuck? In my bathtub?"

The ghost let out another moan. "Listen, lady, it wasn't my idea to get stuck. And what do you mean, *your* bathtub?" He gave her a curious grin. "How could it be yours? I'm the president."

"What? No, you're not! You're dead!"

The phantom took stock of his semi-transparent body, a look of amazement coming over his face, as if he had just discovered he wasn't alive. "Well, I'll be damned. How did I get here? It's not 1910 anymore, is it?"

"Of course not. It's the twenty-first century."

"Hmm, then I suppose you have a point. I do appear to be dead. And all this time, I thought I was back on the job." He turned his attention to the tub. "Where did this little thing come from? This tub is far too small for me. I had an especially big one put in, you know, so this wouldn't happen again. Confound it, they must have taken it out. When the dickens did they do that?"

Patty shrugged. "How the hell would I know?"

"Hmm, I don't suppose you would," said Taft. "I think there's been a terrible mix-up here. A thousand pardons, ma'am. I'll be getting out of your way now."

Patty considered screaming, but before she could utter a word, the outline of his vast form flickered. A second later, he was gone, and so was the bathwater.

She dashed out of the bathroom with her head swimming and grabbed the bed frame for support.

She could call the Secret Service, but the ghost had disappeared. Who would believe that she had just seen William Howard Taft in her bathtub—naked as the day he was born—and that he had just vanished into the ether? What would they think?

She ran to her phone and called Mr. Twiggs. Moments later, the chief usher appeared at her door.

"Mr. Twiggs," she said, still struggling to breathe. "I hate to bother you at this late hour, but I seem to be...I mean, I just saw..."

"You just saw what, Madam President?" the old gentleman asked, his brow furrowed with concern.

Twiggs was the grandfatherly type. Maybe the sweet old guy would understand. "You've been working in the White House for many years. Have you ever noticed anything odd around here?"

"Odd? What do you mean?"

"I mean...like...ghosts?"

Twiggs chuckled. "Oh, you mean the Potusgeists?"

He knew about them! Patty could confide in him without worrying that he'd think she was nuts. "You've seen them then?"

Twiggs turned his head left and right, as if afraid to be overheard, and whispered, "No, I haven't seen them myself. But my predecessor did, or so he claimed."

Twiggs told of an incident years ago when the previous chief usher had been working late. He heard someone knocking at the front door of the Entrance Hall. His office being just on the other side of the wall, he could hear the sound clearly. The man went out to the hall and saw that there were no guards on duty there, which by itself was most unusual. He opened the door, and standing before him was the glowing outline of a boy, perhaps eleven years of age. The chief usher could see right through him, like a thin cloud.

Patty gasped. "What did the boy want?"

"He claimed he was Willie Lincoln—you know, the Lincoln son who tragically died here. He had seen the lights on upstairs and wanted his father to stop working so hard and come downstairs and play with him."

"What did the head usher do?"

"He didn't know what to do. He closed the door in the boy's face. But that didn't stop Willie. The boy just walked right through the door and scampered up the stairs. He was never seen again."

"Do you believe the story?"

Twiggs rubbed his cheek. "I don't know if I do or not. If there are any ghosts rattling around here, they've mercifully left me alone. To tell you the truth, if I did see a ghost, I'm not sure I'd tell anybody, Madam President. People might think the wrong thing."

"Like you're crazy or something?"

"Yes," said Twiggs. "No president wants a crazy chief usher.

For that matter, it's not wise for anyone with an important job to admit seeing ghosts."

Certainly not the President of the United States.

Patty thanked Twiggs for coming and said goodnight.

She looked at her haggard reflection in the mirror above her dresser. "There are no such things as ghosts! There are no such things as ghosts!"

If only saying it over and over would make it so. Patty went to bed, tried hard not to think about ghosts, and after four hours of thinking of nothing else, finally fell asleep.

THE PREVIOUS NIGHT'S weird goings-on hung in Patty's mind like a bad dream. Undeterred, she had her breakfast and went about her busy schedule the next day as planned. A president didn't have time to fool with ghosts.

Her first appointment was a morning meeting with the French ambassador. He was coming to prepare the way for President Dubois before the upcoming state dinner, to ensure that there would be no embarrassing surprises.

"Greetings, Mr. Leclerc," said Patty cordially to the tall, white-haired Frenchman standing in the Diplomatic Reception Room.

Ambassador Leclerc, nattily dressed in a gray suit with a blue tie, possessed an air of refinement and dignity appropriate to his position. As they sat down on the room's yellow brocade chairs, Leclerc admired the antique wallpaper mural, with its sweeping blue and green panorama of scenes from American landmarks. "This is an interesting wall, is it not? Tell me, where are these places?"

Nigel knew all about the mural, noting that the wallpaper itself was French, produced by Jean Zuber in 1834. "There you can see New York Harbor, and over there West Point, and Niagara Falls, and Natural Bridge in Virginia."

Leclerc traced his finger over the wallpaper. "It was superbly done. I read somewhere that the streets of Washington were laid out by a Frenchman," he said with an impish smile. "On the way over here from the embassy, I saw you even have the bad French traffic to prove it."

"Quite so," Nigel replied cheerfully. "Pierre L'Enfant left his mark on this city. The avenues of Paris inspired his design. Consider yourself right at home, Ambassador."

Leclerc broached some key points of disagreement that needed to be ironed out before the French president arrived. He summarized his views, emphasizing the economic importance of the cheese industry to France, the great pride the French people took in it, and what a terrible shame it would be to let a little thing like cheese spoil over two centuries of friendship between the two countries.

As he spoke, Patty's eyes were abruptly drawn to the mural behind him.

"Is there something wrong?" Nigel asked.

"Uh...uh...no."

Her eyes grew wide.

A red liquid, with the color and consistency of blood, trickled down the walls. It seemed to come out of nowhere, dripping down from the crown molding.

It's not blood. It can't be. It's just your imagination. Relax.

Fingers of red stained the opulent mural with a macabre hue. Inch by inch, New York and Niagara Falls were soon engulfed in horrid red drips.

Patty's fists tightened. She felt like screaming, but no one else in the room seemed to see anything amiss.

Nigel, who was facing the mural directly, was unfazed. As the blood oozed, he conversed nonchalantly with Monsieur Leclerc, assuring him that the Pitypander administration was fully committed to resolving the trade dispute as soon as possible.

Monsieur Leclerc responded politely that he was much relieved to hear that.

Wasn't anyone aware of the chilling tableau unfolding behind the ambassador?

Press Secretary Colleen Cook, equally oblivious, diligently transcribed notes on her tablet, her brow folded in concentration. The Secretary of State, Milton Borders, was staring at Leclerc, unperturbed.

How was it possible that nobody else was seeing this?

Patty stifled her fear. She must remain composed despite her desperate unease.

A loud laugh echoed through the room, followed by the mournful howl of a wolf. The chandelier swayed overhead. The hands on the grandfather clock spun counterclockwise.

All this was happening without anyone noticing anything.

Meanwhile, blood continued to trickle down the walls, forming a grotesque pattern on the carpet at Patty's feet. In horror, she lifted her shoes off the floor.

"Are your feet bothering you, Patty?" Nigel asked.

She rubbed her calves. "Oh, no, I'm just getting some circulation going. All this sitting down in meetings cramps my legs sometimes."

Will this meeting ever end?

Leclerc, Borders, and Nigel finally stopped talking, agreeing on the principle that both sides would prefer to remove all trade barriers to both French cheese and American wheat.

At last, the meeting was over.

Forcing a smile, Patty thanked Ambassador Leclerc for his cooperative attitude and assured him of her commitment to maintaining excellent relations with France. The envoy departed.

She stole a fleeting glance at the blood-stained walls, which were still glistening bright red. There was the maniacal laughter again, taunting her.

A chorus of unnerving voices issued from the walls. "Mrs. Pitypander! Oh, Mrs. Pitypander!"

My God! Now the ghosts are calling me by name.

But that was impossible. There were no such things as ghosts. Blood did not drip from the walls. What Patty was seeing wasn't really there.

Let it go, Patty. Let the stress go.

She took in a deep breath, exhaled, and stumbled down the hall, heading to her next meeting. Nothing out of the ordinary was happening to her, and she absolutely, positively wasn't going insane.

CHAPTER 13
THE VIOLINIST

A**DEAD PRESIDENT IN** her bathtub, blood dripping down the walls—Patty wondered what she should expect next from the Potusgeists. What were they trying to do to her?

Her young ghost hunter would have some ideas. She called Clint to the Oval Office and asked what he had found in his investigation.

He told her the only ghosts he had detected so far were the ones Cain and Abel had sensed in the Lincoln Bedroom and Yellow Oval Room.

"Nowhere else?"

"Not yet, but that doesn't mean they aren't there," Clint replied.

Ghosts came and went pretty much as they liked, he said, and they didn't reveal themselves to just anybody. They were particular about who they haunted and why. The ghosts wouldn't have any reason to reveal themselves to him. He wasn't the president.

"Where are the ghosts most likely to show up?" Patty asked.

Clint said multiple studies of paranormal phenomena had concluded that ghosts were mobile, within limits. The scientific term was "zonally restricted." Elite ghosts, like the Potusgeists, could have several zones and haunt more than one place, usually houses that they had lived in.

"Then one of their zones could be here? Could the whole White House be a zone?" Patty asked anxiously.

"Well, we know they're not just in the Residence, since you saw a book jumping around right here in the Oval Office. Offhand, I'd say they could be anywhere on the grounds, since they lived on the entire property."

Patty imagined dozens of ghosts wandering across the South Lawn or through the Rose Garden with their arms outstretched like zombies. "Anywhere?"

"Yes."

Patty's heart sank. There was no sanctuary, no running away from these beings—not unless she wanted to move out of the White House, which was unthinkable. She had gone through so much to get here. It was her White House now. She would deal with the ghosts somehow.

Should she tell Clint what had happened since the jumping book incident? It might blow his mind to know how many bizarre things she had experienced already. Who else but the ghost hunter would believe her crazy stories?

Most importantly, would he keep her secrets?

She had to confide in somebody. Clint's dark brown eyes sparkled with youthful earnestness. Of course, she could trust him.

She revealed everything she had seen, from meeting Jefferson, Adams, and Jackson in the Oval Office to encountering William Howard Taft wedged in her bathtub to the blood-dripping incident in the Diplomatic Meeting Room.

Clint listened intently and jotted down notes on all of it, never once batting an eyelash. Nothing she described surprised him. He had heard it all in his years of collecting ghost stories from people just like her, all of whom thought they were going nuts.

"Jefferson is the one to focus on," Clint said in an analytical tone of voice, as if he were a doctor advising a patient. "He already told you why he's haunting you. He's been given a job to do. We need to learn more about all the presidents, but especially him."

"I had the same thought," Patty replied. "So, I asked my secretary to find me a historian to fill us in on some White House history. He's here now. I assumed you'd want to meet him." She called her secretary to show David Totten into the Oval Office.

Totten, a silver-haired man with a cleft chin, was a retired Navy captain turned history buff. A member of the White House Historical Society, he had converted his passion for history from a hobby into a full-time job, authoring several bestselling books about past presidents.

Patty asked Totten to brief them first about Thomas Jefferson.

The historian scratched his head. "Jefferson is a deep subject. I could talk about him for hours."

The third U.S. president, Totten explained, was the quintessential Renaissance man of the Enlightenment era. A polymath, he spoke or read eight languages, dabbled in architecture, agriculture, archaeology, horticulture, geology, linguistics, music, paleontology, and political philosophy, and invented a slew of practical things such as a letter copying device and the swivel chair. He began studying ancient Greek at five. He read the original texts of ancient Greek philosophers and poets for sheer amusement.

"Basically, Jefferson's mind was an intellectual vacuum cleaner," said Totten. "There wasn't much that didn't fascinate him. He was the most brilliant of our presidents. John F. Kennedy once told a room full of Nobel Prize winners that they were the most extraordinary collection of talent and human knowledge that had ever been gathered together at the White House, with the possible exception of when Jefferson dined alone."

Totten ticked off a list of Jefferson's political accomplishments. He served as a member of Virginia's House of Burgesses, delegate to the Continental Congress, governor of Virginia, ambassador to France, Secretary of State, Vice President, and President. He wrote the Declaration of Independence, doubled the size of the United States with the Louisiana Purchase, passed a groundbreaking law separating church and state, proposed the U.S. decimal monetary system, and, in his old age, founded and designed the University of Virginia down to the last brick and nail. That was only appropriate, as the man himself was a walking university.

"Those are just the highlights," said Totten. "Jefferson was a complicated fellow, full of contradictions. Although he was an aristocrat, he was also a champion of the common man. He condemned slavery and tried for many years to get enough political support to abolish it but failed. He did succeed in stopping the importation of slaves and the spread of slavery to the new territories of the Northwest, but he didn't free many of his own slaves. He couldn't maintain his Epicurean lifestyle without them. To make matters worse, he was a spendthrift. He enjoyed the good life a bit too much and died heavily in debt."

"When did he die?" Patty asked.

"In 1826, on the fiftieth anniversary of the Declaration of Independence. By a strange coincidence, that was the same day that his old friend John Adams passed away."

Patty hadn't really thought much about Jefferson in human terms. She knew basic facts about him but had always viewed him as a cold white statue, the man of marble she'd seen standing inside the Jefferson Memorial, not as a real flesh-and-blood person.

"My friend Clint here collects ghost stories," Patty said. "Do you know of any involving the White House?"

Totten's eyes brightened. "Oh, yes, quite a number of ghosts have been seen here. Some people claim this is the most haunted house in America. Harry Truman wrote to his wife that he could hear ghosts walking up and down the hallway and saw drapes moving back and forth. He joked that she'd better return pronto and protect him before the ghosts carried him off."

"Really?"

"Yes, he believed the place was haunted. He imagined the dead presidents coming out of their picture frames to give him advice."

Patty raised an eyebrow. She wasn't the first president to be pestered by meddlesome ghosts?

"Whose ghosts have been seen here?" Clint asked.

"Many of the ghost stories are about the Lincolns," Totten replied. "They say Old Abe shows up whenever he thinks the country is in danger. Mrs. Coolidge saw Lincoln's ghost. So did Queen Wilhelmina of the Netherlands and Winston Churchill. Ronald Reagan's dog Rex wouldn't go into the Lincoln Bedroom but would just stop at the door and bark, like he was seeing something inside."

Patty and Clint traded glances. Dogs wouldn't enter the spooky old room in Reagan's day either!

Totten told them Mrs. Lincoln herself believed in ghosts and held eight séances in the Red Room to communicate with her two dead sons, Eddie and Willie. She claimed she heard Andrew Jackson stomping around and swearing in the halls. William Henry Harrison had been heard banging around in the attic, looking for something he had left up there before he died.

"Have there been any sightings of Jefferson?" asked Patty.

"Yes, there was one ghost story back then about Jefferson playing his violin. Mrs. Lincoln used to remark that she heard him frequently."

Clint leaned forward. "Did she say what room he was in when she heard him playing?"

"I believe it was the Yellow Oval Room," Totten replied. "Why do you ask?"

"Oh, no reason. Clint loves to hear those little details," Patty replied before the ghost hunter could answer. "It's his hobby."

"It wouldn't surprise me a bit if Jefferson was playing his violin here," said Totten with a grin. "He was an accomplished violinist and owned an extensive collection of sheet music at Monticello. His taste in music included American folk tunes, but he was especially fond of playing sonatas by Vivaldi and Corelli, which I'm told require a lot of skill. Jefferson practiced three hours a day whenever he could. He had a pet mockingbird named Dick that would perch itself on his shoulder and sing as he played."

Jefferson had three hours to himself to play his fiddle? Life was a lot slower back in the old days. How the presidency had changed!

"Is there any information in particular you're looking for?" asked Totten. "Maybe I can help."

"No, thank you," said Patty. "That will do for now. Living here has gotten me interested in history. It seems there's a lot of it around here."

"Love of history is infectious," Totten replied. "Like William Faulkner said, 'The past isn't over. It isn't even past.' I guess that goes double for ghosts."

Patty showed Totten and Clint out, with a warm feeling of relief. She wasn't going crazy after all. The ghosts were real. Even Harry Truman had seen them.

★ ★ ★

PATTY RESOLVED TO keep a watchful eye on the Yellow Oval Room. If the historian was right, Thomas Jefferson was likely to show up there, and when he did, she would give him a piece of her mind.

Every morning, on her way to the Oval Office, she peeked inside and then checked again in the evening on her way back through the Residence. Tiptoeing around the furniture, she fully expected a phantom to leap out of the woodwork at her at any moment, but each time, the space was empty, with no hint of any ghosts standing at the windows or lurking around the fireplace or lounging on the sofas and chairs.

With every day that passed, Patty's frustration mounted. Ghosts, it seemed, were not only rude and intrusive but unpredictable and inconsiderate, like house guests who overstayed—for centuries. They showed up on their own schedule, anywhere, anytime, acting like they had some kind of superior claim to a place just because they had lived there first.

Late one afternoon, Patty's patience was rewarded.

She was strolling down the hallway when her ears picked up the sound of a violin melody. It seemed to come from the Yellow Oval Room.

At last! She turned around and hurried to the door.

It was open. She tiptoed toward the threshold, but as soon as she reached it, the music paused.

Her eyes scanned the room. No one was there—at least, no one she could see. Afternoon light gushed in through the windows, painting the walls a pale yellow. The golden drapes adorning the three tall windows were still. The brass chandelier split the sunlight into a rainbow of colors on the ceiling.

"Jefferson, are you here?" she called out.

No answer.

"I could have sworn I heard music," she muttered, shaking her head. "But I guess not." She left the room and closed the door.

The music immediately started up again.

Jefferson must be teasing her.

She took a deep breath, walked back in, and slammed the door behind her.

"No need to make so much noise, madam. You might disturb someone," said a voice. "Especially me."

There, in front of a window flanked by brass candelabra, sat the shimmering image of Jefferson, holding a violin in one hand and a bow in the other. A wooden birdcage, set on a nearby table, contained a gray mockingbird.

"Do you by any chance play a musical instrument?" asked the specter, wearing an insouciant smile as sunlight from the window streamed through his body. "If so, we might perform a duet, if you have the time and inclination."

The bird chirped loudly, as if in protest.

"Excuse me, Dick, I meant a trio," said Jefferson to the bird. "Please excuse my little pet, Mrs. Pitypander. He seems to be jealous of you."

Patty approached the ghost, almost holding her breath. "Sorry, I don't play any instruments," she answered in a hushed tone.

"I thought not," said Jefferson. "You might consider taking it up. I found playing my violin so relaxing when I was president. Music furnishes a delightful recreation for the hours of respite from the cares of the day."

He had laid out some sheet music on an ottoman. She could just make out a word in the title: C-O-R-E-L-L-I.

Jefferson really did play Corelli, like Totten said.

He followed her eyes to the page. "It is one of Corelli's Violin Solos, Opus Five. Have you heard any of his works?"

"Uh, no, I'm afraid I haven't," Patty admitted.

"More's the pity," said Jefferson. "Arcangelo Corelli was a most sublime composer of the baroque style. One of the best of the Italian virtuosos, in my estimation. His work is more refined than Vivaldi's, though not as expressive. Would you like me to play one of his sonatas for you now?"

"No, thanks."

"Ah, I perceive you are not in a musical mood at the moment. Very well then." Jefferson set his violin and bow aside. "What can I do for you?"

"I've been looking for you."

"So I assumed. I tried to make myself easy to find, and find me you did. Well done." He gestured to her with a flourish of his hand.

Patty gave him a stern look. "You and your ghost buddies have been haunting me. I won't put up with it."

Jefferson looked down at his mockingbird. "She says she won't put up with us, Dick. What do you think of that?"

The bird trilled excitedly.

Jefferson laughed. "Yes, my thoughts exactly." He remained calm, his eyes glowing. "Well, it sounds like we may have made progress, madam. At our first meeting, you refused to acknowledge us at all. Now, we've at least made enough of an impression to stir you to anger."

"I want you out of here, all of you," Patty shot back. "Go haunt someplace else."

"Madam, I don't think you understand," Jefferson replied. "We are bound to this place and were here long before you were born. We aren't going anywhere. We come with the property. You've inherited us by becoming president. This is our house too, you know."

"But why are you bothering me?"

"As I told you before, I have been given a task to perform—to guide you in how best to lead this nation."

"And I told you I don't want your help!"

"Do you not at least concede that we exist?"

Did the Potusgeists exist? They must if she was talking to them. Harry Truman thought they existed, and he was a no-nonsense guy. "All right, you exist. So what? I don't see that it matters if you do or don't because I can just ignore you and pretend to everyone that you don't."

"Oh, no, you will not be able to ignore us, madam," said Jefferson with a chuckle.

"That's not true. I can pretend I don't see you. In fact, I already have."

"We have been invisible to everyone but you," said Jefferson, "but we don't have to be. We have the power to make ourselves visible to anyone. You have no idea who you are dealing with."

"Are you threatening me?" Patty's eyes flashed with anger. "Listen, you ghoul, I was elected by the people—living people—to remake America, and no dead presidents from ancient history are going to stop me. Not you, not John Adams, Andrew Jackson, or that fat jerk with the mustache who showed up in my bathtub."

"Fat jerk? Do you refer to President Taft?"

"Whoever!"

Jefferson smirked. "Well, if it took seeing Old Bill in his natural state to command your attention, madam, it was a tactic I do not in the least regret."

"Oh, I'll make you regret it!" Patty thundered. "Just watch me."

Jefferson crossed his arms and laughed. "And just how will you do that?"

It was a bluff. How did a living person make a ghost regret anything? Or do anything, for that matter? They existed on different terms, in another dimension, and couldn't be threatened with death or enticed with money. What motivated a ghost? What did they live—or exist—for?

Jefferson threw his head back. "You are a most foolish woman, Mrs. Pitypander, and even more obstinate than I feared. How did you come to be so perverse and intractable? Are you a hater of men? Is it the fault of your ill-breeding? I do recall reading that you were raised in Boston. Yes, that must be it. It's the Yankee in you."

That was enough. Patty wasn't going to put up with being insulted by a phantom. "You are the foolish one, you old ghost, if you think you can push me around just because you lived here once a million years ago. This is my house and my century. I want you and your weird little pals to clear out. Now!"

With that, she whirled around and bolted out of the room, leaving Jefferson to fiddle by himself. She didn't give a damn who heard him.

CHAPTER 14

THE INVESTIGATORS

SARTINI, RECENTLY BACK from a state funeral for the Prince of Liechtenstein, entered the Cabinet Room and found his nameplate on the long mahogany table. He took his assigned seat, trying to hide his dismay. He wasn't next to the president or next to the person who was next to the president. Six chairs away, he was as far from her as one could be and still be seated at the table.

That morning, Sartini's wife had unsuccessfully tried to console him that at least he was being invited to Cabinet meetings. In the distant past, the vice president wasn't considered important enough to attend them. Things had changed over the years. Some presidents had seen fit to give their veeps serious responsibilities. But not President Pitypander, not yet.

That was because she hadn't been in office very long, Sartini reassured himself. She must have plans for him. Maybe she would soon give him an assignment that would make him more visible to the media.

It couldn't come soon enough. There had better be more

to the vice presidency than attending funerals, smiling at ribbon-cutting ceremonies, and waiting in the wings in case she died. The smartest boy ever to come out of Licking County, Ohio, would not be kept on hold for long.

His future was not exclusively up to her, Sartini realized. Other powerful people in the Cabinet Room would influence his destiny. He eyed Nigel Windborne, sitting at the president's right hand.

As in every administration, top officials jockeyed for the president's favor, but in this one there were serious doubts about who was effectively in charge, Patty or Nigel. Who had decided where everyone should sit today? That had to be Nigel. He was the power broker.

The chief of staff set the agenda for the president's meetings, arranged her schedule, and decided who had access to her. He controlled most of the information reaching her. That, along with the Englishman's domineering style and steel-trap mind, was enough to make the inexperienced president putty in his hands.

Could Patty act independently of the indispensable aide who had made her president? Would she dare? Sartini didn't think so.

The president seemed to be an empty pantsuit. Although she sat in the big chair, she didn't even run the Cabinet meeting. The man who knew everything did that.

Windborne shuffled some papers, glanced at Secretary of State Borders, and asked him to brief everyone on the latest developments in the French cheese crisis. Borders reported on the recent anti-American riots in Paris and noted the damage the crisis was doing daily to Franco-American relations. President Dubois's state visit couldn't come soon enough.

Sartini followed Patty's eyes to a far corner of the jam-packed room, near the portrait of Harry Truman—the only spot where no one was seated. She appeared to be irritated.

"Shoo! Get lost! No, don't do that! Stop that! Not here!" she shouted, waving her hand.

All eyes turned toward Patty.

She quickly recovered her presence of mind and looked around the table. "Sorry, I was...swatting at a fly. Go on, Milton. Sorry to interrupt."

As Borders resumed his briefing, Patty kept her eyes fixed on him, as if straining not to look to the side. After a few seconds, she peered into the corner. Immediately, her face tensed up and she bit her lip.

What was she seeing?

"Stop! No, get lost! Get out of here!" Patty's eyes swiveled from side to side. "Sorry, it's that darn fly again. Gosh, he won't leave me alone."

Sartini scanned the faces in the room. Others seemed to notice the president's odd behavior as well. The Secretary of Labor, Anita Cowles, raised a quizzical eyebrow. The Secretary of Commerce, John Hoagland, gave Patty a sidelong glance.

"You all right, Patty?" asked Nigel.

She squared her shoulders and pulled herself upright. "Yes, go on." Five seconds later, she was staring at the corner again.

She let out a deep breath, jerked away from the table, and jumped out of her chair. "I'm not feeling well," she announced, bolting toward the door. "Go on without me."

Nigel looked confused but continued the meeting.

When it ended, Sartini approached Cowles and Hoagland. "Did you guys see that? What the heck was that all about?"

Hoagland shrugged. "I dunno. There's something going on, though. She was acting pretty strange."

Cowles looked around the room for a fly, checking the windows and ceiling lights. "I didn't see anything buzzing around her, did you?"

"No," replied Hoagland, pointing to the corner. "And she kept freaking out about something over there."

"She also looked kind of spaced out. Is she on drugs?" Cowles asked.

"God, I hope not," Hoagland replied. "We can't have a drug addict running the country."

"We need to keep a lid on this, guys," Sartini admonished them. "We don't want to start any rumors that the president is acting weird. No leaks, okay?"

They all agreed: no leaks. As far as they were concerned, the president's behavior was totally normal. Nobody had seen a thing.

Sartini thought back to his conversation with Benny Pitypander. What had the casino magnate called his wife's mental condition? *Fantasy-reality confusion.* She had been having conversations with a character in one of her novels.

The Cabinet might have just witnessed the president having a similar kind of psychotic episode, seeing someone who wasn't there. Was she actually crazy or just flaky, like most people thought?

This wasn't something Sartini could overlook or pretend he hadn't witnessed. Whatever was going on with the president, it wasn't just her problem. If she was going nuts, it would soon be the country's, and his too.

He had to know the answer.

SARTINI RETURNED TO his office late the next evening to pick up some papers when he noticed two women outside his door. One was vacuuming the floor. The other was ambling down the hallway, inspecting her work.

"Can I help you, Mr. Vice President?" asked the latter.

Phaedra McBride, a small woman in her fifties, was the usher in charge of the housekeeping staff, the person who made sure the White House was spotless. Her twenty employees cleaned the mansion and the West Wing. They even did the president's laundry.

The staff went everywhere and had access to every room. At any hour, if the president needed fresh towels, a couple of aspirin, or sandwiches from the kitchen, a housekeeper would be at her door in minutes delivering them. Most importantly, if anything unusual was going on in the Residence, the house-keepers would know it.

"Yes, as a matter of fact, I think you can help me."

He led her into his office, closed the door, and directed her to a chair. "Please understand," Sartini said somberly, taking his seat behind his desk, "a serious matter has come up, involving national security. I must ask that you not repeat a word to anyone about what I'm going to say."

McBride glanced around the room in confusion. "National security? Why, Mr. Vice President, I don't understand what you mean. I'm just an usher. What would I know about national security?"

Sartini cleared his throat. "I know this will sound strange to you, and I'm well aware that this is outside your normal scope of work, but quite simply, I need to borrow the eyes and ears of your housekeeping staff."

McBride tilted her head. "I don't understand. Our eyes and ears? What do you mean 'borrow' them, sir?"

Sartini lowered his voice to a whisper. "This is strictly confidential, Mrs. McBride. I'm afraid there may be something wrong with the president, something very serious involving her mental health. Your people are around her more than anybody when she's in the Residence. I want to protect her and the country, but to do that, I have to know what's happening over there. That's where your staff can help me."

The usher's face tensed up. "But what exactly are you asking us to do?"

"I want you to tell your staff that if they happen to see anything strange about the president's behavior, they should report it to you immediately. In turn, you will inform me."

McBride recoiled, eyeing the door as if she were thinking of running out of the room. She drew in a deep breath. "Mr. Vice President, being new here, you may not know this, but that simply isn't allowed. The White House domestic staff is sworn to keep the president's personal life private. It's a long-standing tradition. I can't go to anyone with information about her. I would be fired by the chief usher if I did, and rightly so."

"But I'm the vice president, and what I'm talking about here is a matter of national security. Isn't that more important than the president's privacy?"

"National security or not, it makes no difference. The domestic staff does not spy on the president. There are lots of other people around here who are paid to worry about national security. You should talk to them about your concerns. It's simply not our job." McBride turned to go.

"Wait." Sartini folded his arms, his eyes narrowing. "You work for Mr. Twiggs, right?"

"Yes."

"Mr. Twiggs looks pretty old. He must be near retirement, isn't he?"

"Yes, he's about seventy-five, I think. What's that got to do with this?"

"When Twiggs retires, we'll need a new chief usher. Who knows, I might be president myself someday. If so, I will be the one to decide who replaces him. That could be you."

McBride shot him a blank stare and tilted her head back. "I'm a truck driver's daughter from Wheeling, West Virginia, Mr. Vice President. That's all I am, but I have the great privilege of working at the White House. I've been here since I was eighteen, I started as a housekeeper, and I've seen six presidents and their families come and go. As much as I might want Leo's job, I wouldn't want to get it that way. And if you ever do become president, sir, I will protect your private life as carefully as I do President Pitypander's. I'm sure you wouldn't want it any other way. Good evening."

With that, Phaedra McBride stood up, spun around on her heels, and walked out.

JOHN ADAMS, LURKING unseen in a corner of Sartini's office, stroked his chin in amazement upon hearing Mrs. McBride's words.

Adams grinned and thought to himself: *Well, now—there's a woman with spunk. Good for her. So there are still some people with principles working here. Maybe there's hope for this country yet.*

CHAPTER 15

THE STATE DINNER

THE RESIDENCE BUSTLED with activity, and everywhere Patty went, staff members scurried to and fro, making last-minute preparations for the state dinner.

Thank goodness for old Twiggs and his skill at planning big events. The former rear admiral had coordinated the White House's hundred-person domestic staff, the State Department, and the Secret Service with military precision, overseeing everything from the guest list to the menu to the flowers to the housekeeping.

Patty gazed into the full-length mirror in her bedroom, dismayed by her white Oscar de la Renta gown. It had been made for the occasion, so why didn't it fit? She inhaled, then exhaled, then inhaled again, checking in the mirror from every angle as she struggled to squeeze the folds of her soft fifty-six-year-old body inside.

There was no time left to have the gown fixed. It would have to do.

Tension welled up within her, as if she were a schoolgirl dressing up for her high school prom. It wasn't like she hadn't thrown a lavish soirée before. She had done many, and with much longer guest lists than this one, but those were nothing compared to a White House state dinner. This was no mere mega-party for the ultra-rich but a high-pressure affair, full of tradition, pomp, and, most terrifying of all, class.

Patty could do pomp better than anyone. That only required gobs of Benny's money. It was pretending to be classy that set her teeth on edge. Despite her vast wealth, she had rarely mingled with high society.

Only an hour earlier, Nigel had ratcheted up her self-doubts about her social graces several notches with an unsolicited lesson on state dinner etiquette, leaving her head spinning with dos and don'ts. Protocol must be strictly observed, he had warned, or she would commit a diplomatic *faux pas*. Merely picking up the wrong salad fork could cause an international furor. She must do this and then that, and never that before this, or the press would report that she had conducted herself like an ignorant bumpkin. Her plebeian roots would be laid bare before the world. Thank God her buffoonish, soup-slurping husband Benny wouldn't be there to embarrass her.

Being a queen wasn't supposed to be this hard. The stress of keeping up appearances spoiled all the glamor and glory.

At six o'clock, Patty tossed her insecurities aside, marshaled her self-confidence, and called for the Secret Service to escort her down the Grand Staircase to the State Floor. At the Entrance Hall, she spotted Twiggs, who led her to the front steps of the North Portico and told her where she was to stand on the red carpet: in front of twenty-five handsome Marine guards, smartly clad in black and white uniforms. She clumsily planted her feet where instructed and grinned bravely at the cameras.

As the French president emerged from his limousine, the Marine band struck up "La Marseillaise."

A lone Marine, positioned at the bottom of the steps, snapped to attention and saluted America's honored guest.

"Bertrand, welcome to Washington," Patty gushed, right on cue, wearing the most authentic smile she could muster.

Dubois grinned, ascended the steps, and gallantly planted a kiss on her cheek. "My pleasure, Madam President."

The pleasure was actually hers. Patty was overcome with a giddiness she hadn't experienced in ages. No man as debonair as the curly-haired Frenchman had ever kissed her. Certainly, no one had ever done it so diplomatically, with such aplomb.

Patty beamed as she strode proudly alongside him through the Entrance Hall, past a line of American and French flags, and down the Cross Hall. From there, they entered the State Dining Room, where a hundred and thirty dinner guests—the Cabinet, Nigel, Sartini, congressional leaders, top military brass, campaign donors, various notables, and their spouses—awaited them in tuxedos and resplendent evening gowns.

After introductions were made, Twiggs conducted the two presidents to the head table.

Servants glided silently through the big room, bearing hors d'oeuvres on silver trays. On each table, silver serving plates overflowed with the banned French cheese that had caused so much trouble: Époisses de Bourgogne, Munster, and Camembert.

Dubois laughed with delight. "Mon Dieu, Madam President. I see zat you do not hate our cheese nearly so much as I was told."

"Not at all," Patty replied, daintily spearing a piece of Munster with a fork. "I would gobble it up all day long to keep your friendship, Mr. President. And please, call me Patty. We don't always have to be so formal, do we?"

"Very well, then, Patty." Dubois raised a glass of champagne. "To our friendship."

She raised her glass as well and invited everyone in the room to join her in a toast. "To you, Bertie, and to France, America's oldest ally."

Patty looked down at the gilt-edged menu card with the fancy gold script. Old Twiggs had scored another home run. The dinner would be scrumptious, featuring rack of spring lamb, buttermilk biscuits, Carolina rice jambalaya, and crème fraiche ice cream.

As the crystal chandelier glittered above the guests, a band of musicians at the end of the room played a gentle waltz. Patty turned to admire them.

"How lovely. A string quartet," someone said.

"Quartet?" Patty craned her neck to take another look. She counted five heads, not four.

The fifth, she realized, didn't belong there. Semi-translucent and glowing, he was a tall ghost dressed in a waistcoat and knee breeches. The phantasm was looking at her, smirking as he drew his bow back and forth across his violin.

Patty shrank in her chair. *It's Jefferson! Oh, no! Not here!*

There was a loud creak as a door to the room swung open. The ghost of John Adams floated into the room.

No, not him too!

Adams paced around the tables, looking each guest up and down, as if inspecting them to see if they met with his approval.

The mournful cry of a wolf pierced the windows. Patty cringed.

She swung to her right. Blood began oozing down a wall, curdling around the portrait of Abraham Lincoln above the fireplace mantel.

All the while, the guests carried on with their conversations, blissfully unaware of the ghosts around them. A waiter strolled past Jefferson without noticing him. Another walked right through John Adams.

Wasn't anybody besides her seeing this?

She caught the stares of Nigel, Sartini, and Speaker Underdown, sitting at tables nearby, their eyes fastened upon her like lasers. They, too, were seemingly oblivious to the wraithy party crashers.

Patty gulped, her throat tightening.

She needed to get a grip on herself. There was no reason to panic. If nobody else noticed the ghosts, why did they matter?

The Potusgeists were a nuisance—nothing more. They existed only in the mind and only if one admitted seeing them. The important thing was to control herself, pretend nothing was amiss, and maintain her poise.

The ghosts be damned.

She would go ahead with her plan to entertain Dubois with small talk. Plucking a piece of Camembert off a tray, she downed it with a swallow of champagne, keeping her eyes securely riveted on Dubois. "Tell me, Bertie, how is the weather in Paris this time of year?"

Dubois replied that, being April, it was still too chilly and rainy for his liking, but the flowers were blooming everywhere in great profusion, and they were spectacular. "Springtime, eet eez zee time for love, eez eet not, Patty?"

What was she to make of that? Had she heard him right? The time for love? Was the champagne taking its toll on her? Did the dashing French playboy mean springtime is a lovely time, or was he propositioning her? It was hard to tell. His English was not so good.

Patty would fill the communication gap with her rusty high school French, hoping Dubois would be charmed by her effort to speak his language. She stammered out some words: *"Les jardins...let me see here...I think I have it...les jardins de Paris sont belle comme tu es."* ["The gardens of Paris are beautiful as you are."]

Proud that she had managed to construct an entire French sentence on her first try, Patty looked wide-eyed at the French president, anticipating an appreciative response.

Instead, Dubois seemed vaguely uneasy and protested in a voice just above a whisper, *"Madame, ce n'est pas l'endroit pour flirter."* ["Madam, this is not the place to flirt."]

Patty didn't understand but sensed from Dubois's look of chagrin that whatever she had said must have come out wrong. She tried to remember the French words for saying she was sorry. *"Je regrette...no, that's not it...let's see...je suis desolé."*

Dubois smiled and patted her on the arm. "Zat eez okay."

Goodness! He touched me! What did that mean?

Patty gulped another swig of champagne and glanced at the portrait of Lincoln. Andrew Jackson was reaching above the fireplace mantel, turning the painting upside down. She shut her eyes, waited a second, and looked again. This time, Lincoln's face was right side up, and Jackson had disappeared. She looked over at Jefferson, still stroking his violin joyously, his face lit up with puckish glee.

The Potusgeists, seen and unseen, were goading her, tormenting her, laughing at her, in a clear attempt to drive her over the edge. And they were succeeding.

CHAPTER 16

THE ASSAILANT

A MOTHER COULD TELL when her child was upset, no matter how old the child or how hard she pretended to be fine. During their weekly phone call, Patty's mother, Olympia, knew from the frenzied tone of her daughter's voice that all was not well at 1600 Pennsylvania Avenue.

The old woman packed her bags at the Horizon House retirement community in Fort Lauderdale, told her pickleball team she'd be back in a week, and flew to Washington to see what ailed her little girl.

Olympia had some idea of what the problem was, as she had anticipated it for years. Patty had to be president, and as nothing much could ever stand in her way, she had become president. Her late husband Luigi had predicted Patty wouldn't like the job once she had it because often she didn't see things as they really were.

Telling her daughter she wouldn't like being president was like telling an eagle not to fly. You could give Patty advice until you were blue in the face. She wouldn't listen.

Luigi, God rest his soul, had wanted to protect Patty from her outsized ambitions, but he had also known it was pointless to try. She wanted so desperately to be important, like she imagined he was. His daughter had never understood how dirty politics was because she had only seen the glamor of his being mayor of Boston, never the frustrations of the job, the corruption involved behind the scenes, and what it took to stay in office.

From experience, Olympia knew her daughter was going to complain that someone evil was mistreating her. Patty was always being abused by somebody she didn't get along with. Washington was full of the sort of contrary people who would set her off. It had taken only a few months for the place to get on her delicate nerves.

Patty was so busy on the night when Olympia arrived that they had no time to talk. The housekeeping staff simply escorted Olympia to the Lincoln Bedroom and brought her dinner on a tray.

She unpacked her suitcase, nibbled at the food, and lay down on the enormous canopy bed to rest for a few minutes. She had almost dozed off when she was startled by a loud knock at the door.

"Who is it?" Olympia asked.

There was no answer. Olympia opened the door.

In the hall outside, a small figure in a black dress floated above the floor, cast in a shimmering light. "Who might you be?" the form demanded in an imperious tone of voice.

"I'm the president's mother," Olympia answered, wondering why the woman was glowing around the edges. "And who are you?"

"Mary Todd Lincoln," the woman in black declared, throwing her head back. "I'm the lady of this house."

"You?"

"Yes, and I don't think you or your daughter belong here," said the apparition. "So, I'm going to send you away."

With that, she pulled a butcher's knife out of the folds of her dress and raised it high over her head as if about to strike the old woman down.

"Aaaaah!" Olympia screamed, jumping back from the door. She scurried to the opposite side of the room and huddled in terror.

A tall, bearded man with a stovepipe hat appeared out of nowhere, lunged forward, and grabbed Mrs. Lincoln by the arm. "No, dear, you mustn't do that," he shouted, pulling her back.

"But they shouldn't be here," cried Mrs. Lincoln to her husband. "They need to be killed. Who else will do it if I don't?"

"Mary, let her be, for God's sake." Mr. Lincoln turned toward Olympia with a sheepish expression. "Please excuse us, ma'am. She doesn't know what she's doing." He picked up his wife and carried her away in his arms, disappearing with her through a wall.

Olympia fell back onto the bed, her hand on her chest, gasping for air. After a moment, she recovered her wits, got up, and ran into the hall, yelling at the top of her lungs for help.

A maid rushed to the door, accompanied by a Secret Service agent.

"I'd like to see my daughter right away," Olympia said. "Could you please call her?"

Minutes later, Patty was in the Lincoln Bedroom, holding her trembling mother in her arms. "Mama, are you all right?"

"Yes, baby."

"What did you tell them?"

"Tell who?"

"The housekeeper and the Secret Service agent."

"I told them I'd been attacked by a crazy glowing woman

with a knife. I thought you were supposed to have security here. How did she get into the White House?"

"That was Mrs. Lincoln. She lives here, sort of. Well, she doesn't exactly *live* here. Hangs around is more like it."

"Oh?"

"Yes, she thinks she owns the place."

"She sure seemed to act like it. And there was this very tall man," said Olympia. "He stopped her from stabbing me and carried her away. I guess you're going to tell me that was Abraham Lincoln."

"Yes, Mama."

"I see." Olympia looked over at her half-finished dinner. "Are they putting drugs into the food here?"

"No."

"Then I'm hallucinating, or maybe we've all gone nuts."

"No, there's nothing wrong with us or the food."

"Then what is going on?"

"The White House is...well, it's got ghosts."

Ghosts? Was Patty kidding? A new home always required some getting used to, but this took the cake. "That's silly. I don't believe in ghosts," said Olympia firmly.

"Neither did I, until recently."

Patty described some of the ghost sightings she had experienced in the past several weeks: Naked William Howard Taft stuck in her bathtub, Abigail Adams drying her laundry in the East Room, and Presidents Polk and Buchanan playing checkers in the Treaty Room.

Both of Olympia's eyebrows jumped. "Ghosts taking baths, doing laundry, and playing checkers? You don't say."

"The ghosts here don't like me very much, Mama. They sent Thomas Jefferson to tell me how to run the country. He jumped out of a bookcase in the Oval Office. I've been trying to ignore him ever since, but it's not working so well."

Olympia paced around the floor. "Have you called your therapist about this problem, Patricia? You know, it's not at all normal to see ghosts. Maybe he could give you some pills or something before the men in white coats come and get you."

"I'm telling you, I'm not crazy. You've got to believe me. There really are ghosts here, lots of them."

Olympia had to admit, the bearded man in the stovepipe hat did look a lot like Abraham Lincoln, except he was glowing around the edges, and she could sort of see through him. Maybe those were ghosts, after all.

Whatever they were, all that really mattered to the eighty-seven-year-old was that her little girl was in big trouble.

Olympia knew little about ghosts, but she would believe in anything if it would help. She offered Patty some motherly advice: "You give those ghosts hell, honey. Find someone to protect you, and send 'em packing."

"Yes, Mama. Will do."

JEFFERSON TOOK HIS seat at the windows in the Yellow Oval Room, his violin and bow in hand. It was half past three. He had arrived later than usual and was eager to get started practicing.

He reached for his satchel of sheet music. "Let's see, what shall I play today, Dick?" he asked, taking the pet mockingbird out of his cage and resting him on his shoulder.

The bird chirped a few bars until Jefferson recognized the tune.

"Pugnani! Yes, that's an excellent choice. We haven't done him for quite a while." He rummaged through the satchel and found his well-worn copy of Gaetano Pugnani's violin concerto in D major.

He had just begun to play when the door to the room flung open and the president burst in.

"There you are!" Patty shouted, looking daggers at him from across the room. "I've caught you!"

Jefferson lifted his eyes, startled. "I beg your pardon, madam?"

She stormed toward him, wagging her finger. "Yes, you should beg my pardon. Attacking my mother with a knife. How dare you? How could you do a thing like that to an old woman?"

Jefferson laid his violin and bow down gently on the settee. "Madam, I was just speaking with Mr. Adams about that unfortunate incident, and we want to assure you that we had nothing to do with it. Mrs. Lincoln is given to hysterical outbursts and bouts of melancholy. She was acting entirely on her own."

Patty rolled her eyes. "Oh, she was, was she?"

"Yes, I wouldn't lie to you," Jefferson replied. "We cannot control her. It is all Mr. Lincoln can do to keep her from assaulting the White House staff."

"Well, how about your attempt to ruin my state dinner? I saw you back there, fiddling away. You were trying to distract and scare me, weren't you?"

Jefferson grinned. "Scare you? No, we meant only to get your attention. You need to be trained for the presidency. Your arrogant refusal to cooperate with us has necessitated stronger measures than we would like. I told you that you could not ignore us, did I not?"

Patty's mouth fell open. "What? I'm arrogant? You hijack my state dinner, try to make a fool of me in front of everyone, and you have the nerve to call me arrogant? You could have wrecked our relations with France with your little stunt."

Jefferson was taken aback. How had the ghosts' harmless little haunting of the state dinner provoked such an immoderate response? They were only trying to get her cooperation.

"It was not our intention to embarrass you, madam," Jefferson replied. "That ought to be obvious to you, as you were the only one who saw us there. As for relations with France, if you would but allow me the opportunity, I could teach you a thing or two about dealing with the French. I was Minister Plenipotentiary to the French court for four years, you know."

"I can handle the French just fine if you'll leave me alone."

"That is absurd," Jefferson shot back. "No one can handle the French just fine, not even themselves. You don't know a thing about them. Take your clownish flirtation with President Dubois. The French are masters of flirtation. They regard it even more seriously than wine and cheese. Flirt with them if you will, but do it properly, or you'll earn their contempt. Why, when I was minister to France during the reign of Louis the Sixteenth, you would scarcely believe the heights to which French women took the art of flirting. I was aghast at their morals, I tell you."

Patty exploded, her voice rising to a scream. "I don't care about your flirting with the French! I don't care about Louis the Sixteenth! I want you out of here, all of you, now!"

He restrained himself from laughing. "Or you'll do what?"

She grabbed a vase full of flowers off a coffee table and hurled it at him. It sailed through his shoulder and crashed against the bulletproof window.

"Tsk, tsk, that's no way to treat your gardenias," Jefferson said with a smile.

She stomped on the carpet. "You know something? You're not just a ghost. You're a monster!"

Jefferson tugged on his waistcoat and pulled himself up straight. "Control yourself, Mrs. Pitypander. You are becoming hysterical. If you keep on like this, you will become a raving, nervous invalid like Mrs. Lincoln."

"Aaah, you're impossible!"

The impossibility of being a ghost—now there was an interesting thought. Jefferson's gaze fell to the floor, his mind wandering off into a reverie. "I am indeed. A sentient ghost must seem an impossibility to you. But I assure you, madam, that is what I am—though it is indeed quite impossible."

Cogito, ergo sum. I think, therefore I am. According to the philosophy of Descartes, he existed, despite being a ghost.

He launched into a philosophical soliloquy. "At one time or another, we are all impossible, as it is the nature of all things first not to be, then to be, and again not to be. While we are in a state of not being, we seem impossible. This country, before it existed, and even while we were creating it, seemed impossible to many people. Even you, Mrs. Pitypander, when you were but a glimmer in your parents' eyes, were once impossible—and in a few short years, when you are gone, you will be again."

"I'll be impossible? What the hell are you talking about? I don't understand you!" she shouted.

"I didn't think you would. The living never do. The cycle of existence and non-existence is one of many things one must die to understand." He watched impassively as Patty got up and stormed out of the room.

Dick began to warble.

"I couldn't agree more, Dick," replied Jefferson with a deep sigh. "I've never understood females either—dead or alive. Oh, well, we shall never find a solution for that." He picked up his violin and bow and resumed practicing.

HOUSEKEEPER BLANCA SANCHEZ pressed an icon on her phone and played back the video. There was the president, just as she was five minutes ago, yelling at nobody, waving her fist like a maniac at the settee in the empty Yellow Oval Room, and hurling a vase at the window:

> "I don't care about your flirting with the French! I don't care about Louis the Sixteenth! I want you out of here, all of you, now!"
>
> "You know something? You're not just a ghost. You're a monster!"

With trembling hands, the maid turned off the recording and discreetly stowed her phone in her purse. She entered the room as she had intended before stumbling upon the president talking into space.

It wasn't her imagination. President Pitypander had gone loco. She was talking to nobody and throwing things.

Blanca collected the vase's remains in a trash bag, relieved that the president had damaged nothing else in the room. As she went about sweeping her vacuum cleaner back and forth across the floor, the thought kept returning that she was only a housekeeper. She needed this job to feed her two kids, and what the president said or did was none of her business. Housekeepers were not supposed to see such things. For her own good, she ought to simply ignore what she had witnessed and delete the recording.

But how could she? President Pitypander, the most powerful person in the world, had completely lost her mind, and somebody in a position of authority ought to know about it so they could help the poor lady.

"The president is loco," Blanca kept saying to herself. "It is not good."

Maybe Mrs. McBride would know what to do.

LEO TWIGGS HAD been at the White House so long he could tell which of his ushers was walking toward his office by the sound of their shoes. The tempo of Phaedra McBride's footsteps was hurried and precise, almost like those of the Marine guards in the hallway.

He peered at her over his bifocals. The housekeeping usher, punctual to a fault, was on time for the appointment she had made with him.

Her eyes wandered away from his, indicating her distress. Whatever the problem was, she couldn't handle it on her own, which was unusual for her. Of all the ushers Twiggs supervised, McBride was the most self-sufficient and would normally bend over backwards not to involve him in the day-to-day problems of managing the housekeeping staff.

She took a seat across from his desk, drew in a deep breath, and asked, "Mr. Twiggs, in all your years at the White House, have you ever heard of there being any ghosts around here?"

McBride looked at him earnestly. She or someone on her staff must have heard or seen something strange. Twiggs tightened his lips and looked up at the ceiling. "Yes, I have heard some stories, but I never believed them. Have you seen a ghost, Phaedra?"

"Oh, no, sir," she quickly replied. "I don't think I believe in ghosts either. I've never seen one. Not yet, anyway."

"That's good," said Twiggs. "You had me worried there. From the look on your face, I half expected you to tell me you had. It wouldn't be good to see ghosts, you know. A thing like that could embarrass the president. It would be considered the president's private information. And you know our policy about that."

"Right," McBride replied. "We never discuss the president's private life."

The White House code of silence regarding the president's personal affairs was absolute. Life would be intolerable for any president if the domestic staff, who saw so much, could not be trusted to keep what happened there secret. Presidents would be exposed to constant press stories about the most intimate details of their lives.

McBride had taken the hint. Whatever she knew about the ghosts, she wasn't going to tell him. That was just as well because Twiggs had absolutely no interest in hearing it. There was nothing he could do about them.

He thought back to his first run-in with the Potusgeists, fifteen years ago.

There had been a loud knock at the front door of the White House, steps away from his office. He had opened it to find the ghost of a young woman, Anna Surratt, begging for clemency for her mother, Mary, sentenced to be hanged for her role in the Lincoln assassination. "I must see President Johnson at once," said the ghost, her eyes blazing like hot coals. "Only he can spare my mother's life."

Twiggs fell back on his heels as the tormented spirit cried in the doorway. Terrified, he could think of nothing else to do but slam the door in Anna's face.

He had happened upon the Lincolns several times. Once, walking by the Lincoln Bedroom, he caught Old Abe himself sitting at the foot of the bed, pulling his boots on. In the Red Room, he heard Mary Lincoln wailing about the loss of her husband. Glancing out a window, he glimpsed Willie Lincoln happily climbing a tree.

Then there was the time a groundskeeper rushed to his office and reported seeing a strange form on the tennis court. Twiggs ran to investigate and saw the ghost of a teenage boy swinging a tennis racket. The youth was Calvin Coolidge, Jr., who had died of blood poisoning from a blister on his toe after playing tennis there.

Twiggs had long since gotten over the shock of encountering the White House's spooky inhabitants. They were like the mansion's antique furniture—they came with the place. They must have gotten used to him, too, and knew he wouldn't bother them.

The problem wasn't the ghosts but what the world would think if it knew about them. The world couldn't be allowed to know.

The anguished look on McBride's face as she got up to leave disturbed Twiggs. He hadn't helped her at all, he realized. Someone on her staff had seen something, and she needed to tell him about it, but that was impossible. In the supercharged atmosphere of the White House, the Potusgeists weren't a subject fit for discussion.

CHAPTER 17
THE TRAP

HAVING HEARD NO news about France for several days, Patty called Nigel into the Oval Office for a progress report. Had the riots in Paris ceased? Were the French amenable to lifting their ban on American wheat?

The chief of staff lowered his lanky body into a chair across from the Resolute Desk, his eyes gleaming.

"The cheese crisis is almost over," he announced triumphantly, a self-satisfied grin spreading across his face. "I've managed to solve the problem myself."

Patty smiled back at him. "Splendid. I told you we didn't need the State Department. They just get in the way."

Diplomacy, Patty was beginning to think, was best done without diplomats. Officials who made their living by fomenting international squabbles couldn't be expected to resolve them.

Nigel explained how he had broken through the impasse. He had called the head of the FDA and casually mentioned that the president was extremely fond of stinky French cheese and that the Office of Management and Budget was looking for agency budgets that needed trimming.

The FDA chief got the message. New test results came out later that day, showing that there was nothing wrong with stinky cheese, besides its stench.

The agency withdrew its cheese ban. In return, the French promised to end their threat to outlaw American wheat.

Voilà! With one masterful stroke, Camembert was saved. So were Patty's sagging poll numbers in the Midwest and America's strained relations with France. It was a victory for both Patty and Dubois, who could face their constituents and claim to have defused the crisis with their skillful diplomacy.

Patty sipped her coffee. "That's nice. I never wanted to fight with Bertie anyway. You see, Nigel? The state dinner did help, after all. When you're in a pinch, it never hurts to throw a party. You never know what problems a party can solve."

"Speaking of the state dinner," said Nigel, "what was going on with you and Dubois? Was everything all right?"

"What do you mean?" Patty replied, knowing perfectly well what he meant.

"I looked across the room at your table, and you seemed very tense and distracted when you were sitting with him, like you were ready to jump right out of your skin. Was something wrong?"

She might as well come clean. There didn't seem to be any point in pretending. Her behavior had betrayed her.

"Well, if you must know," she replied, "the answer is yes. It was the ghosts. They were trying to upset me, and they succeeded, too."

"Not again," Nigel moaned, rubbing his temples. "We've been over this. Please tell me you're not seeing them again."

She let out a long sigh, dreading another fruitless argument with him about whether ghosts existed or not. "Yes, as a matter of fact, I am seeing them, and this time they were all over the room. Thomas Jefferson was behind the whole thing. He was playing his violin with the string quartet. John Adams was there, and Andrew Jackson, and who knows who else. Blood was running down the wall, and well, I told Jefferson they must never do that again, but he just won't listen. He's a very stubborn ghost, you know."

Nigel threw his hands in the air. "Patty, how many times must I tell you that there are no such things as ghosts? It's all in your head."

"There he goes again. He says we're all in her head," said a voice out of nowhere.

Nigel looked around. "Who said that? Who's there?"

"Let's get all in *his* head. That will teach him," replied another voice.

The curtains behind Patty started swaying back and forth. Nigel's chair rocked violently. "What is this? What's going on?" He clamped his hands on the armrests to keep himself from falling onto the floor.

Slowly, inch by inch, his chair rose straight up, reaching four feet into the air and hovering there. Nigel thrashed from side to side, holding on for dear life. "Bloody hell!"

Patty remained behind her desk, spellbound at the sight of her chief of staff levitating in midair. "My God!"

The chair started spinning clockwise.

"Call security!" Nigel cried as he whirled around. "I'm getting dizzy!"

Patty sprang from her desk and started for the door.

She stopped and thought for a second. If the Secret Service came in, she would have to explain this. That would make things much worse. The agents would think both of them were crazy.

Patty shut the door and shouted at Nigel's chair. "Cut it out, you guys. You've scared the poor man to pieces. Now leave him alone."

The chair stopped spinning.

"All right, I guess we've made our point," said a voice from nowhere. "Let him down easy, Polk."

The ghosts of two elderly men dressed in three-piece black suits appeared, holding up the chair. One had a big mane of hair. The other stared at her with deep-set eyes. They lowered Nigel slowly, setting him down on the floor with an unceremonious thud that almost pitched the Englishman headfirst on his knees.

Nigel yelped, his hands shaking. "Just who the hell are you?"

One ghost introduced himself as Andrew Jackson. The other one claimed to be James Polk.

Old Hickory walked around Nigel's chair, looking the chief of staff up and down. "No such thing as ghosts, you say? Those are slanderous words, sir. Mr. Polk and I are deeply offended. If I were alive, I would challenge you to a duel. I may do it yet."

"A duel? You mean, with guns?" Nigel asked, his voice trembling.

"Of course, with guns, man!" Jackson replied. "What else would we use, swords?"

"Nothing...I mean...I haven't the foggiest idea."

"Do you need another ride in the air, sir, or are you sufficiently persuaded to recant your position regarding our existence?"

Nigel pulled out his handkerchief and wiped the sweat off his brow. "No, that won't be necessary. I...I believe you. But how... what are you doing here?"

Jackson's lip quivered with contempt. "Why we are here is no concern for a sniveling coward such as yourself, sir. A better question would be, why are *you* here? Normally, I would brook no business with a filthy Englishman like yourself, except to send him either by musket or sword straight to hell, but as we have made our existence clear enough, I don't think any violence will be necessary. Come, Polk, I believe we have done what has been asked of us."

With that, both ghosts rendered themselves invisible.

Nigel looked about the room in confusion, touching his hand to his chest to make sure he was awake. "Where...where did they go?"

Patty had returned to her desk, nonchalant about what had just happened, as if seeing chairs levitate had become part of her normal routine. "Who knows? I'm never sure they are really gone."

"I'm gobsmacked! There really are ghosts in the White House!"

"No fooling. I've been telling you that all along."

She had never seen such humility in Nigel's face. He shrank before her, his eyes cast down in embarrassment.

He stared blankly at the chair he had been sitting in. "And to think you've had to handle this all by yourself. I'm sorry. I should have believed you."

At last, he understood what she had been going through. "It's all right. I forgive you. I wouldn't have believed me either."

"What do you know about these ghosts?" Nigel asked.

She told him that Jefferson was their ringleader, along with Adams, and that they claimed to be sent by the Council of White House Ghosts to teach her how to be president. She had refused their aid, and the more she resisted them, the fiercer and more intrusive they became.

"You mean the whole place is infested with them?"

"Yes, they can pop up anywhere, anytime. They pass through walls and floors like they aren't there. I'm at their mercy, even in my bedroom. And they're getting worse by the day. At first, they were just haunting me, but now they're going after the people around me. They're out of control. What do you think we should do about them?"

Nigel's face went pale. For once, her know-it-all aide didn't have all the answers. "First, we have to keep a lid on this thing. If word gets out that we're talking to ghosts, your presidency will be finished. We'll be laughed out of Washington."

"Let's call Clint. Maybe he can think of something we can do."

"Call in the ghost hunter?" Nigel grimaced at the thought. "Yes, I suppose we must. Who else would know?"

IT WAS POINTLESS to try to scare the Potusgeists out of the White House, Clint told the president. Ghosts who had enjoyed the run of a house for centuries couldn't be driven out. They weren't evil spirits that had invaded another body, so they couldn't be exorcised. They were already dead, so they couldn't be exterminated.

The only surefire way to control a bunch of rampaging ghosts was to capture them, one by one.

That was easier said than done. Ghosts were mostly metaphysical energy, and special electromagnetic tools were needed to find, catch, and hold them. Clint, with his electrical engineering background, was an expert in making and using such devices.

Whatever it took to stop the ghosts was fine with Patty and Nigel. They didn't understand a word of Clint's explanation about paranormal physics but were willing to give him whatever he needed.

Clint lugged a red canvas gym bag full of special equipment into the Residence. The Secret Service let him pass, notified by Nigel that the FBI was conducting a top-secret mission approved by the president. He was to be given access to every part of the White House and its eighteen acres without exception and with absolutely no questions asked.

The devices in Clint's bag were electronic sensors and traps of his own design, which he had cobbled together by hand in his office from components he had ordered online. One sensor, the size and shape of a phone, contained a thermal camera that detected abnormal fluctuations in temperature. Another, similar to a radar gun, measured disturbances in electromagnetic fields within fifty feet. His infrasonic generator, used for attracting ghosts, emitted low-frequency sound waves audible to spirits but not living persons.

Clint's most important tool was his new photonic force-field ghost trap. Only the size of a man's wallet, it could suck in a ghost and hold him or her in its powerful force field, theoretically forever. The trick was to lure the ghost close enough to the device to trigger it.

This would be its first test.

Clint would need to be strategic about where to deploy the few sensors and traps he had. He would start with the Yellow Oval Room, hoping to nab Jefferson.

He opened the door to the big chamber. To his surprise, a ghost was already sitting there: a man in a waistcoat and knee breeches, bathed in ghostly light, lounging at the window.

The apparition, his violin beside him, was turning a page of sheet music, lost in thought as he studied the score. After a few seconds, he looked up and noticed the young man, froze like a statue, and dropped his bow on the settee. In an instant, his form flickered, and he was gone.

My God, that really was Thomas Jefferson.

A rush of excitement came over Clint. Until this, he had only sensed the presence of the Potusgeists. Now, he had beheld one with his own eyes!

How could he be sure Jefferson had actually left the room? The specter might have made himself invisible. To check, Clint switched on his electromagnetic radar gun and waved it around. No paranormal activity showed on the gun's tiny screen.

Jefferson could return at any moment, so Clint had to work quickly. He set up his thermal camera on a table and aimed it at the settee. He put his radar gun on another table a few feet away to monitor the same spot.

The two photonic traps must be concealed where Jefferson was most likely to go. Clint placed one on the windowsill, directly behind the settee, the other in the bookcase.

He rearranged a bookshelf, making space for three new books: *The Complete Works of Aristotle in Ancient Greek, The Revolutionary Philosophy of John Locke,* and *Violin Sonatas of Vivaldi.* If the insatiably curious Jefferson grabbed any of these tempting volumes, the trap would activate and vacuum him up like a dust bunny.

Having baited his trap, Clint slinked out of the room and went to his office, where he waited for three hours, returning to the scene with great anticipation.

He pulled the new books from the bookcase, looked at the trap, and could hardly believe his good fortune.

The trap's red light was blinking furiously. That meant a ghost was inside, held prisoner by the photonic force field.

"Yes!" he shouted, pumping his fist.

Amazingly, his invention had worked on its first trial. It was as improbable as hitting a hole in one on the first tee.

This is unbelievable! I've caught Thomas Jefferson!

He could hardly wait to tell the president, thinking of how thrilled she would be to hear that the troublesome ghosts could be stopped.

Clint slipped the blinking trap into his gym bag, quickly gathered up his other equipment, and triumphantly carried Jefferson out of the Yellow Oval Room, confident that the phantom would never be able to disturb the president's peace again.

★ ★ ★

THE SIGHT OF the blinking ghost trap on the Resolute Desk and Clint's account of how he had managed to lure Thomas Jefferson into it had Patty thinking her paranormal problems might be solved, but she had a few questions, and Nigel many more.

The trap wasn't even as big as Patty's purse, so she struggled to understand how it could contain a ghost who stood six feet two inches in his stockings. "Didn't you have to shrink him first to get him into that little thing?" she asked, her eyes narrowing.

"No, ma'am," Clint replied. "Size doesn't count with ghost traps. Since ghosts are made of metaphysical energy, not matter, they can be densified into an infinitely small space. A ghost trap as little as your thumbnail would work just as well as one the size of a toaster oven."

Patty imagined herself caught in a tiny trap and how claustrophobic and uncomfortable she would feel. "Are you sure he can breathe all right? I don't want him to suffer."

Clint assured her that the trap wasn't cruel. "Don't worry, he doesn't need to breathe. He stopped doing that two centuries ago when he died. He has no body and can't feel physical pain anymore."

"That's good. Well, can he still think if he's that small?"

"Yes, ma'am, he's probably thinking lots of deep thoughts right now, knowing him."

"Like how he's planning to get out of there?" Nigel asked.

"Probably," Clint replied. "That would be my first thought if I were a ghost caught in a trap."

"And I'll bet he's pretty mad at us for putting him in there," said Patty, fascinated by the trap's flashing red light. "He might decide he'd like to kill us the minute he gets out."

Nigel nodded. "Right you are. Which is why we can never let him out. A ghost like Jefferson is far too dangerous."

"We can't let him out? Ever? Oh, dear." Patty hadn't thought much about what it was like to be a ghost, but imagined it wasn't as much fun as it appeared and probably no fun at all if one was caught in a trap. "Don't you think we should give him a second chance? Doesn't Jefferson have any rights? He wrote something about all of us having inalienable rights, didn't he? Wouldn't that apply to ghosts too?"

"Be serious," Nigel replied. "Jefferson was human once, but he's dead now. Besides, ghosts don't have rights, not the way we do."

That didn't sound very nice. "I disagree," said Patty firmly. "Even dogs and cats have rights. It doesn't seem very humane to me."

"Think about it," said Nigel. "If we ever let Jefferson out of that little box, we'll never get him back into it. We won't be able to fool him twice."

He pointed out that catching just one ghost wouldn't solve their problem anyway. There were dozens more of them in the White House. Holding Jefferson hostage might scare the Potusgeists into leaving Patty alone, or it might enrage them. Who knew what havoc a mansion full of vengeful ghosts might wreak?

Clint had no answers to such complicated questions, only informed guesses, and he didn't pretend otherwise.

"Will you be able to trap the other ghosts the same way?" Patty asked.

Clint's eyes gleamed with confidence. "Yes, ma'am. If I can trap Thomas Jefferson, I can trap them all. It's just a matter of luring them in, one by one."

"You'll have to trap them all, and quickly," said Nigel, giving the ghost hunter a foreboding look. "When they learn we have Jefferson, the others will come after us twice as hard. They might regard what you've done to him as an act of war."

A war with ghosts—what a terrifying thought! There were so many of them, and they could come at her from anywhere. They were watching her constantly from behind the walls, lying in wait, and now they had been provoked.

War or no war, it couldn't be helped. The ghosts wouldn't leave her alone.

CHAPTER 18
THE ESCAPE

JOHN ADAMS WAS not surprised to find the ghost den unusually quiet for a Friday morning. It was, after all, Homegoing Weekend, and some Potusgeists had already left the White House to haunt their other homes. There was no Council meeting scheduled or any other pressing business to disturb Adams's peace. At last, he could get some reading done.

He sat on a crate, took his spectacles out of his waistcoat, and found the page where he had left off with Edward Gibbon's *The History of the Decline and Fall of the Roman Empire,* re-reading it for the forty-sixth time. He never ceased to be amazed by how the Romans had allowed their great empire to degrade—first by degrading themselves, and then their institutions, until the chaotic end came and barbarity once again ruled the world.

Adams had made it almost through the tumultuous reign of the first Emperor Theodosius, when James Monroe appeared in the middle of the room.

Monroe had always struck Adams as a sober-minded fellow—unpretentious, reserved, and dignified, with the steady disposition expected of a president. Meticulously dressed in a black topcoat and white necktie, with his tall forehead and prominent nose, he normally projected reasonableness and calm.

Except this morning. The fifth president ran his hand through his hair, his eyes searching around the ghost den. "Say, Mr. Adams, have you seen Mr. Jefferson by any chance?" he asked in a voice laden with anxiety.

Adams replied that he had not laid eyes upon Jefferson for two days and asked what the problem was.

Monroe's expression darkened. "Mr. Jefferson and I were to meet in the Rose Garden, but he did not appear. While there, I happened upon Dolley Madison, and she told me that Mr. Jefferson also missed their weekly get-together to inspect the condition of the garden."

That was odd—and very unlike Jefferson.

"And that's not all, Mr. Adams. Earlier, Mr. Jefferson was scheduled to be on the South Lawn to give a little talk about recent advances in American paleontology. I was among the disappointed attendees. We waited for him and waited—"

"He didn't show up there either?"

"No, sir. Not a trace of him," said Monroe grimly. "Mr. Jefferson is a punctilious man, with the most regular habits of anyone I know. It is not like him to miss three appointments. He would have told us if he planned to return to Monticello for Homegoing Weekend. Given the contentious state of his relationship with Mrs. Pitypander, I suspect he may be the victim of foul play."

"And you think it is her doing?" asked Adams.

"I fear she has made good on her threat to retaliate and ordered her ghost hunter to arrest Mr. Jefferson. Who else could cause his absence?"

For years, there had been troubling reports from other haunted houses that the living had developed some ingenious means to incarcerate ghosts. Some Potusgeists had foolishly dismissed the idea out of hand, thinking it couldn't happen to them because no living U.S. president would dare engage in such disrespectful behavior.

That was sheer arrogance, in Adams's view. The living had sunk to such a state of moral decay, destroying the statues and monuments of great men, that there was no telling what they might do with their newfangled technology. Those who would topple statues wouldn't think twice about rounding up and dishonoring dead presidents, even the greatest, like Jefferson. The living, lost in their self-righteousness, had lost the capacity for humility, self-reflection, and shame.

Adams had heard enough. He laid down his book and slipped his spectacles back into his waistcoat.

"Where are you going, sir?" asked Monroe as Adams walked away.

"To the source of the trouble—Mrs. Pitypander. I shall have a word with her."

ADAMS WALKED INVISIBLY past the president's secretary and through the wall into the Oval Office. Seated around the coffee table, the president and her chief of staff were meeting with a corpulent, short-haired woman whom Adams did not recognize.

"Iris, listen, can't we at least get something—*anything*—done on my Better America agenda this summer?" Patty asked in an imploring tone. "I need to show the voters my administration is moving the ball forward."

The fat woman gritted her teeth. "I've told you guys a hundred times, this stuff won't fly in Congress. There's no money for it in the budget, and we're not blowing up the national debt any further to fund your crazy ideas. We're already sixty trillion dollars in hock as it is, inflation is out of control, and with all the interest we're shoveling out, we can barely fund the Defense Department. If we spend any more, the dollar will be worthless, the economy will be in shambles, and the Republicans will take over. Is that what you want?"

"I don't think we're getting anywhere," said Nigel with irritation. "If you don't help us, this administration will be an abject failure. We'll have nothing to show for our time in office."

"And that will be entirely your fault, not mine," the woman shot back. "Don't even try shifting the blame to me. You people just don't listen. Call me when you get an idea that won't explode the budget." She rose from the sofa and waddled over to the door. "Ha! Like that's gonna happen."

As soon as the woman had left, Adams slammed the door shut and became visible. "I would have a word with you, madam."

Patty's fingernails sank into the armrest of her chair. "My God, it's John Adams again. What does he want now? Look, you ghost, when are you going to leave us alone?"

Adams drew nearer to her. "Where is Thomas Jefferson? What have you done with him? Tell me this instant."

Patty sneered at him. "We've got him where he won't bother us anymore. What business is it of yours?"

"Jefferson is my good friend, that's what. More than that, he's a leader of the Council and deserves proper respect. Now, where is he?"

Patty crossed her arms. "How dare you talk to me about respect? You ghosts didn't show me any respect, did you? I've had just about enough of you. I'm not telling you where he is."

"You won't, eh?" Adams glanced at the fireplace, where Cain and Abel were curled up. The two corgis jumped up, ran over, and yapped at him.

Her little dogs! That's it.

Adams closed his eyes and counted to ten. Pressing his heels together, he transformed himself.

In a flash, he became an enormous black dog, as big as a Newfoundland, standing on all fours.

The two corgis quailed at the sight of him, drew back, and whimpered. He growled menacingly at the tiny dogs, as if he might gobble them up.

Nigel's jaw dropped. "My God, he's...he's...he's turned himself into a dog! I didn't know ghosts could do that."

"The Potusgeists are no ordinary ghosts," said Patty, shaking. "They're monsters."

Adams lunged at Abel and clamped his jaws on the little dog's neck, lifting him into the air. He waved the corgi up and down in his mouth, its arms and legs flailing as it squealed in pain, trying in vain to bite the phantom. Cain fled in terror toward the fireplace and dove under a wing chair.

"Please don't hurt him!" Patty screamed. "I'll tell you where Jefferson is! Just let him go, please!"

Adams spat Abel out of his mouth. The little dog crashed to the floor, scrambled away, and huddled next to Cain.

Adams transformed himself back into human form. "Very well, madam, now where is he? Or do I need to bite you too? What kind of monster must I become to persuade you? How about a fire-breathing dragon? I can do that just as easily."

"No, don't!" she said in a tremulous voice. "I'll tell you. Jefferson is caught in a ghost trap. The ghost hunter has him in his office downstairs in the basement."

"You sent your ghost hunter to trap Thomas Jefferson?" Adams thundered. "You fool! Do you have any idea who you are trifling with?"

As Patty and Nigel cowered on the sofa, Adams rendered himself invisible and walked through the door.

HELD FAST BY a barrage of light rays that enveloped him like an electronic cocoon, Jefferson thrashed and squirmed, but it was no use. He tried to move left and right and up and down, but found he could barely budge, and then only with great difficulty. Switching back and forth between being visible and invisible had no effect on the trap. Rivers of energy flowed around him from all sides and restrained him like unseen ropes.

Jefferson had no idea where he was and could see nothing but blackness and hear only a constant buzz. Yet he could still think and sense the force of energy and was conscious that he was being contained inside some kind of strange apparatus.

The last thing he remembered was reaching for an interesting new book about Aristotle on the bookshelf in the Yellow Oval Room. That was the bait. The young ghost hunter had done this to him.

Jefferson pulled and pushed this way and that, but nothing helped free him from his electronic cage. He was utterly bewildered.

Minutes became hours, and hours stretched into what seemed like days. He lost track of time.

After an undetermined period, he was thrusting his right arm sideways and then up and down when he noticed something odd about the mysterious confining force: Whatever the strange envelope of energy was, it was not uniformly distributed around him. In some places it was strong, and in others weak. In the force's weak spots, he could move more freely. If he could just apply enough strength to a weak area, he might be able to break free of the trap. It was worth a try.

Jefferson became invisible, concentrated himself into a corner of the force field, and pushed against it with all his might.

Suddenly, the awful buzzing stopped.

To his amazement, he found himself standing outside the walls of a flat, rectangular box. He gaped at it for a moment. It appeared to be made of metal. A green light on the box was blinking on and off.

He looked straight up at his surroundings. He was on the floor of an office that looked bigger than a cathedral, and everything around and above him was huge: a desk, a chair, and a young giant, whom he recognized as the ghost hunter.

As his own head was no higher than the sole of the ghost hunter's shoe, Jefferson estimated he was hardly half an inch tall. He flapped his arms to see what would happen. Suddenly, his body expanded itself to thousands of times its previous volume, back to its normal size, inflating like a balloon.

He bent down to inspect the small device that lay blinking at his feet. This was the thing so powerful it could grab and hold him?

What wonderful physics the living had discovered in the past two hundred years, that they could ensnare an incorporeal being like a ghost in something no bigger than a snuffbox! How could such a thing work?

Jefferson looked down at Clint, engrossed in his computer screen, unaware that his erstwhile prisoner had just broken free and was standing unseen beside him, only an arm's length away. It occurred to the specter that he could lash out and strike Clint down with a single blow to the head. Some ghosts undoubtedly would.

Jefferson resisted the temptation. Revenging himself on the ghost hunter would do him no good. Far from being resentful at being kidnapped and shrunk to the size of a thimble, Jefferson was overcome with curiosity about how the young fellow had performed such an astounding feat. He scrutinized him with a mixture of awe, amusement, and alarm.

In another setting, at another time, Jefferson mused, this would be a splendid chance to engage in an hours-long scientific discussion with his captor. There were a thousand questions he would love to ask, but this was not the moment to pose them. The ghost hunter's ingenious traps constituted a grave threat to the other ghosts, many of whom lacked the resourcefulness and ability to elude the devices.

The Ghost Council must be warned of the new danger at once. Jefferson marched through the wall of Clint's office and into the hallway in search of Adams.

He had only taken a few steps down the hall when he turned and saw a short, portly ghost in a frock coat hobbling toward him with a huge smile on his face.

"Aha! What was lost has now been found!" Adams shouted with delight. "How good to see you, Thomas!"

"Oh, you have no idea how happy I am to see you, Mr. Adams," replied Jefferson, hugging his old friend.

CHAPTER 19
BURYING THE MEMO

MAX PERKINS PRIDED himself on having seen it all in his twenty-five years with the Defense Intelligence Agency. The beefy Assistant Deputy Chief of Threat Assessment had fought in Iraq and Afghanistan and had even lost an arm to a roadside bomb. He was tough as leather, and everyone knew it. The DIA analysts who worked for him at Joint Base Anacostia-Bolling feared coming to the hard-bitten veteran with half-baked information, knowing he would chew them out.

Decades of working in intelligence had made Perkins wise in the ways of bureaucracy. He had seen a lot of B.S. and had become jaded, even gruff at times, but no one denied he had a caring heart. He was especially kind to the young employees, like Jane Williams.

A new analyst in his unit, Jane hadn't been around long enough to know the ropes. She walked into Perkins's glass-lined office and handed him one of the silliest briefing memos he had ever seen.

The memo said the CIA had discovered some intelligence about a supposed surge in paranormal activity at the White

House, and Jane, bless her little heart, actually believed every last word of it. Perkins restrained himself, doing his best not to ridicule her.

There's been an upsurge in ghost activity in the White House? Ghosts? Is she kidding?

Perkins read the memo as the young woman sat across the desk from him, eagerly awaiting his response. It was all he could do not to burst out laughing.

The whole CIA dispatch was nonsense, but the part that really floored him was its last line, which proposed that the DIA "immediately review the adequacy of the nation's current threat level, pursuant to DEFCON Boo guidelines."

"DEFCON Boo? That sounds really cool. What is that? Do we investigate ghosts too?" Jane asked in complete seriousness, sweeping the long brown hair off her pretty forehead.

"It's...well, never mind what it is," said Perkins gently, taking a sip of coffee. "It's top secret. You don't have a need to know. Leave it to me. I'll handle it."

"Okay." Jane smiled at him and went flouncing back to her gray, cloth-covered cubicle, leaving the bureaucrat laughing quietly in his office about how the young analyst had fallen off the turnip truck.

It's like they're hiring them younger and younger every day. They'll believe in anything—even ghosts.

Jane reminded Perkins so much of his twenty-year-old daughter that he couldn't bring himself to come down hard on her. No problem. In time, she'd learn what was what.

His more experienced analysts would have recognized that the memo was rubbish. It had to be. The CIA didn't share critical material with the DIA. It hogged information and used it for the agency's own clandestine purposes. Jane was too green to know that.

The memo was probably required by one of Homeland Security's well-intended regulations aimed at getting the intelligence agencies to cooperate with each other instead of competing. Except things never worked that way in the real world.

The CIA didn't have a clue about what to do with their ludicrous "discovery," so rather than deal with it themselves, they were passing the buck to the DIA, which they assumed would file it away and forget it. If the CIA were actually worried, it would treat the information like gold, rush it to President Pitypander, and take full credit for warning that she was in mortal danger from ghosts. Since they hadn't done that, their memo had to be garbage.

In the intelligence business, how you handled information was often more important than the content itself, Perkins knew. You offloaded what you didn't want to deal with and let somebody else waste their time on it. That's what the CIA had done.

Ghosts in the White House? That's a good one! Oh, yeah, we'll get right on it! Thanks for giving us the tip, CIA—you lousy SOBs!

Even if there were ghosts there, what was the Defense Department supposed to do about it, send Navy SEALS to chase them out of the East Room?

DEFCON Boo. Gimme a break.

No senior DIA official with any career ambition would risk breathing the words DEFCON Boo to his supervisor. Perkins wasn't about to be the first. He was due for a promotion and didn't want to be a GS-14 forever. He had tuition bills to pay. His daughter's college cost eighty grand a year.

The memo wasn't going anywhere, and neither was the news it contained. As soon as Jane had left, Perkins shuffled over to his filing cabinet. With his remaining arm, he dropped the CIA memo into a special manila folder, the one where he stored documents he intended never to lay eyes on again.

"Ghosts! Ha!" Perkins said with a snicker, closing the filing cabinet.

CHAPTER 20
THE CONSPIRACY

THERE WAS A knock at Sartini's office door. The vice president opened it and found housekeeping usher Phaedra McBride standing before him, looking anxious.

"Could I have a word with you, Mr. Vice President? Privately, I mean."

"Certainly." Sartini directed her to a chair and shut the door.

Her face was drawn and sullen, like she had been losing sleep. "I may not have been entirely fair to you, sir, when we talked last. Something has been bothering me."

"Oh?"

McBride sat up straight. "Some peculiar things have happened in the Residence lately, and I think somebody ought to know about it. I really don't know who else to turn to. Mr. Twiggs would order me to keep quiet about it, but I can't. I think it's a matter of national security, like you were trying to tell me before."

"National security. My goodness," Sartini said in a solicitous tone. "What is it?"

"Please understand, Mr. Vice President, I'm only concerned for the country," replied McBride. "It wouldn't be good if something was really wrong with the president and nobody here in a position to know about it was willing to step up and face the problem honestly, would it?"

"No, absolutely not," replied Sartini, "but what is it that's wrong with her?"

The usher's eyes shifted left and right. "The president...is seeing ghosts." She settled back into her chair, pressed a hand to her chest, and exhaled, as if she had gotten the weight of the world off her shoulders.

"Ghosts? Really? Are you serious?" Sartini began to laugh but stopped himself. He scrutinized McBride's face. She seemed sincere.

"Yes, and she's not just seeing them," said the usher. "She's even talking to them, like they're really there. Now, mind you, there have always been spooky tales about ghosts hanging around here. But nobody ever really believed them. They were just fun ghost stories that we all loved hearing but never took seriously."

"But how do you know she's seeing ghosts? Do you have any proof?"

McBride told him how one of her maids had happened to walk in on the president as she was hallucinating all by herself in the Yellow Oval Room. The usher pulled out her phone and played back the video recording of Patty talking to nobody.

"There. See what I mean?"

"Yes, I sure do," said Sartini, slack-jawed.

McBride replayed the video and stopped it partway. "Look there, how she's standing by herself, without another soul in the room."

The video was unmistakable. The camera panned from one side of the room to the other. The president was talking into space and chucking a vase of flowers into the window.

"And it's not just that," said McBride. "She's even brought in a ghost hunter from the FBI. He's been snooping around the Residence at all hours, looking for ghosts, setting up his equipment and placing traps to catch them."

"An FBI agent? They do ghost busting?"

"Apparently so. His name is Clint Cranberry. She believes in him and has given him the run of the whole White House. I hear he takes her ghost stories seriously."

Sartini rubbed his chin. "Hmm, or maybe he just pretends to."

The FBI agent's intentions might not be all they seemed to be. The supposed ghost buster could be a predator, humoring the impressionable president so he could gain access to her, playing to her delusions to influence her, like a modern-day Rasputin. That would definitely be a threat to national security.

McBride slumped back in her chair. "So, you see why I can't just stay quiet, don't you? The president's husband is never around to see how crazy she's become and do something about her. She has no family in the White House, so that leaves us, the ushers and housekeepers. We're the people who see her the most. Well, I thought to myself, somebody has to step forward and intervene somehow. The President of the United States can't be crazy. The country simply can't afford that."

"Absolutely not." Sartini folded his hands and told McBride she had done the right thing by coming to him.

She gave him a pleading look. "You won't tell Mr. Twiggs I told you any of this, will you? He'd fire me on the spot if he knew I've blabbed the president's secrets to you."

Sartini assured her he wouldn't tell.

A tear flowed down McBride's cheek. "Please forgive me, Mr. Vice President. I shouldn't blubber like this, but this has been such a terrible strain. I didn't know what to do, but I just knew I had to tell somebody who's in a position to do something about her. You came to me asking about her behavior, so I thought—"

"Yes, I understand." Sartini helped the usher to her feet, patted her on the shoulder, and escorted her to the door. "I'll take care of it, Mrs. McBride. Don't you worry."

CLINT SAT AT his workbench amid the clutter of his tools and spare parts, inspecting the delicate components he would need to build a better ghost trap. This one, he hoped, would generate a force field that no ghost, not even one as clever as Thomas Jefferson, could slip out of.

President Pitypander had looked distraught when he told her that Jefferson had escaped. Her would-be tutor was once again at large and might resume trying to educate her at any time.

In a voice tinged with desperation, she had asked Clint how the Potusgeists could be brought under control if the ghost traps didn't work. The White House couldn't go on functioning like this, with the president afraid of her own shadow. There had to be some way to end the harassment.

Under pressure to find a solution quickly, Clint puzzled day and night over what to do about his trap's flawed design. At last, while measuring the strength of the force field, he found the defect: The trap's electromagnetic emitters were slightly misaligned, creating unevenness in the force field that resulted in weak spots. Jefferson had discovered one of the weak spots and simply pushed through it. He would teach the trick to the other ghosts, rendering Clint's current trap design ineffective.

Correcting the flaw would be a daunting technical challenge. Clint needed to devise an entirely new adjustment mechanism, one that would ensure perfect alignment of the force field emitters.

He was considering various engineering options when there was a knock at his office door. The vice president stood in the doorway.

"Are you Clint Cranberry?" asked Sartini.

"Uh, yes, sir," the startled agent replied.

It was unheard of for someone of the vice president's rank to visit a junior FBI agent with no prior notice. When the president wanted to talk to Clint, her secretary always called first to summon him to the Oval Office. Clint surmised that Sartini didn't want to be seen with the ghost hunter in his own office, for fear of being thought to believe in the paranormal. Ghost phobia was a common problem among the uninformed.

"I won't waste your time, Agent Cranberry," said Sartini. "I have some questions for you. They tell me you've been doing an investigation here in the White House. Would you mind telling me what it's all about?"

Clint felt a lump in his throat. Sartini knew perfectly well that FBI agents were forbidden to tell people about their investigations. On top of that, the President of the United States had sworn him to secrecy. But did a lowly junior agent dare stonewall the vice president?

He had to. If he leaked the president's secrets and she complained to FBI headquarters, his budding career would be over. Everything he had gone through to become a special agent—his training at Quantico and his months on the job—would have been a waste. Ghost-hunting gigs with a steady paycheck weren't easy to find. Worst of all, he would lose his once-in-a-lifetime opportunity to learn more about the Potusgeists. "I can't say," he replied. "Please understand, sir, my work is classified."

"Are you looking for ghosts, by any chance?" Sartini asked.

There was no point in lying. The vice president clearly knew who he was. "I'm from the FBI's paranormal unit. I guess they told you that."

"Yes, they did. Who asked you to look for ghosts in the White House?"

"I'm not allowed to say, sir. My work is classified."

"Classified. Hmm." Sartini's eyes zoomed in on Clint's worktable. "What is that?" He reached over, grabbed a radar gun, and pulled the trigger. The gun's screen lit up.

Clint jumped out of his chair. "Please be careful with that, sir. It's fragile. You might break it."

"Is this some kind of ray gun? Do you shoot ghosts with this thing?" Sartini aimed it at the wall as if he were blasting an alien invader. "This little screen here is reading four hundred milligauss. What the heck's a milligauss?"

"It's a measure of the intensity of a magnetic field, sir."

"Why would you want to measure magnetic fields in the White House? Do we have a magnetism problem around here?"

"I wish I could tell you, sir, but that's classified too. Sorry."

"Come on, you can tell me. I'm the vice president. I work for the president too, you know."

Too? What did he mean by that? Was Sartini trying to trick him into admitting that he was working directly for the president? And that she was seeing ghosts?

Clint bit his lip.

Sartini laid the radar gun back on the worktable. "You know, I can call the FBI Director and ask him these questions instead. He, or somebody under him, must know you're here. I just thought you might want to tell me yourself, in your own words, so I won't have to make that call and embarrass you for not cooperating with me."

Clint looked him squarely in the eye. "Sorry, sir. I have my orders."

Sartini smirked. "All right, you have a job to do—I get it. I'll leave you alone. Say, can I count on you not to tell anyone I was here?"

"We never met, sir."

"Good man." Sartini winked, patted him on the shoulder, and left.

★ ★ ★

SARTINI RETURNED TO his office, convinced that the president was a raving lunatic. He had solid proof, backed by a witness. The fact that Pitypander had brought in a ghost hunter only added to his certainty.

Everything was falling into place. The vice presidency was going to pan out. He wouldn't have to keep playing second fiddle to Pitypander or attending endless state funerals and ribbon-cutting ceremonies.

With the president out of her mind, Sartini was in a prime position to reach for the brass ring and take over. Under the circumstances, he would be crazy not to.

Ousting Pitypander would be a stunningly bold political move. It might fail, but Sartini had a plan for that too. He was only thirty-eight. At his age, he still had a million options, both in and out of politics. He could run for the presidency later or go into business, get on a few corporate boards, and make some real money. If nothing else, the vice presidency had given him connections to the right people. They would be his safety net in case his plan bombed.

To pull off his coup, he would need powerful allies in both the Cabinet and Congress. He had already met with several Cabinet members about their shocked reactions to the president's bizarre behavior. Winning over Congress would be the more formidable challenge.

Sartini asked his secretary to get Speaker Underdown on the line.

"It was fabulous seeing you at the state dinner, Iris," Sartini barked into his speakerphone. "We should get together more often."

Underdown sounded characteristically gruff and standoffish. "I'm pretty busy today, Tony. We've got a bill that's up for a vote in a few minutes, and I need to go down to the House floor. What have you got?"

Sartini reminded Underdown about how strangely the president was acting at the state dinner. "I found out what's been going on with her. She's seeing ghosts."

There was a long pause. Sartini could almost hear the gears turning in Underdown's head.

"Ghosts, as in dead people?"

"Yes."

"You got solid proof of this?"

"I do now. I have a video recording of her going nuts in an empty room, talking to them. She's gone bonkers."

"How do you know the recording isn't a fake?"

"I'm one hundred percent sure of what I saw, Iris. I know the source of the information personally. She's totally reliable. The evidence she's given me is rock solid."

"So what? What are you going to do about her?"

"As vice president, I have a duty to take over the presidency under the Twenty-Fifth Amendment, on the grounds that Pitypander is mentally unable to execute the duties of her office."

"What? You're planning to remove the president from office against her will? The Twenty-Fifth Amendment has never been used for that. Things could get very messy if the president refuses to go."

That was exactly the reaction Sartini expected. "It's a first,

I'll admit. That's why I'll need you to back me. Getting the Cabinet on board won't be enough to satisfy the voters. The country will want to see Congress behind me too, to show we have broad support. Otherwise, it'll look like we're staging a third-world palace coup. Also, if she refuses to go, as I expect, Congress will have to decide who's president, so either way, you'll be directly involved."

"I don't like it," said Underdown. "This is political dynamite you're playing with. It could blow up in your face—and mine. I'm not risking my political career so you can be president. I won't be a part of that. Now, I've really gotta get down to the House floor—"

"Wait, Iris, don't hang up. Please."

"Look, I've heard enough. I'm not helping you push her out, and that's flat."

"Iris, when I take over, there will be an opening for a new vice president."

There was another long pause.

"Are you offering me the vice presidency, Tony?"

"Sure, why not? You're third in line for the presidency now. Why not be second in line? Later, you might end up as president yourself. President Underdown—that has a nice ring to it, doesn't it? "

Sartini let that sink in for a moment. There was nobody of any importance on Capitol Hill who didn't yearn to be president, whose ego wouldn't be tempted by the opportunity.

"Hold that thought, Tony. I'll call you back in an hour, as soon as the vote is over."

Sartini put down the phone and lay back in his chair, his head resting on his hands. Underdown was in the bag.

★ ★ ★

A PLOT TO overthrow the president!

Lurking in the corner of Sartini's office, invisible, John Adams was stunned.

Everything Adams had suspected about the vice president since the inauguration was true. Sartini was a devious snake, a conniving scoundrel, and a would-be king.

Adams had foreseen the vice president's treachery, so he wasn't as much surprised as he was profoundly disappointed. For a president to be forced out of office in such a high-handed manner was appallingly un-American. To think things had come to this!

The people, not some small cabal of insiders, should decide who their leader was. Taking their rights and freedoms for granted, they had let knaves seize the reins of their government.

Sartini was the symptom of a disease eating away at the body politic. Tyranny had come to America, as it had to ancient Rome, in the form of a man with overweening ambition, in a time of weak leadership and widespread institutional corruption. Americans were lost in ignorance and individual self-absorption. Turning against their own past, their identity erased, they had forgotten who they were and had ceded control of their future to unworthy stewards.

Throughout history, this was how democracy had been lost.

The Council must be convened as soon as possible to discuss how to respond to Sartini's scheme. Jefferson would have some interesting thoughts about that. Adams hurried through the wall and made his way to the Residence to find him.

He had just passed into the Red Room when a woman's voice echoed behind him. "John! John!"

It was Abigail, rushing toward him with a distressed look on her face.

"I've been searching for you everywhere," she said breathlessly. "Have you seen Quincy?"

"Quincy?" Adams rubbed his chin. "No, come to think of it, not for...let's see, it would be going on three days now."

"Nobody else has seen him either. I'm worried. Quincy wouldn't leave for so long without telling somebody."

Could this be the work of the ghost hunter? Quincy, like Jefferson before him, might at this very moment be caught in one of his fiendish traps, desperately struggling to escape.

The traps were yet another matter for the Council to deal with. Adams rushed with Abigail to the ghost den.

CHAPTER 21

THE PRISONER

CLINT WALKED DOWN the dimly lit steps to the basement of the Residence, his heavy gym bag of sensors banging against his knee.

Until now, he had left the lowest level of the mansion unexplored, venturing downstairs only once to do a cursory inspection of some storage rooms, thinking it unlikely he would find anything. Ghosts preferred to haunt the places they had frequented in life, and the Potusgeists, who had resided on the upper floors, had no reason to inhabit rooms three stories below.

In the interest of thoroughness, Clint reconsidered. The ghosts could roam anywhere in the White House, to nooks and crannies where no one would ever expect to discover them. He decided to do a broader search and sweep the whole basement.

He started in one of the larger storage rooms, where tables, chairs, and supplies for major events like state dinners were kept. Seeing nothing of interest there, he entered a small utility room filled with electrical breaker panels. His radar gun showed no sign of anything out of the ordinary. His thermal sensor detected no drop in temperature.

Wandering down the hall, Clint methodically inspected one area after another, coming to a larger utility room roaring with the Residence's air conditioning equipment. Near it, he noticed a dingy door with faded paint in the northeast corner of the basement. He pressed on it, but it stuck tight to its jamb. Pushing his shoulder against it, he gently kicked the bottom. The door shuddered open, its rusty hinges creaking loudly.

He flicked on the light switch and looked up. Old wooden crates lay atop one another, covered with a thick coat of dust. Cobwebs stretched across the dark corners near the ceiling. A sweet, musty odor pervaded the space.

A thick book lay on one of the crates. He read the title: *The Decline and Fall of the Roman Empire.* Inside the cover was scrawled the name "J. Adams, Esq."

Clint's hands trembled. *John Adams has been here.*

He lay the book down, stepped farther inside the room, and was seized by an eerie coldness.

As he turned around, he felt his wrists being grabbed and yanked behind his back. His gym bag dropped to the floor.

"What the heck?"

He wrenched his head as far back as he could and caught a glimpse of the shimmering forms of two ghosts wearing suits and black silk neck scarves.

"Who are you?" Clint asked, his voice cracking with fear.

"William Henry Harrison, if you must know," said the specter on his left, staring at him sternly. "You're in a lot of trouble, young man." Harrison looked at the other ghost. "Do you have a tight hold of him over there, Mr. Tyler?"

"I do, sir," the other ghost replied.

Harrison and Tyler? Oh, my God. It's Tippecanoe—and Tyler too.

Those were the two Whigs who won the 1840 presidential election, Clint remembered from his research.

William Harrison, nicknamed Tippecanoe, was the Indian-fighting president who succumbed to pneumonia, which he contracted while giving a two-hour inauguration speech on a bitterly cold day. He passed away just a month later—the first president to die not only while in office but in the White House itself. Tyler, his running mate, was the first vice president to take over after a president's death.

It made perfect sense that Harrison should be a White House ghost. His life had been cut short here at a critical time, right after he took office. Cheated out of his opportunity to lead the nation, he had unfinished business.

But what was Harrison doing in the basement? According to White House ghost lore, he was supposed to be haunting the attic.

This must be a special room, Clint realized. It was the Potusgeists' den, their club room. Ghosts liked to hang out together, and this forgotten storage area was the perfect spot to do it—the one place they wouldn't be bothered by the living. The room had been abandoned because of its sticky old door, which no one had bothered to fix.

The two ghosts dragged the young man behind the wall of crates and bound him fast with ropes to a large vertical drainage pipe in the corner.

Clint tilted his head up and screamed, "Help! Help!"

"Hush," said Harrison angrily. He glanced at Tyler. "Close that door and put something in his mouth."

Tyler found an old white rag inside a wall cabinet and began to tie it around Clint's head.

"Wait, let's question him before you gag him." Harrison peered into Clint's eyes. "Where's John Quincy Adams? What have you done with him?"

"I don't know what you're talking about," Clint replied. "Is he missing?"

Harrison's lips flared. "Don't play dumb with us, boy. You know damn well he is. You'd better think up a better answer than that, and fast. John and Abigail Adams are coming here, and they'll skin you alive when they learn that you're the rascal who kidnapped their son with one of your infernal traps."

"But there are no ghosts in my traps. I checked them no more than an hour ago."

"A likely story!" Harrison raised his fist at him. "Have it your way. Go ahead and gag him, Mr. Tyler. Some time to think about being torn limb from limb might improve his memory."

It wasn't an idle threat. Even an average ghost had many times the strength of the living and could kill him easily. There were ancient tales of ghosts wreaking their revenge on the living with medieval methods of torture, such as slowly pulling their victims apart, piece by piece.

Clint grunted as Tyler wrapped the rag around his head. He closed his eyes, his body shaking as he imagined the agony of being dismembered.

A HUSH FELL over the ghosts as John Adams arrived at the Council meeting with Abigail, their faces consumed by worry. The frightful news that Quincy had been missing for three whole days had sparked an uproar in the ghostly community.

The very idea that such eminent leaders as themselves could be hunted down like rats was outrageous. If the Sage of Monticello and now the honorable sixth president, John Quincy Adams, had been snatched, there must be no limit to the ghost hunter's impudence. Who would be next to fall victim to his diabolical mechanisms?

Jefferson's hair-raising account of what it had been like to be sucked in by one of the ghost hunter's mysterious contraptions and held fast in its merciless electronic grip so inflamed Adams's fears that he began to pray in silence.

Abigail was equally distraught. Adams tried to restore her hope, reminding her that somehow Jefferson had gotten free and maybe Quincy could do the same. "We must trust in divine Providence, my dear."

Mr. Harrison and Mr. Tyler came rushing up.

"Good news, Mr. Adams!" said Tyler excitedly. "We have just caught the ghost hunter red-handed."

"There's your man, sir." Harrison pointed out the tall young fellow tied fast to the big drain pipe in the corner, grunting with a gag in his mouth. "We apprehended him not an hour ago, prowling around here as if he was looking for something. We found him toting a bag full of some strange equipment. He pretends not to know what he's done with your boy. We left it to you to beat the truth out of him. We thought you'd want the satisfaction."

Adams approached Clint, inspecting the FBI agent up and down with a cold stare.

As much as he wanted to believe this was the perpetrator, he perceived that something was amiss. The old codger had defended plenty of riffraff in his law practice and prided himself that he could tell an innocent man from a felon at thirty paces simply by observing his expression. This was no felon.

The ghost hunter lacked the desperate, wanton eyes of a kidnapper. There was a streak of virtue in his young face. He seemed more like a common tradesman than a criminal.

Adams grew uneasy with doubt and removed the gag. "Speak, boy. Have you seen my son?"

Panting, Clint labored to catch his breath. "No, sir. I haven't captured any ghosts this week. I've checked my traps, and there are no ghosts in any of them."

Adams harrumphed and pointed the end of his cane at him. "That's not for want of your trying! How dare you set traps to seize us! Who do you think you are? More to the point, who do you think we are? Kidnap my son, will you? I don't think so!"

Clint clenched his teeth, preparing to be dismembered, as the furious ghosts pressed closer.

Adams waved them back. "No, this is not the time to exact revenge." He turned to Clint. "We'll deal with you later. Right now, we have even more important business to discuss. Mr. Harrison, would you and Mr. Tyler please be so good as to escort him out of here for a while? What I am about to say is not meant for his ears."

Harrison and Tyler untied Clint and led him away.

Adams stepped onto the speaker's box. "Ladies and gentlemen, please listen. I bring you news even more distressing than the heinous kidnapping of my son."

He explained that he had been monitoring Sartini closely since the inauguration, watching the vice president's every move. "He is assembling a cabal within the Cabinet that will be legally empowered to oust Mrs. Pitypander from office and replace her with himself. It is a most traitorous scheme, which I fear could lead to much political strife and tear the country asunder."

His warning was met with baffled looks from the ghosts. What was the problem with Mrs. Pitypander being ousted? A palace coup would be their chance to get rid of her without lifting a finger. Why not just let events unfold by themselves? Let the living rule the living, someone said.

Teddy Roosevelt, peering through his pince-nez eyeglasses, raised his hand to speak. "Mr. Adams, with all due respect, I am thoroughly confused as to your views on Mrs. Pitypander. It was only recently that you and Mr. Jefferson urgently convened a Council meeting in which you asserted she was the worst president ever to set foot in office. We must intervene, you insisted, to prevent her from wrecking the country with her fantastically bad ideas. Are we to understand that this is no longer the case? Has Mrs. Pitypander reformed her thinking with no help from us?"

"Sir, I stand by what we previously told you," replied Adams. "Mrs. Pitypander is the most abominable president we have seen to date, as unfit as ever, but her vice president poses an even greater threat. Mr. Tony Sartini is an ambitious backstabber with the heart of a ruthless tyrant, whereas Mrs. Pitypander is merely a foolishly stubborn do-gooder advocating a ruinous Utopian agenda."

"This is our choice, a despot or a fool?" asked Roosevelt. "They both sound horrendous. Perhaps they deserve each other. Are they not equally bad?"

"No, they are not," said Adams. "Mrs. Pitypander's faults are located in her thick head, where education and reason could cure them, if she would allow it, while Sartini's are written on his blackened soul, from which they can never be expunged, save by the grace of God. Therefore, he now poses the greater danger to our republic and ought to be the present focus of our efforts."

James Madison, standing on a box of his own, spoke up. "I object. If we take on Sartini, we'll become mired in his problems, forced to get ever more deeply involved with him, as we have with Mrs. Pitypander. Soon, you'll want to depart from the Rules to get rid of Sartini. Do we wish to become so embroiled in the business of the living that we choose their leaders for them? We never have before."

"It cannot be helped, Mr. Madison," said Adams. "The times are perilous and require our active participation—that is, unless you all prefer to stand idly by and watch our glorious republic being dismantled by a dictator. During the Revolution, I put my life on the line to prevent such a calamity. In death, I can do no less."

Someone in the crowd shouted, "Hear, hear! Well spoken, Adams!"

"What would you have us do?" Madison asked. "How broad a scope of intervention do you advocate? If we are to permit further involvement, we deserve to know before voting."

"I was coming to that." Adams grasped the lapels of his waistcoat. "I propose the least intervention possible: Let us give Mrs. Pitypander fair warning of Sartini's plot, that she may prepare herself in time to thwart his coup attempt. Give her fair warning, I say—no more help than that."

"Fair warning? That's all?" Madison regarded him skeptically. "As much as I would like to believe things would stop there, experience tells me we are headed toward fighting her battles for her. I thought you said Mrs. Pitypander was stubborn. Has she paid attention to any guidance we have offered her thus far?"

Adams looked at Jefferson. "In truth, no—not the slightest attention, I regret to say. Mrs. Pitypander is singularly obtuse and will not listen to reason."

"Not singularly, sir," Jefferson interjected, "but plurally, as she has plenty of company in her frailties. She is a woman, after all, and like all members of the fair sex, reflexively and resentfully opposes any advice thrust upon her by men, even well-intentioned gentlemen like ourselves."

"Then, if she will not listen to us, how are we gentlemen to convince her of her peril?" asked Madison.

"The warning the Council proposes to send her need not be conveyed by a man," Jefferson replied. "A woman would have a distinct advantage over any man here in efficacy of persuasion. Women, I have observed, listen to each other. Why they do so, I cannot say, but it is plain that they do."

"Very well, then." Adams cast his eyes about the room for a volunteer. "Would any of you ladies be willing to act as the Council's ambassador to inform Mrs. Pitypander about Sartini's treasonous intentions?"

Abigail Adams and Dolley Madison raised their hands.

"Ah, two lovely ladies!" said Adams. "Excellent. With two of you on the job, we should expect Mrs. Pitypander to be twice as persuaded. Mr. Madison, by lending our wives to this cause, I fear we risk being shown up, for they are far more capable than we are."

"Fear not, Mr. Adams," Madison replied with a grin. "The world has known that for centuries."

A ghost slipped into the meeting at the back of the room. Adams squinted at the figure, hardly able to believe his eyes.

"Quincy!" Adams shouted with joy. "Is it really you?"

"Yes, Father," Quincy answered with a wave of his hand. "Sorry, I'm late. I was detained at our old place in Massachusetts. Did I miss anything?"

The ghosts turned around, astonished. They peppered Quincy with questions about where he had been for three days and why he hadn't told anyone he was planning to be gone. Quincy responded that he didn't expect to be away so long but found upon his arrival at Peacefield, the Adams's family farm, that he had to do some emergency haunting to scare off some incompetent restoration contractors who were about to ruin the historic property. He hadn't foreseen that his absence would cause such distress.

"All's well that ends well," said the senior Adams with a broad smile. "Now we have but one piece of unfinished business left."

As God had granted his son's safe return, a spirit of warm generosity washed over him.

The Potusgeists had no reason to hold the misguided young ghost hunter hostage any longer, as no actual harm had been done, Adams argued. "The quality of mercy is not strained, gentlemen. So says Shakespeare, and so say I."

The ghosts had given Clint a taste of his own medicine by scaring him out of his wits and ought to release him, if he would behave himself and do no further mischief to them.

Adams proposed three conditions for Clint's freedom: "You must promise not to reveal where our meeting room is, you will never attempt to trap us again, and you will deliver a message to Mrs. Pitypander to appear alone tomorrow night at eight o'clock in the Treaty Room, where she will encounter two ghosts."

Clint, much relieved to know he would not be flayed alive or torn limb from limb, readily agreed to these easy terms, and the Potusgeists let him go, unhurt.

CHAPTER 22

Fair Warning

PATTY ENTERED THE Treaty Room, wondering why the ghosts wanted to meet her there. The place didn't seem particularly spooky.

With its massive chandelier, long table, and matching chairs, the room was where the treaty to end the Spanish-American War had been signed. Its most striking feature was an elegant gilded mirror with intricate neoclassical detailing, complemented by a white marble mantel.

Tonight, the antique mirror looked different somehow. An otherworldly glow ringed its frame with light from the chandelier. Patty sat down and beheld her image in the glass, becoming mesmerized by the aura around the mirror. She found herself unable to turn her eyes away.

This was no ordinary mirror, she realized—it was haunted. The longer Patty stared, the stronger the glow grew. After a few seconds, the mirror started pulsing rhythmically, as if mimicking the beat of her heart.

The bells in a clock on the wall tolled eight times. A deep

voice boomed out of the ceiling: "Mirror, mirror, I see you. Be the one to show these two."

Two indistinct circles suddenly appeared in the mirror's glass, side by side. Slowly, they came into sharper focus.

They weren't circles, Patty realized. They were faces!

Two ghosts were peering back at her. One was a severe-looking lady wearing a white lace bonnet, and the other a woman with rouged cheeks and a friendly smile.

"Good evening, Mrs. Pitypander," said the figure in the bonnet. "So nice of you to join us. My name is Mrs. Abigail Adams. Here by my side is Mrs. Dolley Madison."

"Um, hello," Patty replied, not sure how to address women the age of her fourth great-grandmother. Should she say "madam" or "ma'am" or "Mrs. Whatever"?

"We do hope you are enjoying the White House," said Mrs. Madison with a gentle Virginia drawl. "It is such a marvelous place, isn't it?"

Patty acknowledged that it was.

Mrs. Madison, smiling mildly, seemed the amiable type, not the least bit ponderous and self-important like the male ghosts. Mrs. Adams, on the contrary, was sullen and gave off a stuffier vibe, like a no-nonsense New Englander.

"We know you must be busy, Mrs. Pitypander," said Mrs. Adams, "so we won't keep you. We've been asked by the Council to bring you some important information. We hope you won't mind."

In truth, Patty minded the ghosts' meddling in her business very much, but her mounting curiosity about the strange beings outweighed her irritation. She asked the two phantasms what the meeting was all about.

"I will speak plainly and directly, woman to woman," said Mrs. Adams. "The Council has sent us because we've learned that your vice president, Mr. Sartini, is not at all what he pretends to be."

"Oh, what do you mean by that?"

"He is plotting to overthrow you."

Patty burst out laughing. "Tony Sartini? Are you joking?"

Mrs. Adams's face revealed no emotion. "You will find that I rarely joke, Mrs. Pitypander. Mr. Sartini has been using you for his own nefarious ends. He is gathering allies to his side to rise up against you as we speak."

It was a preposterous idea. The cute young congressman with the Roman nose was betraying her? Sartini, not yet forty, was barely old enough to be president. He didn't have the national backing to pull off a coup. The rich donors who pulled the strings of the Democratic party's candidates hardly knew him.

The ghosts were obviously insane, but Patty wanted to hear them out. "Okay, and how, if I may ask, is he planning to go about this supposed takeover?"

"He has obtained evidence that you are seeing ghosts. He will use it against you, asserting that you have lost your mind."

But she *was* seeing ghosts. They were coming through the walls, following her around, and talking to her, right there in this strange mirror!

"What do you want me to do?"

"We were sent only to warn you of the danger you are in, not to render advice," replied Mrs. Adams. "How you deal with Mr. Sartini is your concern. But if you want my opinion...you do want it, don't you?"

Patty sighed. She was going to get Mrs. Adams's views whether she liked it or not. "Sure, what's your opinion?"

Mrs. Adams continued. "You must prevent Sartini's scheme from taking root. He knows that you have surrounded yourself with selfish, unprincipled people. Those are the same ones whom he intends to bribe with favors and turn against you. Start with them. Identify your betrayers in the Cabinet and replace them."

"You want me to purge the Cabinet? Just like that?"

"You must, and quickly. Otherwise, Sartini's plot will unfold, and you will be tossed out of office on your ear."

"Wait a minute! What difference would it make to you ghosts if I did lose the presidency? If you don't think I'm qualified to be here, why do you care what happens to me?"

Mrs. Adams threw her head back indignantly. "You don't do us justice, Mrs. Pitypander. I am a woman too—the first ever to live in this house. Why, the place wasn't even quite finished when John and I moved here in 1800. Many other women have lived here since, but you are only the second to arrive here as president. We women could not stand idly by and see you thrown out of this place by a man, much less a scoundrel like Sartini, without doing anything. We would not be able to forgive ourselves."

Patty scoffed. "I'm sorry, but I don't believe a word of this. Tony wouldn't do that to me. He couldn't if he tried."

"Don't be so sure," said Mrs. Adams. "The presidency is a temptation few men can resist. Hunger for power can drive men to forsake their friends and become bitter rivals. My husband John lost the White House to his vice president and good friend, Thomas Jefferson. Many years passed before they overcame their pride, buried their anger, and renewed their friendship."

What did that have to do with her? "If I take advice from a bunch of ghosts in a mirror, I really will be out of my mind. Why should I listen to you?"

"Why? Because you will learn either from history or from your own regrets," said Mrs. Adams. "We, the dead, have already made every mistake you could make. The future can be predicted by the past. Learn from us. Sorrow is such a heartless teacher."

She was being lectured by disembodied phantoms. It was incomprehensible. "I didn't get elected president by dead people, and I'm not taking advice from a couple of old witches. Get out of here and haunt someone else. I have a country to run."

Mrs. Adams glowered at her. "You call us witches, do you? How dare you! Here we have come to save your presidency, and you insult us for taking the trouble. You silly, ungrateful, insolent fool!"

"Why can't you ghosts get it through your heads that I don't want your help? Get lost!"

"Dolley, we are wasting our time, as I feared." Mrs. Adams turned once more to Patty. "You know, child, they told me you were surpassingly stubborn, but I think you are much worse. You are also spoiled, ignorant, incurious, and arrogant. I am amazed that Mr. Jefferson has shown such patience and concern for your welfare when you showed none for his. How cruel of you to set your ghost hunter after him and ensnare him in a trap!"

Patty yawned at the mirror. Jefferson had been taught a well-deserved lesson, and besides, he was free now. "Oh, spare me the lecture. A ghost cares about me? That's ridiculous."

"I heartily agree," Mrs. Adams replied with a snort. "You are most unworthy of his attention. But enough of this pointless talk. Dolley, we have delivered the Council's message as asked, and it will profit us little to squabble with the likes of her. I bid you good evening, Mrs. Pitypander. May you get the full measure of what you deserve."

A voice boomed from the ceiling again: "Mirror, mirror, we are done. Return to view the living one."

With that, the haunted mirror went dark, both ghosts faded into the blackness, and Patty saw her stunned face in the glass.

THE FIRST LADIES' weekly social was likely to be especially well attended, as the news about how rudely the president had rejected the ghosts' warning spread throughout the Potusgeist community. Anticipating a crowd, Dolley Madison arrived at the ghost den early to arrange the crates and make sure there were enough of them for all the first ladies to sit on.

Even when there was no real news in the White House, which was most of the time, the social furnished a splendid opportunity for the ladies to hear the latest gossip without having to endure the disapproving looks of their husbands. With the unsettling events of the last few days fresh in everyone's mind, there was a mountain of gossip to be traded.

Mrs. Madison had long regretted that she couldn't serve some relaxing libations at her little gatherings, as the disembodied ladies could not consume any sort of drink, including liquor. Some of the women would benefit from being loosened up a bit, even strict prohibitionists like Mrs. Hayes, who had banned alcohol from the White House. A few rounds of mint juleps would surely brighten the ladies' dispositions, but alas, it was physically impossible.

Without the aid of spirits, Mrs. Madison had to fall back on her well-known social graces to warm her guests. She would draw each of them into the group's discussion and make them feel their views were welcome and important. This was harder than it sounded, as the women hailed from such diverse backgrounds and time periods that they naturally clashed.

When arguments did break out, the first ladies blamed their husbands, which they all agreed was only fair, as the men were often the cause of their discord. Certain presidents were bitter rivals, and the women sometimes felt compelled to make a public show of championing their husbands' views, regardless of what they really thought.

In all situations, Mrs. Madison, the consummate hostess, played the peacemaker. She anticipated that today's discussion would be animated but hoped it would remain civil.

Her hopes were quickly dashed when Mrs. Adams began to tell everyone what had happened the previous evening.

"Oh, that Mrs. Pitypander is simply awful!" Mrs. Adams said, telling the group how poorly they had been received by the president. "Why, she is every bit as rude as we were told. Dolley and I went to her last night with the best of intentions, and what does she do but ignore our warning and call us old witches? A disgrace to her office, that's what she is. She has no manners and will accept no advice. Mr. Jefferson is wasting his time with her. The woman is too thick-headed to be taught anything."

Mrs. Lincoln's face became inflamed with rage. "I told everyone she would cause nothing but trouble. I told you she ought at least to be driven out of the White House. But did anyone listen to me? Of course not. No one ever does."

"Oh, Mary," said Mrs. Madison, "you don't mean it. You don't really want to drive her away."

"I do indeed!" Mrs. Lincoln replied. "I would do it myself, mind you, but Abe keeps stopping me. Only hanging can improve that woman, I tell you. Mr. Jefferson hasn't the slightest chance of succeeding with her."

Edith Wilson, a petite lady with expressive blue eyes, put her hand to her cheek. "Mrs. Lincoln, Mrs. Pitypander rubs some of us the wrong way with her indelicate modern style, but she can't have bothered you so much as to justify lynching her. If Mrs. Pitypander did die in office, she would become one of us that much sooner. Surely, you wouldn't prefer to have her here as a ghost, sitting beside you."

"I'm sure she didn't mean it, Edith," Mrs. Madison added, seeking to forestall another disagreeable outburst by Mrs. Lincoln. "Though we each have our opinions concerning the new president and her appropriateness for the job, I think we can all agree at least that it's a mighty fine thing that a woman has been elected once again."

"Even my Woodrow must think so by now," said Mrs. Wilson. "He was initially reluctant to let us have the vote, if you remember. But later, when he had his stroke, and I had to step in and run the country for him for seventeen long months, his views about women in office changed remarkably, don't you know."

Lucy Hayes put down her needlepoint and addressed the matter squarely. "Whatever is proper for a man to do is equally right for a woman. We have as much right and intelligence as men and are not meant to be their slaves."

"I make that clear to John at every opportunity," said Mrs. Adams, "and he pretends to agree."

Mrs. Hayes nodded. "That's a habit with husbands—they readily agree about a matter only when they think nothing will come of it."

"It did take them more than a century to admit us to the Council," said Mrs. Wilson. "But they eventually relented. We must give them credit for that. Men are slow learners, you know."

"What do you think, Julia?" Mrs. Madison asked.

"I believe the question is not whether a woman should be allowed to be president," Julia Grant opined. "Of course we should be. The question is whether Mrs. Pitypander should be. There have been some pretty awful men in the presidency too, and the republic has survived somehow. Aren't we entitled to have a clunker or two from our side?"

"We certainly have a clunker in Mrs. Pitypander," replied Mrs. Adams. "Have you noticed how she ogles that young ghost hunter? We are all just waiting to see what happens when she makes her move on him."

"That will be the day," added Mrs. Lincoln, fanning herself. "I can't imagine a fit young man like him wanting anything she has to offer, but who knows what temptations she may throw in his path? Did you know she was accused of molesting a teenage intern in California?'"

"You don't say," Mrs. Adams responded, looking horrified. "Well, I can believe it. She does have a roving eye. It's scandalous how she gawks at young men."

Eleanor Roosevelt sighed. "I think we are all much too quick to criticize Mrs. Pitypander. Rather than point out all the ways she should be better than she is, we should be better than we are and make the best of her presidency. The poor woman is in danger. Let's forgive her flaws, pitch in, and help her out, shall we?"

Several seconds of icy silence followed. Mrs. Adams made a grim face. Mrs. Lincoln pouted, fanned herself harder, and mumbled under her breath, "Well, I never."

"Isn't it wonderful that Quincy was found unharmed?" Mrs. Madison asked the group, desperate to change the subject. The ladies had to agree with that.

A hush lingered in the air. For a moment, no one knew what to say. With Mrs. Roosevelt so ready to douse the flames of their ill humor, Mrs. Adams and Mrs. Lincoln clammed up.

"Yes, of course it's good that Quincy is safe," said Mrs. Hayes, at last answering the question.

Mrs. Madison recalled Mr. Lincoln observing once that if you looked for the worst in people, expecting to find it, you surely would. The same was true in looking for the best.

That was why it was always such a bad idea to gossip with a woman as full of good-hearted kindness as Mrs. Roosevelt. She would always see the best in people, which spoiled all the fun.

CHAPTER 23

THE MYSTERIOUS FRIEND

PATTY PEEKED AT the mirror in the dining room and cringed, half expecting to see a ghost appear before her. Too many rooms in the White House had mirrors. After last night's upsetting exchange with Mrs. Adams, they were suddenly everywhere.

Ghosts weren't the only scary things that lurked in mirrors. In this one, she saw herself, looking more alone and vulnerable than she could ever remember. The mirror revealed too much. She got up from the table and turned her back on her disturbing reflection.

She headed down the colonnade joining the Residence to the West Wing, while thoughts of Tony Sartini and his alleged treason intruded.

What the ghosts had told her about Sartini's treachery was too important to be ignored, and yet she felt desperate to do just that. Her mind filled with reasons why the warning couldn't be true and just as many why it might be.

A coup attempt by a lightweight like Sartini didn't seem

plausible, but it wasn't out of the question. Sartini's loyalty was the issue. She wasn't nearly as sure about it as she had pretended to Mrs. Adams.

The truth was that Patty didn't know Sartini well enough to be sure of anything about him. The two were political partners only, and he had been added to the presidential ticket at the last minute, right before the Democratic convention. What little time they had been together on the campaign trail was spent doing photo ops.

Who was Tony Sartini, really?

Her motives for making him her running mate were no purer than his for accepting the position. She had picked him because she needed to win Ohio, and his political obscurity all but guaranteed that he would not overshadow her. The young man with the shapely Italian nose was also easy on the eyes and, when placed beside her on campaign posters, made her seem ten years younger. His youthful looks would boost her appeal to voters under forty.

So Sartini was ambitious. That was no surprise. Nobody ever took the vice president's job without a covetous eye on the Oval Office. But being ambitious and treasonous were two different things. No vice president had ever formed a conspiracy to wrest power from the president, and Tony Sartini was not well positioned to be the first.

She puzzled over what Mrs. Adams meant about Jefferson being concerned about her. He had done nothing but insult her and disrupt her meetings. The idea of a ghost caring about her seemed absurd.

Yet Jefferson did profess to care about the country. That meant he had emotions. Could they be the same as those he had while alive? Who could understand how a ghost felt? It was too much for any living person to fathom.

Upon walking into the Oval Office, Patty noticed a sealed envelope waiting for her on the Resolute Desk. On the front, the words "Madam President" were written in script.

She assumed it was just another of Jefferson's irritating educational letters. It would be about some arcane and tedious topic, like democracy or the limits of her constitutional powers.

When Patty opened it, she realized it was no such thing. All that was inside the envelope was a brief note, penned in a jumbled hand, much less compact and consistent than Jefferson's, with letters that were hard to decipher:

Dear Mrs. Pitypander,

Please accept this message in the helpful spirit intended. What you have been told by Mrs. Adams about Sartini's plan to replace you is true. After your last Cabinet meeting, the vice president shut the door and met secretly with nine of your Cabinet members to secure their cooperation in ousting you from office. The time for you to do something is short. It is extremely urgent that you take action now to protect yourself from being overthrown. You must fire your Cabinet immediately.

Regards,
Your Friend

Patty flipped the page over, looking for more writing on the other side, but there was nothing more. The author had to be a ghost, but which one? None of the ghosts had been coy about revealing their identities to her so far.

One thing was clear: The Potusgeists were trying awfully

hard to convince her that something terrible was about to happen. Was it a trick or were they actually trying to help her?

It didn't seem logical that they would be on her side, given the contempt they had shown, but why would they go to the trouble of tricking her?

She decided to hold off on telling Nigel about her most recent meeting with the ghosts. He wouldn't believe the warning about Sartini any more than she did.

Clint understood ghosts. He could investigate the letter.

She called him to her office and swore him to secrecy.

"I know this sounds crazy, but the ghosts are warning me about a coup," Patty explained. "I don't know whether to believe them, but I need to find out fast."

Clint read the letter and gasped. "Whoa! Sartini's plotting a takeover? This is incredible."

"Can ghosts be trusted? If I'm going to take action against the Cabinet, I have to know I can trust whoever's warning me."

"Ghosts are the same as people," Clint replied. "Some are good, some bad. Whether you can trust this one depends on who he is and why he's doing this."

"Right—that's what I figured. So, make a copy of this letter and find out who wrote it," said Patty. "I need to talk to him right away."

NOT LONG AFTER Clint had gone, Patty glanced through a window at the Rose Garden and did a double-take.

Behind a row of boxwood stood two ghostly forms conversing with each other. One of them was a man, tall and lanky, who looked like he might be Jefferson. He was pointing at some roses and seemed to be smiling.

She kept her eye on him until he finally turned toward her. It was Jefferson, all right.

The other ghost was a woman in a silky white dress, hair turban, and pearl necklace, with her back to the West Wing. The ghostess bent over to inspect a rose bush, revealing her reddish face and curly hair. That one was Dolley Madison.

They might be able to give her some answers.

Patty grabbed the mystery letter off her desk, rushed out the door, and told her Secret Service detail she wanted to go outside, alone, to enjoy the nice spring weather.

Jefferson stiffened upon seeing her. Mrs. Madison flashed a welcoming smile.

"Why, Mr. Jefferson was just talking about you, Mrs. Pitypander," said Mrs. Madison sweetly. "It's so wonderful of you to join us. Isn't this a splendid morning? Mr. Jefferson was showing me what a bounty of roses the Lord has blessed us with this spring."

Jefferson looked down at a mass of velvety red blooms, which he identified as the Pat Nixon roses. Leaning over to smell them, he drew back with a frown. "Can't smell anything anymore—how is it that I keep forgetting? Oh, well, they are still delightful to look at. Over here, as I was telling Mrs. Madison, we have some marvelous white Pascali varieties, while over there—"

Patty raised her hand to interrupt. She motioned with her finger for the two ghosts to follow her along the garden's edge. Halting behind a leafy Japanese red maple, she looked to make certain she could not be seen talking to them.

Patty showed them the letter and asked if either of them knew who had penned it.

Neither ghost had any inkling who its author was.

"I can confirm its message, however," Jefferson said. "Sartini has persuaded a majority of your Cabinet that you are unable to discharge your official duties. He has bribed the speaker to get Congress on his side. Next, he must convince the public of your incapacity. To accomplish that, he will plant slanderous stories about you in the press. You must prepare to be most viciously calumniated."

Calumniated. That meant they were planning to smear her.

"If you are wondering how I know this," said Jefferson, "it is because I have seen the tactic used many times before. I myself was shamefully slandered while in office. Once, a disgruntled journalist even falsely accused me of keeping one of my slaves as a concubine. No president has ever been immune from the taint of slander, not even George Washington, whose conduct was above reproach."

Patty asked if there was anything she could do to protect her reputation.

"No, it is the awful price we Americans pay for our freedom of the press. Better to have newspapers without a government than a government without newspapers. You must simply endure their lies and have faith that truth will win in the end."

Patty comforted herself that she had been smeared before and had become so thick-skinned that she was beyond feeling embarrassed. Nonetheless, though she had survived political attacks, she still felt pain when the arrows hit.

The lies that stung the worst and were hardest to refute were the ones that contained a grain of truth—such as the lie that she was talking to ghosts, which was true but implied that she was crazy, which was false.

The lines separating true from false—and sane from insane—were supposed to be sharp and clear, but in Patty's mind they never were, and with every day that passed, they blurred still more.

If Jefferson was right and the plot to oust her was on the verge of being set in motion, what should she expect to happen?

Would the American people accept a president who thought she was seeing ghosts?

She already knew the answer. No, the publicity would make her a laughingstock and doom her presidency. Patty laid her palm across her forehead, looked at Jefferson and Mrs. Madison, and cried out in anguish, "And this is all because of a bunch of ghosts who won't mind their own business!"

Mrs. Madison reached out her hand. "You may well blame us, my dear, but surely you must realize by now that we are your friends, not your enemies. If we were hostile to your interests, we would not bother to reveal these troubling facts to you."

That made a kind of sense. The Potusgeists weren't haunting her like before. Now it seemed they were looking out for her, in an odd, roundabout way. Something had caused them to have a change of heart.

What had turned them around? They must have decided Sartini was worse than she was.

Yet if the ghosts expected her to take action against the vice president and purge the Cabinet to prevent his coup, she would need solid evidence that the conspiracy was really happening.

"What proof do you have that I can show the public?" Patty asked.

Mrs. Madison raised an eyebrow. "Proof? Why, Mrs. Pitypander, how can you ask such a question? Mr. John Adams himself has borne witness to Sartini's treachery and informed the Council. He is a most honorable man. His word is all the proof anyone should require. Even my husband, a cautious man and a diehard Republican, would accept Mr. Adams's word at face value."

"As would I," said Jefferson. "For all Mr. Adams's faults, he has a noble soul. He would never lie. He's too prideful to stoop to that. His conceit will not permit it."

"But I can't give the word of John Adams as proof!" Patty protested. "No one will believe me."

They looked at her in bewilderment.

Only a lunatic would trust the word of a ghost, even if he was Adams or Jefferson or any of the other spooks who inhabited the White House. "I've got to have something better than that," she muttered.

Patty bade them a good day and wandered back to her office, wondering whether even Nigel would believe that a palace plot to overthrow her was afoot.

CHAPTER 24
THE POKER GAME

CLINT FIDGETED AT his desk, unable to concentrate on the handwriting samples on his computer screen. None of them matched the mysterious letter written to the president, and he had run out of clues as to who its author might be.

The ghosts might know, and he could just ask them, if he dared. They could answer many other questions as well.

The letter was the excuse he needed to go to the ghost den and meet with the Potusgeists again. Would the ghosts react angrily at being disturbed a second time? After some consideration, he decided he didn't care. He would never forgive himself if he missed this chance to learn more about them.

Setting his fears aside, Clint tucked the letter into his pocket and made his way downstairs to the ghosts' hideout. Hearing some male voices inside, he placed his ear against the door.

"Deal the cards," said a voice.

Clint shoved the door open and switched on the light.

A piece of plywood had been set on a box to make a tabletop. On it was a deck of playing cards and poker chips. Other playing cards were floating above crates surrounding the table.

"Look, it's that darn ghost hunter again," said a second voice. "I thought we got rid of him. What in tarnation does he want?"

Clint closed the door behind him. "Please, sir, I just came to talk."

"I'll take two," said the first voice. Two cards floated face-down through the air in the voice's direction.

"He says he wants to talk," said a high-pitched voice. "Why don't we see what the boy needs?"

"Confound it, can't he leave us alone? I came to play poker, not to jabber with him."

"Oh, the boy means no harm, Jackson. Let him talk."

"All right, have it your way. Speak your piece, young man."

Clint stepped toward the voices. "If it's not too much trouble, sirs, could you tell me who I'm speaking to?"

"Of course! Where are our manners? Let's make ourselves visible to him," said the high-pitched voice.

A ghost appeared before Clint. It was Abraham Lincoln, with his famous craggy face, stovepipe hat, and beard.

Three other ghosts showed themselves: Andrew Jackson, whom Clint recognized from the twenty-dollar bill, and two phantasms who were unfamiliar.

One of them, a ghost with a long, pointed beard, introduced himself as James Garfield. A short, stern-looking wraith with thinning hair announced that he was William McKinley.

"Welcome to the Pot Shot Poker Club, young man," said Lincoln. "We'll be happy to deal you in, if Five-Card Draw is your pleasure. I must warn you, though, this is a wily bunch. Nobody bluffs like Jackson here. He'll have you thinking he's holding a royal flush when all he's got is a pair of deuces."

"And he's the luckiest damned cuss you'll ever meet," said Garfield.

"You can depend on that," Lincoln echoed.

Jackson flashed a wry smile at them. "No luck involved. Just brains."

The Pot Shot Poker Club? Clint thought about it. Here were Lincoln, Jackson, Garfield, and McKinley. What did all four presidents have in common? All of them had been shot at. All but Jackson, whose attacker's two pistols miraculously misfired, had died of their wounds.

"No, thanks, Mr. President," Clint replied, pulling up a crate and sitting down next to Lincoln. "I just wanted to ask some questions, if you guys don't mind."

"Sure, we've got nothing to hide. Fire away, boy—figuratively, that is," Lincoln said with a wink.

Garfield laughed. "Nothing to hide? Now, Abe, you know that's a damned lie. We all have secrets. I'll take two cards."

"I will concede that, Jimmy boy," Lincoln replied, tossing two cards to him. "It's just that most of our secrets ain't important enough anymore to account for much. We have little to reveal that would interest anyone these days."

That wasn't true. Everything about the ghosts fascinated Clint. So many questions flooded into his mind that it was hard to know where to begin. "Let's see. If you guys are the Pot Shot Club, why aren't other presidents like Kennedy and Reagan here? They got shot at too, didn't they?"

Lincoln stretched out his long legs and propped his feet up on a nearby crate. "Kennedy? Oh, yes, he's one of our members, but he spends most of his time haunting his fancy beach house on Cape Cod. He's not much of a poker player. With him being a Harvard man and all, it irks him that we rubes always clean him out. As for Reagan, he's not here yet because he's only been dead a couple of decades, you know."

That wasn't long enough? Clint had wondered why he hadn't

seen any of the more recently deceased presidents. "How long does someone need to be dead?"

"Fifty years is our new rule," said Lincoln. "You see, in the White House's early days, we welcomed presidents and their first ladies as soon as they died, but there got to be so many of us around here that some of the older ghosts complained. To reduce overcrowding, the Council imposed a fifty-year time-in-coffin rule. If a new ghost shows up before being formally initiated, he's shunned."

McKinley took another card and sighed. "We needed some entrance requirements. There's no nuisance like a greenhorn ghost. New ghosts were showing up here fresh out of the coffin, lacking basic skills. They were still in complete confusion about being dead, and they didn't know how to change form, pass through walls without getting stuck, or move objects without dropping them. Those things may sound easy, but they take time to master. Now, the new ones learn the ropes of ghosting at their other houses long before they get here."

According to Garfield, there was a more compelling reason for the time-in-coffin rule that nobody liked to admit: Some of the more recently expired presidents and first ladies were unacceptable to the older Potusgeists because of their strange modern ways of thinking. To the elders, big government was anathema, the very thing they had fought to free America from. Presidents were supposed to be upstanding leaders, men of integrity, not entertainers or creatures of America's decadent popular culture. The time-in-coffin rule helped keep the peace.

Garfield rubbed the bullet wound in his lower back. "Can you imagine what will happen when people like Nancy Reagan or Bill and Hillary Clinton pop up here as ghosts? God help us, old Adams will be fit to be tied. You think he's on fire about Mrs. Pitypander? Just wait until Donald Trump walks back in here as a ghost. Then you'll see some sparks fly."

"I sure don't want to be hanging around here when that happens," said McKinley.

Jackson took a card and raised an eyebrow. "I bet seven dollars."

Lincoln mulled over his cards and rolled his lips, as if trying to contain a smile. "I'll see your seven dollars and raise you four."

Garfield looked at his hand, frowned, and decided to fold. McKinley did the same.

"Are you the only ghosts here who play poker?" Clint asked.

"No, several others do as well. For presidents who died of natural causes, we've also got a Dropped Dead Poker Club," said Lincoln. "William Harrison, Warren Harding, and Franklin Roosevelt are in that one. We play the Dropped Deads sometimes, just to vary our routine and mix things up socially. You'd best watch out for Harding—a very calculating man, he is. He knows poker, yes, sir, indeed he does, but you must watch his cards carefully because he's also been known to cheat."

"We never let Harding deal," said Garfield firmly.

"Not on your life," echoed McKinley. "He'd get a royal flush every time. Honesty's important when you can make cards appear and disappear at will."

Clint asked the group why it was that all presidents became ghosts. Were they being singled out for something?

The Potusgeists did not know, according to Lincoln. Some thought they were being punished for bad behavior, as all had been politicians. Others believed that being a ghost must be an atonement for the injustices they had permitted to occur while in office and that their penance was to witness what happened to the country they had led so they could face the consequences of their decisions and repent before moving on to heaven or hell or whatever fate awaited a politician's soul.

"Repent? Ha! I'll be damned if I ever repent," Jackson declared.

"You'll be damned if you don't," Lincoln replied with a smile.

That was another vexing issue about being a ghost: No one knew whether their time in that mode of being was finite or eternal. Not a single Potusgeist had ever been released from what they called their "peculiar condition."

"Old Mr. Adams was the first one here, and he's still serving time," said Lincoln. "Of course, he is a mite crotchety."

"And hasn't improved at all in over two centuries," added McKinley. "I don't expect he ever will. Ghosts get pretty set in their ways after two hundred years."

As Clint had assumed, the Potusgeists could move within the White House grounds but not an inch beyond the iron gates that separated them from the rest of Washington. An invisible barrier surrounded the property and repelled them if they tried to cross it. They could transport themselves at will back to where they came from, or to their coffins, but nowhere else.

"No, my boy, you don't want to be a ghost," Lincoln warned, his face long and pensive as he examined his cards. "We live in a limbo between life and death, imbued with awareness and feelings but unable to act as we did while living. In a limited sense, we are still here, but excluded from reality in every other way. We see, we hear, we think, we feel, but we can barely experience the sensory world we once knew. It is frustrating beyond all imagining. Being undead is a hard and unprofitable existence, which I would not recommend to anyone."

Jackson was more upbeat about his spectral state and even claimed to enjoy ghosting. "No matter how crazy the world gets, I'll take hanging around up here over spinning in my grave watching the living screw up the world any damn day.

The view is much superior, and the society more congenial. I do not enjoy the company of worms and moles."

McKinley pointed to the paper in Clint's shirt pocket. "What is that you have there, son?"

"The letter! Oh, yes, the letter," said Clint, so fascinated by the Potusgeists that he had forgotten why he had come to see them. "The president wants me to find out which of you wrote this to her." He unfolded the letter and showed it to them.

None of them recognized the handwriting, but all agreed that its advice should be taken seriously.

"That Sartini fellow is up to no good," said Garfield. "I agree with Adams on that point."

Jackson pushed the rest of his chips into the middle of the table. "I'm all in, Lincoln. What do you have to say about that?"

Lincoln stroked his beard and shuffled in his chair. "I call you, General." He slid his chips into the pile.

Jackson laid his cards face up on the table. "A straight flush! Read 'em and weep."

Lincoln threw down his three queens in disgust. "Dad-gummit!"

Jackson pulled in a mountain of chips to add to his growing stack. Garfield and McKinley groaned.

"What's the use in playing?" asked Garfield. "Can't shoot him. Can't beat him at cards. Jackson always wins."

CHAPTER 25
THE RUMOR

SARTINI WATCHED THE nine handpicked men and women filing into the Cabinet Room as they gathered around the long mahogany table.

He had recruited one more Cabinet secretary than he needed, in case someone got cold feet. If any of the nine were even thinking of going wobbly on him, now was the time to find out.

The meeting, arranged in secret only two hours earlier, wouldn't take long. With the president in New York at a political rally, Sartini could gather his closest supporters and sound them out before taking the first irreversible steps to remove her.

As the Cabinet secretaries took their seats, Sartini rolled his shoulders against the back of the president's chair and rubbed his hand along the soft leather armrest. The big chair fit his body nicely. He could get used to this.

First, they needed to discuss leaks. Sartini reminded everyone that, for obvious reasons, nothing they heard in the room should be repeated outside. "Any leak could cause your immediate dismissal by the president before we have a chance to take action against her. I'm a constitutionally elected officer, so she can't get rid of me, but she can fire the rest of you on a whim. She doesn't need anybody's approval to do that. Once we start this thing, we have to move with lightning speed. Everybody understand?"

Heads nodded around the table. The president could strike before they did.

As he reviewed his plan for invoking the Twenty-Fifth Amendment, several of the secretaries traded nervous glances.

Secretary of Defense Buster Codd, a stocky man with a booming voice, was the first to object. "Tony, you can't do things this way. It's too arrogant and pushy, and it will look bad for everybody here. And it's not fair to the president. You're tossing her out without first giving her a chance to resign. She might bow out gracefully and spare us all this trouble."

Sartini had thought of that but dismissed the idea. "You really think Pitypander might consider resigning? Are you kidding me? You know her better than that. She'd sooner cut off her right arm than give up this job."

Codd didn't care. Sartini's plan wasn't the way things ought to be done, he said. Pitypander was the president, after all, and no matter how crazy she was, she deserved some respect for that reason alone. Several other secretaries agreed.

"At least give her the opportunity to save some shred of her dignity," Secretary of State Borders implored. "Who knows? She might decide to quit, and then her removal won't look half as bad to the public. And we won't look as bad either because people will see she's consenting to leave on her own. Her resignation could keep this whole thing from blowing up in our faces."

They were losing their nerve and didn't want to look like bullies. Sartini, sensing that he wasn't going to win the argument, gave in. They would first approach the president with the request that she step down. After she rejected that option, they would lower the boom on her as he had planned.

Sartini took a vote. "Is everybody on board with this? If so, raise your hand. If not, now's the time to back out."

Nine hands went up.

It was time to cross the Rubicon.

PATTY LOOKED OUT of Marine One at the Washington Monument as beads of rain trickled down the window. The helicopter cleared the trees and descended, landing softly on the South Lawn.

The door to the outside flung open. She walked gingerly down the steps and returned the salute of the Marine at the bottom. A Secret Service agent held an umbrella over her head, escorting her through the damp grass toward the West Wing, near a group of reporters standing behind a rope line.

"President Pitypander, is the rumor about the ghosts true?" shouted one of them.

Patty pretended not to hear and kept walking. As soon as she entered the Oval Office, she called Nigel in and asked what the reporter was referring to.

He hadn't heard the rumor, only that there was one being floated around, and that some big news was about to break. "Something strange is definitely going on."

"I know," she replied. "The ghosts warned me about it."

Nigel's eyes widened as he looked at her skeptically. "What did they tell you?"

Patty revealed that Mrs. Adams and Mrs. Madison had appeared to her in a mirror to alert her that Sartini was planning to steal the presidency out from under her. "I wanted some time to clear my head and think about whether I believed it myself. I decided I do believe it."

"But that's ridiculous," Nigel said. "He couldn't mount a coup against you. This is not some banana republic. Presidents don't get overthrown here. The Twenty-Fifth Amendment was written to take care of medical emergencies, like when the president has an operation. It's never been used to stage a coup."

"That's what I told the ghosts," Patty replied. "And then I got a letter from one of them saying Sartini has gone behind my back to meet secretly with the Cabinet. They say he's buying them off with favors."

"Sartini? I just find it hard to believe he would try that. He doesn't have the political heft to pull it off."

"I thought the same thing, at first. But then, after hearing them out—"

Patty's secretary knocked at the Oval Office door, bearing an urgent message from Nigel's secretary to turn on the news immediately.

Nigel scurried across the room and switched on the television. A blond reporter was standing outside the White House with a microphone in one hand and an umbrella in the other.

The reporter wore a hangdog expression. "The New York Times and Washington Post are reporting that the president has been acting bizarrely. A rumor is swirling around the capital that she may be suffering from a rare anxiety disorder called phasmophobia, or fear of ghosts. Sufferers from the disorder believe they are seeing ghosts and, in some cases, experience fits of paranoia, thinking they are being hounded and pursued by them."

The caption at the bottom of the screen read: "BREAKING NEWS: President Pitypander, Stricken With Rare Mental Illness, Sees Ghosts."

"Is there any treatment for phasmophobia, Karen?" asked the anchor. "Like drugs or therapy?"

"Sadly, no," the reporter replied as the rain pelted her umbrella. "The disorder is progressive, and the patient becomes more and more convinced that she really is seeing and interacting with ghosts, becoming totally immersed in the world of the paranormal. It's a kind of psychological escape for them from the stresses of the real world. And, of course, no one is under more stress than the President of the United States."

Nigel jumped out of his chair. "That's a damned lie! You aren't suffering from a disease. This place is teeming with ghosts. I've seen them myself."

He paced the floor. It was all a setup. Someone had leaked the story to the press with the obvious intention of smearing her.

Not just someone, Patty realized. It was Sartini, or someone working for him.

She was being calumniated, as Jefferson had forewarned. "What do we do?"

"We deny every stinking word, of course," Nigel replied. "You can't allow that story to go unchallenged for even a day. The public might believe it."

"It's the truth. I am seeing ghosts, and talking to them too."

"But you aren't sick in the head like they're saying. And the truth doesn't matter if Sartini can't prove it. How can anybody besides you know what you're seeing?"

"The ghosts said he has solid evidence."

"Have you seen it?"

"No."

"Then as far as we know it's nothing but a baseless rumor, and that's how we'll play it. We'll have Colleen go before the press this afternoon and deny the whole bloody thing."

★ ★ ★

SITTING NEARBY IN the Oval Office, Patty and Nigel watched Colleen on television as she lugged her three-inch binder into the Press Briefing Room. She laid it on the podium, eyeing the rows of seated reporters like she was facing a pack of ravenous wolves. She riffled through some pages and let out a deep breath.

"You can do this, Colleen," Nigel said to the screen. "Just tell them it's all hogwash, everything will blow over in a few days, and we'll all be fine."

The press secretary swept the long black hair out of her eyes and read her prepared statement: "Before I take questions, let me put an end to today's wild rumor. The president is not suffering from a mental illness called phasmophobia. She has never been diagnosed with any such disorder. The rumor is simply false. She has not been seeing ghosts in the White House or anywhere else."

A reporter raised her hand. "But, Colleen, isn't it true that President Pitypander has a history of seeing things that aren't there? Isn't it true that she went to a psychiatrist in Southern California about having delusions before she became president?"

"No, that's just another part of the same false story," Cook replied. "The president is not having delusions. She is in full control of her faculties and always has been."

"Does the president suffer from hallucinations?" shouted a male reporter.

Cook stared him down as if he were a disrespectful schoolboy. "What kind of question is that? What makes you think she is having hallucinations?"

"I'm just asking," he replied. "Is she or isn't she? It's a simple question. Why can't you just answer it? What are you hiding from us?"

Cook resorted to one of her favorite dodges: Instead of answering a question, she would make tangential statements that pretended to answer it. "The president is a very level-headed and practical woman. I've never seen her have a hallucination."

That was plausible, yet irrelevant, even if true. "Well played, Colleen," said Nigel.

The reporter was undeterred. "Are there ghosts in the White House? Haven't there been stories about ghost sightings here, going back well over a century?"

Cook refused to confirm or deny the stories. "Whether or not there are ghosts here, it's not the president's policy to see them."

Of course it wasn't Patty's policy to see ghosts. It wasn't anybody's policy to see them. Another irrelevant truth.

The reporter countered by feigning a look of surprise. "Whoa! Whether or not there are ghosts here? So, are you saying, in effect, that there *might* be ghosts?"

Cook bared her teeth. "No, I didn't say that at all. Look, Sam, don't put words in my mouth. I meant the president does not see things that aren't there. Nobody at the White House is seeing ghosts. Nobody. We're all seeing things that are real, all the time, because we're very sane people here, got it?"

Another falsehood. They weren't very sane people. They were politicians. Politicians who were seeing ghosts.

Patty looked at Nigel skeptically. "Do you think they're buying this B.S.?"

"Not for a second." He grabbed the remote and turned off the television. "They're smelling blood. The more she denies it, the harder they press her for answers. But under the circumstances, there's nothing we can do but lie our asses off and pray that the public doesn't care about any of this nonsense."

★ ★ ★

MINUTES LATER, THERE was a knock at the Oval Office door.

Vice President Sartini marched in, followed by Secretary of Defense Buster Codd and Secretary of State Milton Borders. Seven other Cabinet secretaries filed into the room, hanging their heads in mournful silence.

"What is the meaning of this?" Nigel demanded, as if he didn't know. "Are you the ones putting the rumor out there?"

Sartini, wearing a somber expression, stepped forward and crossed his arms. "Look, Patty, there's no use pretending anymore. We know you're seeing ghosts. We've all noticed your behavior, and we're very concerned about your mental health. For the sake of the country, it's time for you to step down. The job is obviously too much of a strain on you."

The Cabinet members looked sad but stoical, as if attending a funeral. They had bought Sartini's lies and become willing stooges in his cunning plot.

"Why, you slimy little snake," she said, pitching her head back. "Hell no, I won't resign."

"It's no use, Patty," Sartini replied. "The jig is up. We know what's going on around here. We have proof."

"I don't care what you have," she shot back. "I'll be damned if I'll desert my supporters. You didn't win the presidency, I did. All of you just rode into office on my coattails. You're not stealing the presidency out from under me."

Sartini's lips formed a caustic smile. "I didn't think you would go quietly, but we had to give you a chance." He slipped his hand into his coat pocket, pulled out a document, and handed it to her.

It was written on official White House stationery, addressed to the Speaker of the House and the President Pro Tempore of the Senate, and read as follows:

Pursuant to Amendment XXV, Section 4 of the United States Constitution, we hereby inform you of the President's inability to discharge the powers and duties of the Office of the President and to inform you that those powers and duties shall be discharged by the Vice President as Acting President.

The brief note was signed by Sartini and the nine dour cabinet members standing in the Oval Office.

That's all it took to end her presidency, after everything she had gone through to get here? She looked at Borders in disbelief.

Only months before, he had been a nobody, the relatively unknown junior senator from Maine, with only a three-month stint on the Senate Foreign Relations Committee under his belt. She had raised him from obscurity to run the State Department, and there he was, sticking his knife into her ribs, along with the other traitors.

"You too, Milton?" she asked in dismay.

"Sorry, I'm afraid it has to be," Borders replied, his head bowed. "It's for the good of the country."

"You can't just barge in here and depose the president like this!" Nigel raised his fist menacingly. "This is an outrage! The people will never stand for it!"

Sartini smirked. "They will now. They've just heard the news about what's been going on around here. We have her on video, talking to a ghost like he's really alive. Everybody can see she's totally bonkers."

"Look here," said Nigel. "I don't care if she's having séances with Elvis Presley, John Lennon, and Mahatma Gandhi. She's the duly elected president, dammit. She has rights under the amendment's appeal procedure. We'll appeal this to Congress."

"I expect you to," Sartini replied. "In the meantime, I'm the acting president, and I'm ordering both of you to vacate the West Wing immediately. We're taking over the administration as of now."

"You're throwing me out of here?" Patty asked, shaking her head. "This is incredible."

"Just the West Wing. You can stay in the Residence until the appeal process is over."

She faked a laugh. "You'll let me stay there temporarily, will you? That's awfully nice of you." She was tempted to spit at him.

The Attorney General stepped forward to escort Patty and Nigel out. He gestured toward the door. Patty shoved him away, barely able to keep from scratching his eyes out.

The billionaire's wife was losing everything that mattered to her, the intangible things that sustained her spirit: the presidency, the prestige, and the lifelong certainty instilled by her father that she was destined for greatness. Her pride was being stripped from her by a mere scrap of paper, signed by her duplicitous staff, people she herself had chosen. Unbelievably, they had morphed into a gang of political thieves.

Shuffling to the door in a daze, she looked back at the Resolute Desk, at the flag standing nearby, at the presidential seal on the carpet—at the Oval Office itself. These trappings of power would be hers no longer.

She glanced to her left. Standing at the bookcase was the glowing form of Thomas Jefferson, his arms hanging down, his face in anguish. It almost seemed like his eyes were filled with tears, but that was physically impossible. Ghosts, she had been told, had no tears to shed.

CHAPTER 26
THE CALL OF DUTY

PATTY LAY SPREAD-EAGLED on her bed, the walls seeming to close in on her as the wave of bitterness and anger slowly subsided, replaced by a paralyzing gloom. If only she could think straight, a viable way out of her dilemma might present itself.

The mutiny that had just occurred in the West Wing was so unprecedented that even Nigel, after two hours of hashing over Patty's legal options with the White House Counsel, was unsure how to proceed.

She could appeal her removal in Congress. It would be a messy affair that would drag her public image through the mud, but she would get through it, he assured her.

As she gazed at the ceiling, a troubling question kept nagging at her, one she had never faced before: Did she still want the White House?

Maybe the presidency wasn't worth it. The job was nothing like what she had expected, and she had sacrificed the opulent life of a billionaire's wife to get it.

And for what? Was the presidency a prize or a curse?

She could just turn her back on the whole president thing, as if she had woken up from a terrible nightmare. Images of sunny Southern California and her palatial oceanfront mansion at Durango Beach flashed across her mind. Why not return to that idyllic life? She could enjoy a leisurely retirement and spend her time as before, walking her beloved dogs, reading steamy novels, and watching the pretty surfer boys on the beach. All her cares would disappear.

Why not let Sartini have this crazy place and discover for himself the crushing burdens that came with it? That would be a fitting punishment for his treason. Her punishment, for worshiping the false god of power, would be humiliation.

Patty imagined what her mother would say. Olympia would be distraught, naturally, outraged that her little girl had been pushed out of the job she had wanted all her life. She visualized the fire in her mother's careworn eyes. Olympia would tell her to hang in there and fight the bastards with everything she had.

Benny, her husband in name only, who never believed she could handle the firestorms of being president, would do the opposite. He would turn his back on her and gleefully say, "I told you so. You weren't cut out for the presidency."

What others wanted for her didn't matter. What did *she* want? That was the question.

Hearing three gentle knocks at her bedroom door, Patty breathed deeply, barely able to muster the energy to get up and see who it was.

She opened the door a crack. Standing behind it, six feet tall, was the shimmering figure of an ungainly woman with a toothy smile.

Oh, no. Not another ghost. Not now. I can't take any more.

"Mrs. Pitypander, I'm Mrs. Eleanor Roosevelt," said the phantasm. "May I come in?"

Eleanor Roosevelt!

Patty, pressing her hand to her chest, nodded with excitement and opened the door. Mrs. Roosevelt had long been one of her idols.

The champion of many women's rights causes, from voting to workplace access to health care to education, she had been an early civil rights activist. The most effective first lady ever at using the media, she'd even had a regular newspaper column, which ran in major dailies around the country.

Though no beauty, Mrs. Roosevelt exuded class. Patty appreciated that she had manners enough to knock first, not just fly through the door like some other Potusgeists did.

"What can I do for you?" Patty asked.

Mrs. Roosevelt didn't answer at first but walked to a window, looked out at the South Lawn, and turned around with a glint in her eye. "I spent a great deal of time in this house. It is much as we left it. I confess I didn't always enjoy it, and neither did Franklin."

"He didn't? Did he ever get so tired he thought of quitting?"

"Quitting? Oh, yes, he was tempted to quit, many times," said Mrs. Roosevelt. "We led the country through the Great Depression, with twenty-five percent unemployment, and then World War Two, with fifty million dead. Like you, we were quite wealthy, and we'd had a good life in New York before coming here. It wasn't to protect our egos that we went on suffering the slings and arrows of Washington politics. I will admit, it was Franklin's ego that brought him to the White House, but it didn't keep him here after the shine wore off. And it didn't hold him here when his health was failing at the end of the war, either. Something else much deeper and more motivating did that."

Patty sat on the sofa, transfixed. "What was it that kept him here?"

"Duty, child, duty," the ghost replied. "Duty to the country, duty to our supporters, duty to do what we thought was right and just. Duty is what sustains a president in the darkest hours, not ego. You came here to leave your mark, I suppose, like all new presidents do. Well, some people will leave a mark on this world, sure enough, while others, like Sartini, will leave a stain. If you let that horrid man and his gang force you out so soon, you'll leave nothing at all. Think of how many millions of people you'll disappoint."

"But I don't know if I have the strength left to fight Sartini."

Mrs. Roosevelt crossed her arms. "Why, of course you do, child. I've watched you ever since you came here. As I've always said, a woman is like a tea bag—you can't tell how strong she is until you put her in hot water. Well, you're a far stronger tea bag than you know, Mrs. Pitypander. Overcoming problems for the sake of others, overcoming yourself—that is the path to greatness. You don't need a Resolute Desk for that. Resolution comes from the heart."

"You're the one who wrote me that letter, aren't you?"

"Yes, I wrote it," Mrs. Roosevelt admitted. "I was afraid you would ignore the Council's warning. In the end, it didn't matter because there was so little time for you to prepare yourself for Sartini's putsch."

"Now, what do you think I should do?"

"Fight him with all you've got, child. Your contest with Sartini will be decided by who has the most powerful allies. The millions of women who came out during your campaign in all weather, who believed in you, who sent you to the White House—they will surely be behind you now. Call on them. Get them marching in the streets in every city, banging the drum for you. Get good advice and heed it. You might even persuade

Mr. Jefferson and Mr. Adams to help you. Two hundred eighty years of observing human behavior have made them wise."

"Wise? They're the ones who got me into this mess."

"They can also help you get out of it, if you'll let them."

"How could they possibly help?"

Mrs. Roosevelt smiled. "The ghosts of the White House are more powerful than you imagine. But it is for you to ask them and for them to show you, not me. I have told you all that I came to say, and I know you must be dog-tired. Good luck, dear, and fight well."

With that, before Patty could ask another question, Mrs. Roosevelt disappeared.

CHAPTER 27

THE DEFCON BOO TABOO

SECRETARY OF DEFENSE Buster Codd clutched the DIA memo in his left hand, reread it for the third time, and growled across his desk at the Chairman of the Joint Chiefs of Staff, ready to rip him to pieces.

Codd pounded his desk with his fist. "Dammit, Hack, you're just giving me this information *now*? The entire country has learned that Pitypander's seeing ghosts, she's been kicked out of office because of it, and now you're getting around to telling me there's been ghost sightings at the White House, and someone in the department has known it for weeks? Where the hell were you with this information all that time?"

General Hack Hightower cringed. "I just got the memo about the ghosts from DIA yesterday, Buster. I didn't know about it myself."

Didn't anybody in the Pentagon know anything?

Codd ran his fingers through his hair, wondering why he had agreed to take this job in the Pitypander administration when the one he really wanted was Secretary of State. In his first months, the former Zencorp CEO had observed that "information constipation" was a common ailment at the Pentagon. The top brass often had no clue what was going on in the vast bureaucracy underneath them. Codd suspected that they preferred things that way. They couldn't be accused of covering up what they didn't know.

He glared at Hightower. "Dammit, General, I was totally blindsided by this ghost business. I had to learn everything from Vice President Sartini on the fly. There I was, sitting at the table, looking stupid and helpless. Sartini knew there were ghosts in the White House, but I didn't. I'm supposed to be the Secretary of Defense. For Chrissake, don't we have defense intelligence analysts so they can tell me what's going on?"

"Yes, sir," replied Hightower. "That's the way it's supposed to work."

"Then what the hell caused the delay in getting this information about the ghosts up to me?"

"Well, sir, it was...it was DEFCON Boo."

"DEFCON Boo. And that's another thing. Why the hell wasn't I told about that?"

"Plausible deniability, sir," Hightower replied. "DEFCON Boo...well, it's taboo."

Codd looked at the general like he had two heads. Decades ago, the Pentagon had made contingency plans for a ghost uprising. That was totally insane, as everyone acknowledged, but no one wanted to tackle the issue. Promotions had been lost just by bringing up the subject.

Codd couldn't wrap his head around how anyone could think fighting ghosts was possible. "How do you propose to put the kibosh on ghosts, nuke 'em? Do we shoot vampires too? How about leprechauns and little green men? Tell me, General, where do our war planners draw the line?"

"That's just it—they don't draw it anywhere, sir," replied Hightower. "That's the problem with DEFCON Boo. The guidelines are Hollywood science fiction stuff. No threat is off limits, even ghosts. That's why DIA sat on the ghost intelligence. For a staff officer to suggest moving to DEFCON Boo is like saying he believes in the tooth fairy."

"We have a readiness alert system for fighting ghosts nobody here dares to mention because if they do, everybody will think they're off their rocker?"

"Yes, sir. Staff officers are rated on their judgment and mental stability. Would you give a high-performance rating to a general who went around saying he believed in ghosts?"

"Hell no," Codd answered with a growl. "I'd send him to Walter Reed to have his head examined. Then, if I couldn't fire him, I'd banish him to the least important job I could find, like defending an Aleutian island or something."

"Exactly."

Hence, DEFCON Boo. An alert system that was impossible to implement.

Now Codd would have to sit on the ghost information too, like DIA did, and for the same reason. If he dared to propose raising the Pentagon's readiness level to DEFCON Boo, he would be the one who looked crazy. "I suppose we could do nothing. Then the worst anyone could say about us is that we're incompetent."

"Yes, sir. That's about the size of it. If we go to DEFCON Boo, we look crazy. If we don't, we look incompetent. Which do you prefer?"

Incompetent was the safer choice, Codd agreed, at least until he knew who the president would be. Even at his high level, government officials rarely got canned for doing nothing. It seemed to be tacitly understood to be part of everyone's job description.

"General, I don't want you breathing a word about this DEFCON Boo stuff to anyone, you understand? Not the National Security Council, not the president, not anybody. Mum's the word. If it can't bleed, we don't shoot at it, got that?"

"Understood, sir," Hightower replied with a salute. "No blood, no bullets. A very wise policy. I'll see that it's implemented."

"The Pentagon's not chasing after ghosts if I can help it."

CHAPTER 28

THE RESURGENT

CONFERRING WITH PATTY in her makeshift office in the West Sitting Hall, Nigel explained how the Twenty-Fifth Amendment worked if the president refused to step down voluntarily. It all boiled down to a battle of letters.

Having received Sartini's letter, Patty could appeal by countering with her own, claiming that she was fit for office, whereupon she would immediately take back her powers.

Sartini would then have four days to submit a second letter insisting that she was unable to serve. That would send the matter to Congress, which had twenty-one days to decide the issue. While Congress debated, he would remain acting president.

To prevail, Sartini needed two-thirds of both the House and Senate. One vote less in either chamber and Patty would regain the presidency.

Nigel liked their chances, as it was hard to get two-thirds of Congress to agree on the time of day, much less the fitness needed to be president. "The odds are on our side. Unless the people think you are completely bats, we should win."

They might as well start the exchange of letters. With Patty's appeal in hand, they hurried to the West Wing, brushed past Sartini's secretary, and entered the Oval Office unannounced.

Sartini looked up and grinned, obviously expecting their appeal.

Nigel slapped Patty's letter on the Resolute Desk. "There you go, Sartini. You are hereby removed as Acting President."

Unfazed, Sartini reached inside the desk and handed Nigel a letter insisting that Patty was still mentally incapacitated. The battle of letters had taken less than a minute. The dispute was now in the hands of Congress.

"Now run along, please. I have work to do."

Patty stamped her foot on the floor. "Traitor!"

Sartini lay back in his chair and put his feet on the desk. "Please leave. I'd hate to embarrass you two by calling the Secret Service to have you physically removed."

Patty glared at him. She was the president, not some college kid occupying a campus building. Her forcible ejection from the Oval Office would stir up sympathy, but at the cost of her public image—probably not the best idea.

She was turning to Nigel to ask his opinion when the phone on the Resolute Desk buzzed. "Your next visitor is here to see you, sir," said a woman's voice on the intercom.

"Show him in," Sartini replied with a smirk.

Benny Pitypander waddled into the Oval Office, turned his head, and stopped in his tracks upon seeing Patty. "Uh oh."

She was equally stunned. "What are you doing here?"

Benny's face turned red. "Just dropping in for a visit with the new president, Doll. I didn't expect to see you here. I heard you got canned."

Patty walked up to him and balled her hands into fists. "I can't believe this. Why the hell are you talking to Sartini?"

Benny's pudgy palms began sweating. "Now, Doll, don't get your panties all twisted up in a wad. I'm just here on business. Tony has been helping me work out one of my deals."

Patty searched Benny up and down, her face filling with disgust. "And now you're returning the favor, aren't you, you little snail? Let me guess. You're bankrolling him, right?"

Sartini folded his arms. "Well, as a matter of fact, if you must know, Benny and I do have some mutual friends in Congress. And we're looking to make a lot more soon, aren't we, Benny?"

Benny did not utter a word. He stood frozen in place, his owlish brown eyes pinging nervously back and forth between Patty and Sartini.

"Oh, I see," said Patty. "Just buying some friends in Congress, huh? Like enough to get you two-thirds of the House and Senate?"

"Yes," Sartini replied. "How did you know?"

How? In the thirty years Patty had been married to Benny, he'd never once missed an opportunity to buy powerful people. The upcoming vote in Congress was the biggest chance he'd ever had to scoop up several dozen politicians and add them to his global network of movers and shakers.

Nigel eyed the billionaire with revulsion. "I'm flabbergasted. This is the most selfish thing I've ever seen. You're funding your wife's political enemy to remove her from the presidency? It was bad enough you wouldn't help her get elected. Now you're in cahoots with her enemy to destroy her?"

"Destroy her? Nah, I'm not out to destroy her. It's nothing like that," Benny retorted. "She never should have run for the presidency in the first place, Windborne. I told you a long time ago she wasn't cut out for it, remember? You wouldn't listen to me because you craved power. That's why you talked her into running—so you could be her puppet master and control her yourself, behind the scenes. I'm wise to your game, pal, and I'm going to beat you at it—by ending it once and for all and sending her back to California, where she belongs."

Nigel pointed his finger at Benny. "Nonsense. She's not nuts, and she's not some pawn in a chess game either. You've never accepted that your wife has a mind of her own. It grates on your macho self-esteem that she's independent, that she's outdone you, so you need to pull her down and put her back in her place. Oh, I think you and Sartini will make great partners. You two are the lowest forms of life I have ever encountered. Have you no shame, betraying Patty like this?"

No, they didn't. There was no shame in politics, Washington, her marriage, or any other part of Patty's world. The entire universe was steeped in corruption.

She stormed out of the Oval Office, so mad she could spit nails.

PATTY STAGGERED INTO the Residence, wondering how a man she had been married to for so long could act so callously.

It was bad enough that Benny hadn't lifted a finger to help her get elected president, but a hundred times worse that he was actively participating in the plot to overthrow her. He had to know that Sartini was a two-faced Judas who would dump him as soon as he had robbed her of the Oval Office.

Benny wouldn't care, she realized, as long as he got what he wanted out of the disgraceful alliance. The Casino King was every bit as much of an ingratiating worm as Sartini, having built his global empire of glitzy resorts by cozying up to mobsters and cutthroats, many of them government officials.

Nigel was shocked by Benny's selfishness, but its boundlessness was the only thing that surprised Patty. Her attainment of the presidency had simply amplified his greed, enabling him to be selfish on a far grander scale than when she was governor.

She would put Benny out of her mind for now. Getting even with him could wait. Sartini posed an immediate threat.

Just then, having almost reached her bedroom, she heard a familiar sound cascading down the hall.

It was a violin.

Jefferson!

She turned around, hustled down to the door of the Yellow Oval Room, and closed it behind her.

The ghost of the third president was lounging on the settee, turning a page of his sheet music. He looked up and smiled. "Ah, Mrs. Pitypander, I thought you might be along sooner or later. Your struggle with Sartini is shifting to Congress now, is it? I do hope, madam, that you are bearing up under the strain."

The news had traveled like lightning. The gossipy Potusgeists, living unseen in the walls, had to be the world's greatest eavesdroppers.

"I am all right, Mr. Jefferson, though I'm still shocked," she said. "The worst part is my husband Benny."

Jefferson looked at her with sad, sympathetic eyes. "I heard how he betrayed you. He is a knave of the first order and deserves to be publicly horsewhipped."

"Thirty years I've been married to the man, and the first chance he gets, he backs Sartini against me."

"Hardly the behavior of a proper husband, I'll grant you," said the ghost. "But what's done is done. Trouble yourself no more about him. Allow me to cheer you up and take your mind off your problems. Would you care to hear some music? I find it a tonic for the soul whenever I feel melancholy and oppressed by events."

Patty had a few free minutes. Why not? She sat down in a nearby chair.

"I was just practicing some Corelli," said Jefferson, "but I think you might find that too ponderous today. You need something lighter and more uplifting." He thought a moment, took up his violin, and plucked a string. "In my day, during my campaign for the presidency, we sang a song about fighting tyrants. It's called 'Jefferson and Liberty.'"

Jefferson could sing?

Indeed, he could. In fact, he played his violin with such liveliness and sang with such gusto that she soon found herself clapping and stomping her feet along with the lyrics:

Rejoice, Columbia's sons, rejoice!
To tyrants never bend your knee,
But join with heart, and soul, and voice,
For Jefferson and Liberty!

No lordling here, with gorging jaws
Shall wring from industry the food;
Nor fiery bigot's holy laws
Lay waste our fields and streets in blood!

Here strangers from a thousand shores
Compelled by tyranny to roam,
Shall find amidst abundant stores,
A nobler and happier home.

Here Art shall lift her laurelled head,
Wealth, Industry, and Peace, divine;
And where dark, pathless forests spread,
Rich fields and lofty cities shine.

From Europe's wants and woes remote,

A friendly waste of waves between,
Here plenty cheers the humblest cot,
And smiles on every village green.

Here free as air, expanded space,
To every soul and sect shall be
That sacred privilege of our race,
The worship of the Deity.

Let foes to freedom dread the name;
But should they touch the sacred tree,
Twice fifty thousand swords would flame
For Jefferson and Liberty.

From Georgia to Lake Champlain,
From seas to Mississippi's shore,
Ye sons of freedom loud proclaim
"The reign of terror is no more."

These gifts, great Liberty, are thine,
Ten thousand more we owe to thee,
Immortal may their mem'ries shine,
Who fought and died for Liberty.

Rejoice, Columbia's sons, rejoice!
To tyrants never bend your knee,
But join with heart, and soul, and voice,
For Jefferson and Liberty!

Jefferson laid down his violin. "There you go, madam, a serenade to brighten your spirits, with my compliments. May you defeat the tyrants of your day as we did in ours."

"That was fantastic!" said Patty, awestruck that a ghost could sing.

"Oh, by the way, please don't mention my campaign song to Mr. Adams," said Jefferson. "Hearing it always drives him into fits of rage. He lost that election to me, you know. The old fellow never has quite gotten over it."

Jefferson was as unique an individual as Patty had been told—a man of the highest intellect, a courtly man without pretense, a natural aristocrat who could hobnob with the French court one minute and preach for the rights of the common man the next. Though he was from a wholly different time and milieu, his views on freedom were not so different from hers after all.

"Mr. Jefferson, can you...can you help me?" she asked, her voice quavering.

Jefferson smiled. "Madam, helping you has been my chief object since your first day at the White House, though I admit my efforts have been clumsy and wholly unfruitful. What is it you desire?"

"If the ghosts can haunt me, they can haunt Sartini, can't they? You could go after him in the Oval Office like you did me, couldn't you?"

Jefferson dropped back into the settee as a gloom settled over his face. "Oh, well, yes, we could...but there's a considerable obstacle in the way of that idea. You see, the Ghost Council would have to authorize it and—"

"Oh, do you think they would?" she asked, clasping her hands together as if in prayer.

Jefferson tilted his head as he considered the question. "It is hard to say. We are normally prohibited by our Rules to interfere in the affairs of the living. Your case was an exception, and the Council has not been pleased with the result. Their reluctance to plunge even deeper into the quagmire of your problems has only increased."

"Does the Council prefer Sartini to me?" she asked. "Are they willing to just watch him take over the presidency and do nothing?"

Jefferson frowned. "I say, Mrs. Pitypander, you do ask the most difficult and pointed questions. I can't speak for the whole Council. I'm only one ghost among many, you know."

"But you could ask them, and they would have to listen to you, wouldn't they? They can't ignore you. You're Thomas Jefferson."

He looked down at his slippers. "Yes, I'm quite certain they would at least listen to me."

"Then will you ask them?"

Jefferson paused for a few seconds and gazed into her eyes. "Mrs. Pitypander, I must say I have badly misjudged you. I now see how you came to rise to the presidency. You are one of the most hard-headed and persistent women I have ever known and a great deal more determined than I first realized. The answer is yes, I will bring the matter of haunting Sartini before the Council. But, mind you, I cannot promise that they will heed my words."

Patty smiled. His effort would be enough for her. "And you, Mr. Jefferson, are the nicest and most interesting ghost I have ever met."

"Why, thank you, madam," he replied, bowing his head.

She wished him success in his meeting with the Council and left the room. As soon as she closed the door, the violin music started up again.

How refreshingly different Jefferson was from living men of the present, she thought as she walked down the hall. The contrast between him and her boorish husband could not be more stark. One was a patrician genius who reveled in the world's beauty, the other a dirtbag who worshipped money and his own ego. One was honored by monuments, the other built monuments to himself. Class separated the two even more than centuries of time.

She assumed that someday, in the distant future, when she herself was dead, she would become a Potusgeist too. She would take her place here as a new spirit among much older ones, inhabiting the White House as they did. Jefferson would still be here then.

Better to spend eternity with Jefferson than with Benny—much better. Benny disgusted and degraded her. When talking to Jefferson, she felt her soul uplifted and her mind clear and sane.

She had come full circle, from doubting that a ghost could care about her to wondering whether she could have feelings for a ghost. Though strange, it seemed entirely plausible and could hardly be worse than having an absent and faithless husband. Ghost or husband, they were the same in one respect: she couldn't touch either one.

CHAPTER 29

THE PLEDGE

THE FURNACE FANS kicked on in the room down the hall from the ghosts' lair, producing a low rumble and filling the basement with white noise. Jefferson frowned, wishing he could turn the system off. It would be that much harder for him to project his squeaky voice across the storage room.

Adams banged on a pipe with his cane to get the meeting started. Jefferson stepped nervously onto the podium box, waiting for the ghosts to settle down.

"Ladies and gentlemen, please come to order," Adams yelled over the din. He whacked the pipe again. This time, the noise level dropped, and the ghosts turned to face the podium.

Jefferson shuffled his notes and cleared his throat. "Ladies and gentlemen, allow me to bring you up to date. At our last meeting, we agreed to warn Mrs. Pitypander of the danger Mr. Sartini posed to her, but our warning came too late. Mr. Sartini has seized the powers of the presidency, asserting that Mrs. Pitypander has gone mad, as it has been discovered by the living that she is seeing ghosts."

The Potusgeists looked at each other, stupefied. Seeing ghosts? Of course, she was seeing ghosts, they told each other. How would that make anyone crazy?

Adams struck the pipe a third time. "Order! Order!"

"If I may continue," said Jefferson. "Now, here is the question before us. Mrs. Pitypander has appealed to us to take sides in her fight against Sartini and haunt him. I am here to argue that we are morally bound to come to Mrs. Pitypander's aid, applying the full array of our ghostly powers against Sartini's usurpation, lest his despotism prevail and darkness fall upon the land."

The room erupted into a dozen conversations.

"Order, order!" shouted Adams. "The meeting will come to order."

The ghosts simmered down again.

Theodore Roosevelt stepped toward the podium. "Mr. Jefferson, with all due respect, have we not ventured too far already? Mrs. Pitypander, as you yourself told us only months ago, is herself a danger to the republic and thoroughly unqualified. Despite your best efforts, sir, she remains a danger. Now, her vice president comes along, confirms that she is unfit, and seeks to remove her permanently from that office. Why are we supposed to be up in arms about that? How has this threat to the republic become such a great asset?"

"Hear, hear!" cried Mrs. Lincoln, shaking her fist. "I told you we should have driven her out ourselves months ago! Or better yet, killed her! I would have done it myself if you had let me!" She pulled out her butcher's knife and raised it over her head.

The ghosts drew back in horror.

Abraham Lincoln sprang forward and grabbed his wife by her shoulders. "Come, Mary, we are leaving," he said firmly as he led her out of the meeting, turning abashedly to the ghosts. "Sorry, everyone. Mrs. Lincoln is not herself today."

It seemed Mrs. Lincoln never was herself. Weary of her continual outbursts, Jefferson wondered why Lincoln couldn't pack up his distracted wife and send her off to haunt their home in Illinois and leave the White House in peace. They needed to add something to the Rules about banishing a ghost for disorderly conduct.

Jefferson faced the bespectacled T.R. "Mr. Roosevelt, as Mr. Adams and I explained at our last meeting, Sartini is even worse than Mrs. Pitypander, unless you are willing to put up with having a double-crossing tyrant as the head of the nation. We are decidedly not willing to tolerate him."

James Polk raised his arm. "But she brought in that FBI agent who hunted us down like rats and set traps for us. She meant to jail us all. How can we support such a president? Would Sartini do an awful thing like that to us?"

"Yes, that and much worse. Nothing will stand in the way of a man like Sartini," Adams avowed. "A grasping, power-hungry politician like him wouldn't think twice about getting rid of us. By contrast, Mrs. Pitypander's attitude toward us has softened so much that she now implores us to help save her presidency."

"Then she has made great progress, hasn't she?" said Eleanor Roosevelt in her lilting voice. "She started out insisting we weren't real and now wants our help. That means we have succeeded in bringing Mrs. Pitypander around. If she wants us for her allies, will she not soon seek our advice and counsel? Isn't that the change in her we wanted all along? Isn't that reason enough for us to support her struggle to stay in office?"

The ghosts broke out into conversations again. Mrs. Roosevelt's point had hit its mark. Mrs. Pitypander, many of them agreed, was still an empty-headed ninny, but she was their ninny and didn't seem quite as bad as she used to.

Tyler said the devil they knew was better than the one they didn't. Jackson pointed out that it was best not to change horses in the middle of a stream. Similar justifications for sticking with Mrs. Pitypander were expressed by Garfield and Hoover.

Madison frowned. "It is just as I feared—first, we were in for a penny, but now are in for a pound, drawn ever more deeply into Mrs. Pitypander's business. Now you tell us that as a consequence of our past ill-executed interference, we have a duty to intercede more boldly. Helping Mrs. Pitypander could mean a lot of things, Mr. Jefferson. How do you suggest that we aid her?"

Jefferson laid it on the line. "To convince Congress that Mrs. Pitypander is deranged, Sartini must assert that she is seeing ghosts. I propose that it is only fair that Sartini should see us as well. Let us thwart his sole claim to power by haunting the would-be tyrant out of the White House!"

Madison waved his rulebook in the air. "No! No! A thousand times no! If we do not restrain ourselves, we will become the usurpers, don't you see? It is not for the dead to pick the leaders of the living. Our day is past. We must respect the Constitution, even if the living distort and abuse it. Let them find their own way out of their dilemma. Preventing such brazen and impassioned involvement in their affairs is the whole point of our Rules. These principles have served us well for two centuries. Are we to abandon them so cavalierly in the heat of the moment, for such a fleeting and trivial annoyance as Mrs. Pitypander? I say not!"

Jefferson was stung by his words. It was not often that he and Madison, the closest of political allies, found themselves on opposite sides of an issue in a public debate. He could outwit most of the ghosts but not a great logician like Madison, who knew precisely how his mind worked and could rebut his arguments point by point.

Maybe they could work out a compromise. "What if we set some limits to our haunting of Sartini?" Jefferson asked.

Madison's shoulders slumped. "Limit the haunting as you may, you will still be taking sides and promoting one contender over the other. And you won't respect any limits for long—you'll be back again soon to loosen them, to gain some advantage or respond to some new contingency. That's the nature of conflict—it always escalates."

Adams stepped forward. "If that be so, let us admit our intentions plainly right now, with no more half measures or beating about the bush. I propose that we take the side of Mrs. Pitypander, foursquare against the tyrant Sartini, with no limits whatsoever to hamper us. Who will vote with me to stop the usurper?"

Slightly more than half the ghosts raised their hands while the rest groaned in sullen disapproval. The pro-Pitypander faction had won.

Adams rubbed his palms together. "Then the motion has carried, and the game is on. Let the haunting of Sartini begin."

Madison dropped his rulebook, leaned forward, and laid his head in his hands.

BUOYED BY THE Council vote, Jefferson sat on a crate in the ghost den, considering what to do next. He and Adams had taken on a most daunting assignment, with no clear plan for how to accomplish it. Exactly how were they to go about driving Sartini out of the West Wing? Such a thing had never been attempted before.

The usurper would fight back with every weapon at his disposal, and the task of ousting him would take more than one or two ghosts. What they needed was a small, scrappy band of commandos who could marshal all the ghosts in the building and turn them into an effective fighting force.

The Potusgeists did not lack for leaders. Within their ranks were a number of great military heroes, and some were present at the White House that very week.

Adams jotted down a list of them and read their qualifications. "Let's see, we have Andrew Jackson, victor of the battle of New Orleans. He's never turned down a fight. William Henry Harrison won fame in the Battle of Tippecanoe and the War of 1812. Zachary Taylor served in the U.S. Army for forty years, most recently in the Mexican-American War. Ulysses S. Grant and James Garfield were generals in the Civil War. Theodore Roosevelt led the Rough Riders in a famous charge up San Juan Hill during the Spanish-American War."

All six specters had been men of action, leaders of indomitable will, toughness, and resourcefulness. The mere sight of them, Adams opined, ought to scare any living person silly.

"Excellent," said Jefferson. "Let's ask if they'll do it."

All the former soldiers eagerly responded to the call of duty. Thrilled by the chance to enter the fray and don their old uniforms again, they tossed aside any reservations they had about backing Mrs. Pitypander.

Jackson, sporting gold epaulets on his shoulders, strutted around the Lincoln Bedroom like a peacock. He tied a red sash around his waist and gave it a confident tug. Roosevelt fastidiously adjusted the feather in his "campaign hat," so pleased at viewing himself in the mirror that he had difficulty tearing himself away from it.

Grant donned his muddy boots and lit his cigar. "That's enough fancifying, boys. We aren't dressing up for a costume ball. We're going to war. Now let's get at 'em!"

Jefferson assembled the little squad of volunteers outside the President's Bedroom, lining them up from left to right in historical order, careful not to offend any of the ghosts' delicate egos.

"Where's Eisenhower?" asked Roosevelt, looking around the room. "Shouldn't he be here?"

"Ah, he sent his regrets. Says he can't make it," said Garfield.

Roosevelt was dubious. "He's playing golf in Gettysburg, I'll bet."

Adams smiled at the team with pride. "Look at them, Jefferson. A more fearsome collection of warriors was never assembled on this continent, I think. Their uniforms alone should terrify Sartini."

"They are magnificent, Mr. Adams," Jefferson replied. "I surely would hate to face them in battle."

He knocked three times on the door of the President's Bedroom.

Patty opened the door a crack and fell backward upon seeing the motley crew.

"Mrs. Pitypander," said Jefferson with a bow, "may I present your troops." He introduced them, one by one.

The sight of the soldiers, accompanied by the news that the Ghost Council had voted to back her to the hilt, brought a broad smile to Patty's face. "You have no idea what this means to me."

"Roosevelt, reporting for duty, madam," said T.R. with a salute, standing ramrod straight. "If nothing else, we'll make a bully haunting of it. I can promise you that. He won't forget us in a million years."

Grant growled and chomped on his cigar. "Sartini won't have a moment's peace. We'll attack him from the left. We'll attack him from the right. We'll make his life a bloody, living hell. We'll burn him out of there if that's what it takes."

"That thieving rascal won't deny my existence when I put my boot up his ass," Jackson thundered.

"Oh, my," Patty replied with a delighted smile. "I expect not."

"We're all behind you, madam," said Adams. "If you can't have the Oval Office, we'll see to it that Sartini can't either."

Patty, at a loss for words, wiped away a tear.

Jefferson nodded at Adams with satisfaction. The Potusgeists were ready for battle. Sartini wouldn't stand a chance.

CHAPTER 30

THE ATTACK

A SOLID WALL OF buses parked end to end lined Constitution Avenue, completing the cordon sanitaire that sealed off the White House from the rest of Washington. Though the barrier was meant to keep Sartini safe, it only raised his blood pressure.

With so much hostility toward him brewing outside, could he have underestimated the people's support for Pitypander?

Henry Snoops, Secretary of Homeland Security, had just finished telling him that everything was under control, and yet there were thousands of women in pink hats out there, screaming and holding pro-Pitypander signs. What about them?

"Relax, the demonstrations will blow over in a couple of weeks," Snoops said. "It's just a bunch of crazy women. We have all the people we need to handle the situation."

Sartini was not comforted. They had already called in the D.C. National Guard to man the barricades, and they might need the Maryland National Guard as well.

Secretary of Defense Codd didn't look worried either. "Look, Tony, if things really start coming unglued, we can get all the

Marines we need down here in an hour. There's no shortage of troops around Washington."

Capitol Hill was as besieged as the White House. Thousands of placard-waving demonstrators had camped in tents outside the security fencing hastily erected there.

Speaker Underdown had assured Sartini that the fix was in. A simple majority of both houses of Congress already favored him, and a two-thirds majority was achievable, depending on how next week's hearings went.

To Sartini's dismay, the media were no help. Coverage of the coup remained impartial, as the networks and newspapers were unsure of who had the advantage in the power struggle. Without clear direction from their editors, most journalists reported on the chaotic events without bias.

Looking anxiously out the window at the protesters, Sartini heard a loud moan coming from behind him.

He glanced at Codd, whose eyes were bulging out.

Sartini spun around. Something was slowly emerging from the bookcase, something translucent and glowing around the edges.

It was a human form. A tall, slender man in a frock coat with knee breeches, stockings, and slippers took shape.

He grinned at them.

"My God!" said Sartini, transfixed by the apparition. "What the hell is that thing?"

"I...I have no idea," Codd replied, taking a step back.

"It looks like...it's a ghost!" cried Snoops. "But it can't be."

The thing bobbed in the air, as if suspended on a string, before coalescing into a stable image.

"Who the hell are you?" Sartini demanded.

The form stepped forward and identified himself. "Sir, I am the spirit of Thomas Jefferson, Representative Plenipotentiary for the Council of White House Ghosts."

Sartini folded his arms and laughed. "And I'm the Ghost of Christmas Past. Pleased to meet you, Mr. Scrooge. Oh, please. Gimme a break, fella."

The apparition cocked his head in confusion. "I'm not sure what your request for a break means, sir, but unless I miss my guess, you are expressing skepticism regarding my identity."

Sartini sneered. "Yeah, pal. You got that right. You're an illusion. I don't know who cooked up this little clown show, but it won't work on me. I'm not a gullible fool like Pitypander."

"No, sir, I perceive that you are an entirely different kind of fool," said Jefferson. "And I might have the same reservations were I in your place. But I assure you, sir, I am no illusion."

"Uh-huh. Sure thing."

"Perhaps this will persuade you." The ghost clapped his hands three times. Six more ghosts marched out of the bookcase, one by one, and lined up in front of it, shoulder to shoulder, in parade formation.

Jefferson introduced the members of his ghost squad, from Jackson to Roosevelt. "Do you still doubt us, sir?"

Jackson eyed Sartini ominously. Tippecanoe rattled his sword in its scabbard. T.R. stood perfectly erect, like a statue, his rifle at his side.

Sartini was unmoved. It had to be a trick. "There are no such things as ghosts. You're a fake."

"Doubt us as you like, sir. It's all the same to me," said Jefferson. "I have simply come to inform you that the Ghost Council demands that you vacate the Oval Office forthwith and restore the presidency to Mrs. Pitypander."

"Oh, the Council does, does it? Well, I'm the Acting President of the United States. Tell the Council to stick it."

"Stick what, sir?" Jefferson looked puzzled at first. "Oh, I see. You are expressing contempt."

Sartini crossed his arms. "Yes, I am."

Jefferson looked at his troops. "As I expected. Very well, then, have it your way. Mr. Jackson, please remove these gentlemen from the room."

"Get 'em, boys!" Jackson yelled.

The ghosts rushed forward.

Codd and Snoops, cowering behind a sofa, dashed across the room to a window. Employees in adjoining offices ran to the doorways.

Jackson and Grant caught Sartini near the fireplace and grabbed him by his arms. Harrison and Taylor seized Codd by the throat. Garfield and Roosevelt lifted Snoops, who had fainted, off the floor.

The ghosts dragged the three men out of the Oval Office, past Sartini's astonished secretary, and down the hall, dumping them like sacks of flour on the floor of the Vice President's office, prostrate and gasping for air.

Jackson raised his fist, hunching over them. "No such things as ghosts, eh? This is just a warning, you lily-livered jackals. Go back into that office and we'll show you some real haunting. I'll tear your innards out myself and feed you to the crows to pick over. Let's go, boys. Let them think about that for a while."

Jefferson waved his hand as the signal to leave, and the ghosts dutifully walked through the wall in single file after him.

SARTINI, CODD, AND Snoops, breathing hard, picked themselves up from the floor of Sartini's office and gazed at each other in shock.

"You mean there really are ghosts here?" asked Codd, his chest rising and falling as he struggled to catch his breath.

"No, of course not!" Sartini snapped. "They can't be ghosts, you idiot!"

"Okay, you say they aren't ghosts. Fine, then what the hell are they?" asked Codd. "They sure looked like ghosts to me. There was Jackson, Grant, Teddy Roosevelt, and whoever the other three were."

Sartini swept his hand across his suit, brushing the dust off. "I tell you, they aren't ghosts. They have to be some kind of high-tech thing, something we've never seen before."

"You mean like a computer-generated hologram?" asked Snoops.

Sartini's face brightened. Finally, somebody had an idea that sounded halfway plausible. "Sure, a hologram. That's it. Does the CIA know how to pull off this kind of thing?"

"Nothing like this," Snoops replied. He acknowledged that the CIA once had a skunkworks project where researchers used artificial intelligence to mimic real people with holograms. The technology was intriguing but never got out of the experimental stage. It didn't seem useful for the agency's purposes, so the project was shut down.

"The Russians or Chinese could have developed the technology too, couldn't they?" Sartini asked.

"It's possible," Snoops replied, "but do you think they would actually be crazy enough to use it here, to take over the White House?"

Sartini scowled at him. Snoops must lack imagination. "Are you serious? What better place would there be than this? Look at the total havoc they're creating. They're turning this place upside down."

Snoops pulled up a pant leg and examined the contusion swelling up on his ankle. "Holograms are just three-dimensional images projected into a space. It would take more than images to pick us up and throw us out of the Oval Office. It would take some kind of force."

"An enemy could have made some huge technological advances we don't know about," Sartini suggested.

"Or they're ghosts," said Codd with resignation.

"Stop saying that! They aren't ghosts!" Sartini bellowed.

Codd drew back. "All right, we got run out of the Oval by non-ghosts. I won't use the g-word again, I promise."

Sartini pressed his hand to his forehead. By forming his cabal from the Pitypander Cabinet, had he created a gang of nincompoops? It couldn't be helped. To pull off his coup, he needed willing Cabinet members, such as they were. He could replace them after he was certified as president by Congress.

"Wait, I heard Pitypander brought in somebody from the FBI's paranormal unit to investigate what's going on around here," said Snoops.

"The FBI agent? Yeah, I met him once," Sartini replied with an indifferent shrug. "He's a nerdy young guy with a little office in the basement. I couldn't get him to tell me anything. I don't think he'll be much help."

"Well, if he's an FBI agent, then I'm his boss," said Snoops. "He might open up to me. It wouldn't hurt to ask."

THE THREE DISHEVELED men found Clint bent over his worktable, adjusting the range of his radar gun. The ghost hunter sat up with a start.

Sartini explained what had happened in the Oval Office. "These things, whatever they were, literally threw us out of there. I think they must be some kind of high-tech projections or illusions of some kind. What do you say they are?"

Clint put down his tools and turned to face him. "They're not illusions—they're ghosts," he said without hesitation. "Fully capable fourth-degree paranormal apparitions."

"They can't be ghosts," Sartini insisted. "That's impossible."

"Well, they are. The White House is full of them—several dozen at least. This is one of the most haunted houses in America."

Snoops clutched his chest. "Several dozen? Are all of them former presidents, like the ones we saw?"

"Nope, there are first ladies, too. Also a few miscellaneous family members who died here, like Willie Lincoln. I found him playing outside once in the South Lawn fountain. He's a good kid. Too bad typhoid fever got him."

Sartini looked at Clint like he had escaped from an insane asylum. The ghost hunter wasn't joking. He actually thought he had been seeing ghosts all over the place.

Clint examined the inside of his radar gun, took a miniature screwdriver off his worktable, and turned a tiny screw. "They're harmless unless you piss them off, which it sounds like you did. The ghost you really want to avoid upsetting is Andrew Jackson. He's a badass. They didn't call him Old Hickory for nothing."

"He was one of them all right," Snoops confirmed. "What we want to know is, can they be stopped?"

"Uh, I'd rather not say. I've worked out a deal with them."

"A deal? What kind of deal?" asked Snoops.

Clint smiled. "They let me study them as long as I don't bug them too often. We didn't understand each other at first, but we get along just fine now. I've learned tons about them."

"That's ridiculous!" said Sartini. "Ghosts don't exist! Dead people don't make deals!"

"These dead people do," Clint replied. "And the way they see it, they're not invading your space—you're invading theirs. They've been here for centuries. They just want some respect, that's all. Trust me, you don't want to rile them up. Fourth-degree apparitions have special powers."

Special powers? That was all the crazy talk Sartini needed to hear.

They thanked him and walked down the hall.

"That kid's even battier than Pitypander," said Sartini. He turned to Snoops. "Doesn't the FBI have more senior people than him who could help us, somebody who's rational and doesn't believe in ghosts?"

Snoops proposed bringing in an armed FBI SWAT team to take back the Oval Office by force.

"Whatever it takes, do it," said Sartini with a huff. "Ghosts have special powers? He's nuts. I'm the one with special powers."

CHAPTER 31

DUELING SPEECHES

ARAY OF AFTERNOON light poured into the West Sitting Hall, brightening the room's yellow walls. Patty stood at the big lunette window and gazed wistfully at the West Wing.

"Don't worry, you'll get it back soon enough," Nigel assured her, looking up from the sofa.

There was reason to be hopeful. The ghosts had driven Sartini out of the Oval Office and were holding it for her. Congress was about to debate her fitness to be president and would surely vote in her favor. Across the country, her legions of supporters, the International Ladybugs, had swung into action.

Colleen Cook walked in looking upbeat and reported that she had been on the phone with the organization's leadership for an hour. The Ladybugs were up in arms, incensed that a man they had barely heard of could just swoop in and steal the presidency out from under their candidate.

Two million outraged activists were ready to march in the streets for Patty, from chapters in every city and state. Images of furious women in pink hats turning over cars and smashing storefronts filled the news broadcasts.

"We'll just keep cranking up the pressure, putting the heat on Congress," said Colleen. "I've arranged for you to speak at the weekend Ladybug rally at the Lincoln Memorial. Two hundred thousand pissed-off women are sure to get Congress's attention."

Patty would need the show of support. The Democratic party had split into opposing factions over whether she was mentally competent, and the Republicans were already against her. Behind the scenes, Benny's billions were buying Sartini more votes every day. The usurper had the leadership of both chambers of Congress in his pocket.

Benny's treachery made Nigel even more fiercely determined. Her side had mega-rich donors too, he pointed out, and SuperPAC contributions were pouring in from Silicon Valley. They had received fifty million dollars in the last two days, which they could use to run TV spots against Sartini.

Nigel's phone buzzed. He answered the call and looked at Patty. "It's Mr. Twiggs. Says it's urgent."

The old gentleman trudged into the West Sitting Hall with a mortified look on his face. "I found the leakers," he announced.

Twiggs had called each of his ushers into his office, one by one, and asked if they had anything to do with spreading information about Patty seeing ghosts.

"Phaedra McBride broke down in tears as soon as I put the question to her," said Twiggs. "She confessed to giving Sartini a video recording of you in the Yellow Oval Room. It was made by one of the housekeepers."

The staff had fed her personal information to her political enemy—an automatic firing offense.

The old man's hands hung down at his sides like lead weights. "I've given both of them forty-eight hours' notice. They knew they were not to tell outsiders stories about your personal life. It's the first thing we teach the staff when they start working here."

Patty asked why they had done it.

"They thought they were protecting the country," he replied. "I don't think they meant to cause you all this trouble, and they feel terrible about it. I sincerely regret it, Madam President."

Patty rubbed her temples. "No, Mr. Twiggs, I don't want you to fire them."

"But they're a security risk," said Nigel, his eyes flaring. "You can't have housekeepers who spy on you. Think of what else they could do to undermine us. They could go to the press with their story."

"Firing them won't prevent that," Patty replied. "They did it for the country, and had no way to know I'm not crazy. As long as they've learned their lesson, I don't think it will happen again."

"No, it sure won't, and thank you for understanding, Madam President," said Twiggs, exhaling heavily. He pressed his hand to his heart, turned around, and walked back down the hall with a smile of relief.

THE SEA OF pink hats gathered on the Mall was the largest crowd Patty had ever spoken to. It covered both sides of the Reflecting Pool and stretched all the way to the Washington Monument.

She took a deep breath and made her way slowly down the steps toward the podium as a deafening cheer rose up. She smiled and waved at the multitude.

"Pitypander for President!" they roared. "Down with Sartini!"

Patty stepped up to the podium and gave a nod to the head of the International Ladybugs.

Pulling the microphone down to a comfortable height, she cleared her throat. "People of America, greetings! We have come together here today to celebrate and defend our democracy. I, the duly elected President of the United States, have no intention of surrendering the reins of government to a small group of power-hungry politicians scheming in a smoke-filled room to seize power from me. I won't allow it to happen. And you won't either!"

With that, the crowd erupted in cheers.

"Now, the connivers have claimed that I'm not fit to be president. Last November, you said otherwise, with your eighty million votes. The powerful people who run this city behind your back heard your voices then, but it seems they have forgotten about you. Let your voices be heard again! Let them hear from you, all the way to Capitol Hill." Patty raised her fist in defiance.

A deafening roar ricocheted across the Mall as the crowd raised thousands of fists in the air.

"The connivers say I'm seeing things that aren't there. In a way, they're right. What I'm seeing is the future, a better future for America that will be ours if we simply have the backbone to fight for it. Will you fight for me? Will you fight for your future, America?"

"Fight for Pitypander! Down with Sartini!" the women thundered.

Patty reached into her coat pocket and pulled out a slip of paper. "A friend of mine gave me this little reminder of what we're all about in this country and what we've stood for from the very beginning. I thought you might like to hear it too." She read the lyrics of Jefferson's campaign song aloud:

Rejoice, Columbia's sons, rejoice!
To tyrants never bend your knee,

But join with heart, and soul, and voice,
For Jefferson and Liberty!

These gifts, great Liberty, are thine,
Ten thousand more we owe to thee,
Immortal may their mem'ries shine,
Who fought and died for Liberty.

Rejoice, Columbia's sons, rejoice!
To tyrants never bend your knee,
But join with heart, and soul, and voice,
For Jefferson and Liberty!

"I'll never bend my knee to tyrants!" she called out, raising her fist in the air.

"For Jefferson and Liberty!" the crowd shouted back.

Patty concluded her remarks with a prayer that Almighty God might preserve and protect America from the depredations of usurpers and tyrants, now and for all time.

Nigel, standing off to the side, flashed a big smile. He gave her the thumbs up, and they departed from the scene.

AN HOUR LATER, Patty was back at the White House when word arrived that Sartini was going on live television to address the nation.

Colleen switched on the news. A male anchor with perfectly coiffed brown hair speculated that Sartini would try to calm the country's fears about growing dissension.

The acting president sat in a room Patty had never seen before. It was a fake movie set resembling the Oval Office, complete with a fake Resolute Desk, fake gold curtains, and an American flag.

"My fellow Americans," Sartini began somberly, "I know that many of you are very concerned, as I am, about the precarious state of former President Pitypander's mental health. As you may have heard, the former president has developed a stress-related nervous condition that has gradually worsened to a point where she now believes she is seeing ghosts. She has even been recorded having conversations with them. Yes, that's right—conversations with dead people."

Sartini looked into the camera, grinning like a used car salesman. "Now, folks, we've all known some special needs people like Patty in our personal lives. Lots of families have someone with an issue like this. And, as we all know, there are no such things as ghosts. I hope you'll understand that upon learning of her mental disability, for the country's sake as well as hers, a majority of the Cabinet and I were compelled to step up and do our constitutional duty to relieve the former president of the heavy burdens of her office. Like all of you, we wish the former president the very best and will see that she gets the finest medical attention available, in hopes of her speedy recovery and return to sanity."

Sartini emphasized how important it was that Congress vote courageously to approve his succession to the presidency as soon as possible, for the sake of national security.

As he spoke, his eyes departed from the teleprompter and shifted to his left, as if he was seeing something coming at him. He swung his hand at it, paused long enough to smile at the camera, and looked up to his right, his eyes filling with panic.

"Oh, no!" He ducked his head quickly. "Go away! Get lost!"

He raised his arms as if to block a blow and then dropped behind the podium, falling on his back, his legs flailing in the air.

"Don't do that! No, stop that! Please stop!"

Sartini struggled for fifteen more seconds, until the video went dark. A test pattern filled the screen.

Seconds later, the anchor reappeared. "Uh, ladies and gentlemen, we're not sure what's going on at the White House. It looks like there may be some kind of technical difficulty with the acting president's equipment. We'll return to his speech as soon as they have things cleared up over there."

Nigel leaped to his feet, shaking his fist at the screen. "It's the ghosts! They're bloody well after him."

CHAPTER 32

AT THE BATTLEMENTS

THEODORE ROOSEVELT PACED nervously around the Oval Office and peered out the windows at the South Lawn, expecting a retaliatory raid by Sartini's forces to come at any moment.

The Potusgeists' six commandos had deployed to key locations in the West Wing and Residence, alongside twenty-five other specters, including nine first ladies.

Squinting through his thick glasses, Roosevelt spied a group of twenty armed men in blue FBI uniforms marching toward him across the South Lawn. "There they are, boys. The enemy is coming!" He passed word of the impending attack to Franklin Pierce, who hurried away to summon all available reinforcements.

Ulysses S. Grant appeared by the fireplace, a cigar clenched in his teeth. "They're already in the West Wing! Quick, boys, turn yourselves invisible."

The ghosts vanished and took up positions on both sides of the door, bracing for combat.

Seconds later, three agents clad in bulletproof vests and helmets burst in, waving assault rifles. They scanned the room and stepped warily inside, checking around the Resolute Desk, under the sofas and chairs, and near the fireplace.

"All clear, Maverick, it's not in the Oval," said one of them into a cell phone as he came out of the president's study.

Another agent pulled the curtains back and looked behind them. "It's gotta be here somewhere. I can't believe the officer on duty just left it here unguarded. He could be court-martialed for that."

"Yeah, he must have been pretty damn scared."

The ghosts shadowed them through a doorway to the adjoining office. One of the agents noticed a black leather briefcase with a leather strap lying flat on the floor.

"Hey, isn't that it?" said the agent excitedly.

"Yeah, it's gotta be," replied another.

The agent rushed over and tried to lift the briefcase with one hand, but it was too heavy. He bent down, slipped the strap over his shoulder, and lugged it across the room.

"Get after 'em, boys!" Roosevelt shouted.

"What? Who's that?" The agent looked up, then down, and all around but saw nothing.

Roosevelt and Jackson descended on him, seizing him by the collar and causing the briefcase to slip off his shoulder and fall to the floor. Grant kicked the other two agents in the butt before turning to double over the first agent with a hard punch to the gut.

The three agents ran for their lives down the hallway as Potusgeists streamed through the West Wing's walls in hot pursuit.

Grant watched with satisfaction through the window, puffing on his cigar, as the dazed agents poured out of the White House onto the South Lawn, their eyes filled with terror.

"Damn, I wish Robert E. Lee and his boys had been this easy to lick," he said with a wry smile. "I could have had the Civil War over in twenty minutes."

Grant pointed to five of the ghosts. "You guys go down to the Situation Room and clear it." He motioned to eight of the others. "And you guys take the rest of the West Wing but leave the ghost hunter in the basement alone. He's on our side."

The two groups did as they were told.

Grant spat into a trash can. "God, I miss this stuff! I was never worth a damn at anything else."

Roosevelt picked up the briefcase and heaved it onto a desk. "What is this thing? It weighs a ton."

Jackson flipped it on its side and poked at it with his index finger. "Let's see what's in it." He pressed a brass button, and it snapped open. Lifting its lid, he took one look and jumped back. "What the hell!"

Inside were dozens of odd-looking buttons with letters and numbers printed on them. A small green light was flashing.

Fishing into a side pocket with his hand, he drew out a black book entitled "STRATCOM Retaliatory Options and Procedures" and a small card bearing codes.

The ghosts stared at each other in bewilderment.

"Look at this thing. I wonder what it does," said Jackson, surveying the keyboard. He pressed the letter "H." The flashing green light turned red. Other lights started blinking in a random pattern. Numbers flashed. A tiny screen read "Alert Procedure and Countdown Initiated. Targets Selected. Input Codes to Confirm."

A voice came out of a corner of the briefcase. "STRATCOM here. Bogey One, please confirm signal."

There was a long pause.

"I repeat, Bogey One, please confirm signal."

"The damn thing talks," Jackson muttered. "What should we do with it?"

Roosevelt gave it another hard look. "Let's take it to Jefferson. He'll figure it out. He loves playing with gadgets."

FAR FROM THE White House, deep within Cheyenne Mountain, Colorado, Second Lieutenant Josh Rodgers was busy surfing his favorite pornographic websites when his control panel lit up like a Christmas tree. His screen read "BOGEY ONE MISSILE LAUNCH PROTOCOL INITIATED."

An earsplitting alarm sounded. The other technicians on the Strategic Air Command alert floor turned to look.

The lights on his panel were blinking.

"Oh, my God, this is for real." Rodgers pressed a red button, summoning Major Andy Hopkins and Colonel Tom Martin to his side.

The colonel leaned over the console, the color draining from his face. "It's Bogey One, all right."

"I didn't know we were having a test today," said the major.

"We're not," replied the colonel. "This is the real deal."

"Holy crap."

The colonel called General Osborne.

"You are authorized to send receipt confirmation and request for orders," the general responded.

"Authorization to proceed received." The colonel looked at Rodgers. "Go ahead, lieutenant, do it."

Lieutenant Rodgers took a deep breath and typed in the code. A red light on his control panel turned orange. He gazed up at the colonel with dread. "Receipt confirmation received, communications link established, request for launch orders sent, sir."

They waited...and waited. One minute, three minutes, then five minutes went by without a reply. By now, they should have received either an order to launch, or if this were merely a test of the system, an order to halt the launch sequence. Getting no reply was not supposed to happen.

"No response? What do you mean there's no response?" said the colonel. "Send it again."

Rodgers retransmitted the code and again received no answer.

"There could be something wrong with the football. Verify the GPS location and condition of Bogey One," the colonel ordered.

The lieutenant punched some more buttons. A map came up on his screen. "Bogey One is on the White House grounds, sir. It's undamaged. Battery charge is at ninety-eight percent. All systems nominal. No transmission problems. I don't see anything wrong with it."

The colonel scratched his head. "It doesn't make sense. Where's the Bogey One operator? Get him on speakerphone."

The phone rang five times before it was finally picked up. "Hello, Bogey One, are you there?" said the lieutenant. A few seconds passed. "Bogey One, are you there? C'mon, Bogey One, answer me."

They heard the noise of someone shuffling around in the background and then a voice saying, "Well, I'll be hornswoggled, Jackson. I do believe this thing is trying to talk to me."

"I'll be damned—so it is, general," said another voice.

"General? Who is this?" asked the lieutenant.

"U.S. Grant. Who wants to know?"

The colonel leaned over and shouted at the console, "Look, mister, I don't know who you are or what game you're playing, but we've had enough of it around here. What the hell are you doing with the president's nuclear football?"

No answer. There was a grunt, and the phone went dead.

★ ★ ★

SARTINI SCOWLED AT Snoops, who was slumped in a chair, looking defeated.

"How? That's what I want to know," said the acting president. "How could a trained FBI SWAT team be driven out of here by a bunch of...well, whatever the hell those things are?"

"Ghosts," said Snoops disconsolately.

Sartini slammed his fist on his desk. "They're not ghosts, dammit! Stop calling them that. Ghosts don't exist. Ulysses S. Grant hasn't come back from the dead to defend the White House. That's ridiculous."

"It's not just him. They have Teddy Roosevelt on their side too," said Snoops. "Face it—we're just outmatched. We sent twenty men in there, and they got their butts kicked."

They couldn't be outmatched. Sartini had the awesome power of the U.S. government at his disposal. There had to be some way to use its three million employees to fight...the non-ghosts.

"Codd, didn't you tell me we have lots of troops stationed around Washington? Can't we send them in there?"

Secretary Codd looked at Sartini with a distinct lack of enthusiasm, as if he had been dreading the question. "Tony, be serious. What could troops do that an FBI SWAT team couldn't?"

"Well, first and most importantly, they're troops," Sartini replied, thinking the answer was glaringly obvious. "Aren't they trained for combat? Don't they have tanks, grenades, flamethrowers, and stuff like that?"

"Yes, of course, but it's the White House we're talking about and—"

"Well, what else do they need to get the Oval Office back? F-35s? ICBMs? We have enough weapons to do this, don't we?"

The Defense Department had a trillion-dollar budget. It operated bases on every continent. It was inconceivable that the U.S. military could wage a war halfway around the world but couldn't handle a bunch of pesky...whatever those things were...in the heart of the capital.

The only item they lacked for this battle was an acronym—something to avoid using the word "ghosts."

"All right, Tony, have it your way," said Codd, yielding to his commander-in-chief. "We'll send in some troops to get rid of... those things."

A COLUMN OF camouflage-colored tanks with cannons and guns mounted on them rumbled across Lafayette Square, passed through the White House visitor's gate, and churned down the driveway toward the West Wing. Atop each tank were two soldiers wearing metal helmets. Other vehicles full of soldiers followed the tanks in.

Teddy Roosevelt had seen photographs of such machines before, but nothing nearly so advanced. These were larger and faster by far than anything used in World War I.

The tanks sped around the West Wing, surrounded it, and pointed their gun turrets at the Oval Office.

"Talley ho, boys, it seems they need another lesson," T.R. cried out to the Potusgeists guarding the windows.

Grant's eyes grew big. "What the hell are those, Roosevelt? I've never seen the like."

Roosevelt explained that tanks had been invented to break through enemy trench lines. They could also pulverize buildings with their cannon or wipe out a group of soldiers with their machine guns.

Grant understood, being an expert on trench warfare from his bloody campaigns during the Civil War. "They're magnificent. I surely could have used some of those at Cold Harbor and Petersburg. But there are no trenches here. I can't believe they mean to blow up the White House with their cannon. What purpose would that serve?"

"I don't know, general," Roosevelt replied. "I confess it doesn't make any sense to me."

"It must be a show of force." Grant chomped on his cigar. "That's it—they mean to scare us. Trying to scare a bunch of ghosts, now ain't that a caution? We'll show them what scared looks like."

Troops carrying machine guns appeared on the South Lawn. The sound of boots pounding up the stairs echoed into the Oval Office.

"Turn yourselves invisible, boys," Grant ordered. "Let them come in and take over the building, follow me out of here, and don't make a sound." He dispatched Franklin Pierce with a message for Jackson to meet him on the South Lawn with all the reinforcements he could muster.

The ghosts abandoned the Oval Office, passing through the walls onto the South Lawn, where Grant, Roosevelt, and Harrison lined them up and waited for Jackson to arrive.

Jackson soon showed up with fifteen Potusgeists, including several first ladies.

"Join the line, Jackson," Grant commanded.

The ghosts, now numbering thirty, stood at attention in a phalanx.

"Now, we're going to put the fear of God into those boys over there," Grant said. "I want every third one of you to transform yourself into a lion but stay invisible."

The ghosts did as they were told.

"Every second one of you, transform into a tiger," he said. It was done.

"The rest of you, except for Taft and Cleveland, transform into gorillas." That was done.

"Taft and Cleveland, you're going to be our elephants."

They smiled and made themselves into elephants.

Grant walked up and down the line, inspecting his menagerie of transformed ghosts with a satisfied grin. "I think this will do just fine. Follow me!"

He marched them toward the tanks. "Taft and Cleveland, make yourselves visible."

They did so, much to the surprise of the troops in the tanks.

"Now, destroy those machines," Grant ordered.

Taft and Cleveland made trumpet blasts with their trunks and charged the tanks. Standing on their hind legs, they brought their front hooves crashing down on the vehicles, battering them over and over. Some of the astonished tank crewmen, terrified that they were about to be crushed, slammed their hatches shut. Others jumped out of their tanks and fled as fast as their legs could carry them.

Taft pressed his trunk against the side of a tank and pushed hard, rocking it up and down. Cleveland saw what he was doing and clomped over to help him. Working together, they flipped the tank over. They moved to the next tanks and did the same to one after another. The soldiers, afraid that they were about to be trapped, scrambled out of their vehicles. Soon, all the tanks lay upside down, like turtles flailing helplessly on their backs.

Grant pointed to the West Wing. "The rest of you come with me." He led his invisible band of lions, tigers, and gorillas back into the White House.

In the Oval Office, six soldiers guarded the windows, machine guns at the ready.

Grant picked out Roosevelt and Jackson. "Turn yourselves visible, and get 'em out of here."

Jackson, who had become a gorilla, approached the soldier nearest the Resolute Desk and beat his chest. Roosevelt, a lion, trotted over to some soldiers at the other end of the room, bared his teeth, and roared.

The soldiers, their mouths agape, pointed their guns and sprayed several rounds at the phantoms. The bullets passed harmlessly through Jackson and Roosevelt, riddling the wall next to a portrait of George Washington.

"Stop that, you idiots! They can't be shot! They're not alive!" yelled one soldier.

"Then what are we gonna do?" said another.

"Run for it!"

The soldiers scrambled out the door and into the hallway, with Roosevelt and Jackson in pursuit.

Grant dispatched the remaining ghosts to clear the rest of the West Wing. Soldiers rushed out of the building and ran pell-mell in all directions, the ghosts nipping at their heels. Astonished tourists helped the terrified troops clamber over the White House fence.

With the enemy in disarray, the ghosts regrouped next to the overturned tank battalion and lined themselves up in front of Grant.

He gave the order for them to transform themselves back into human form and disappear.

"Now that's a show of force," said Grant, tossing his cigar butt onto the grass.

CHAPTER 33

THE DESTROYER TRAPS

SARTINI GLOWERED AT Secretary Codd in stunned silence. It was bad enough that the troops' attack on the West Wing had ended in a fiasco. Now, they would have to explain to the media how thirty wild animals suddenly got on the White House grounds, repelled dozens of heavily armed troops, and disappeared without a trace.

He would deny everything. The incident never happened. The press would have to believe him. What choice did they have? They didn't dare report the fantastic stories given by eyewitnesses. People would think they were crazy.

Sartini's press secretary would claim the cell phone videos taken by shocked tourists standing outside the gates were fakes. The truth didn't matter if no sane person would believe it.

Sartini's biggest worry was whether there was any hard evidence left behind, like dead bodies. That would be bad. Bodies had to be explained. The soldiers' families would want to know how their loved ones had perished at the White House. Telling them wild animals did it was a non-starter.

"Was anyone killed?" Sartini asked anxiously.

"No. We did have a few injuries, though," Codd replied. "Scraped elbows, torn hamstrings, sprained ankles from jumping over the fence, minor stuff like that. Nothing that will make the evening news, thank heaven."

The overturned tanks, visible from surrounding streets, had been quickly removed, Codd assured Sartini.

"Tell me again how the tanks got turned upside down?"

"Rampaging elephants flipped them over, sir."

Elephants at the White House. Sure thing. Try to explain that.

"Where did they come from?" Sartini asked.

"Nobody knows. The elephants appeared, and then poof—they were gone."

The beings-who-could-not-be-named had the power to turn themselves at will into other creatures. That was a discomfiting thought. There was no telling what Sartini might be dealing with next. The beings could become whatever was necessary to defeat him.

Like the ghost hunter said, they had special powers.

The dead presidents, if that's what they were, had been skilled politicians in life, so maybe transforming themselves came naturally to them in death. Sartini had changed himself from a congressman to a vice president and lately to an acting president, all by an act of will. It hadn't been hard for him, and he wasn't even a ghost.

"How are we going to get those...things... out of there, Codd?"

The weary Secretary of Defense had anticipated his question. "Ghost traps."

Sartini drew in a long breath. "But there's no such—"

"Not that there are such things as ghosts, of course," Codd quickly added before Sartini could slam his fist on the table in protest. "But just in case, I took the precaution of having the soldiers place ghost traps throughout the West Wing. We got them from the CIA. As I understand it, if they work, the... things... will disappear, and we'll be able to walk back into the Oval Office without firing a shot."

Sartini couldn't fight it any longer. His sanity slipping away, he threw his hands up in resignation. "Okay, ghost traps—whatever you say. Just stop them."

BASKING IN THEIR victory, the Potusgeists gathered in the ghost den to regale each other with accounts of how thoroughly they had thrashed Sartini's troops.

"Mr. Adams, you should have seen me," said Garfield proudly. "I roared at them twice, and the third time they went flying. I have never seen legs move so fast. They practically pole-vaulted over the fence."

"Grant had 'em pegged, didn't he?" said McKinley. "All those soldiers needed was a little terror in their hearts, and they folded straightaway."

"It would have been more sporting if we had all become the same animal, though," said Jackson. "You lions and tigers had an easier time of it. A gorilla can't match a lion for sheer fearsomeness."

"You made up for it with ugliness, Jackson," Garfield replied with a chuckle. "Why, you were so ugly, they took one look at you and ran like the wind."

Adams turned around and saw Franklin Pierce enter the ghost den, his hand clutching his forehead.

"What is it Pierce? What's wrong?" Adams asked.

"Sir, I bear the most awful news. Abraham Lincoln has disappeared."

Pierce told them how he had personally seen Lincoln vanish into a small metal box in the Cabinet Room. He had been hanging around the West Wing with the others after helping chase Sartini's soldiers out of the building. "It was a trap—I'm sure of it. I didn't dare get too near, but I was close enough to see what happened to poor Abe. It was horrible. The thing just sucked him right in, stovepipe hat and all. Mrs. Lincoln is frantic and swears she will kill every living person in the White House if Mr. Lincoln is harmed."

Who had done this? The young ghost hunter had promised he wouldn't trap them again, and he seemed sincere from what Adams could tell. In any case, he was the only one who could help them. None of the ghosts, not even Jefferson, knew anything about how ghost traps worked.

When Adams reached Clint's office, he found him examining a small metal box, running some kind of wand-like tool over it.

"Is that one of the contraptions?" asked Adams. "One of their traps, I mean?"

Clint looked up, startled to see him. "I'm afraid so, sir. I'm glad you assumed it wasn't mine."

"Is it...occupied?"

"Yes, you can tell from this." Clint pointed to a red light blinking at the end of the trap. "It's probably full, but I'd stand farther away from it if I were you. Some traps can suck in more than one ghost."

Adams jumped back. "More than one?"

"I've never seen a trap as powerful as this one, but I've read about them in the science journals," said Clint. "It's the most advanced type—a destroyer trap. It doesn't just trap ghosts. It gradually destroys them."

"My God! How does it do that?"

As Adams listened in horror, Clint explained that a destroyer trap slowly dispersed a ghost's electromagnetic field to infinity, so the ghost couldn't function. The electrical bonds holding the ghost together weakened to the point where the spirit dissipated into nothingness and ceased to exist.

Destroyer traps were designed to exterminate ghosts within twenty-four hours. With enough of them, Sartini could wipe out all the Potusgeists. The soldiers had undoubtedly installed more all over the West Wing.

Clint held the deadly device in his hand and poked at it with a tool that made a beeping sound. "Do you know who's inside?"

Adams could scarcely bring himself to utter his name. "God help us. It's Abraham Lincoln."

BY THE TIME Clint arrived at the Oval Office to look for more destroyer traps, the Potusgeists had evacuated the West Wing. He reached into his red gym bag for his force field detector and waved it around the room.

A reading of ten thousand milligauss was coming from the gold drapes behind the Resolute Desk. Clint pulled them back, revealing a small rectangular ghost trap about the size of a pack of cigarettes, identical to the one that had ensnared Lincoln. He discovered another destroyer trap stuffed under a sofa cushion and a third on the mantel above the fireplace.

It took two hours to hunt down the others. The soldiers, unfamiliar with the habits of ghosts, had done a poor job of locating the devices, placing some where ghosts never went, such as refrigerators and toilet stalls.

To the ghost hunter's great relief, none of the lights on the other traps were blinking. He carried a bagful of the devices back to his office, where he locked them in a lead-lined box for safety.

Clint checked his watch. He would have to work quickly to free Lincoln and prevent long-term damage to his ionic structure.

He turned the trap over. Unlike those of his own design, this one had no on-off switch. There was a seam along the corners of the casing but no way to pry the casing apart without generating a sudden catastrophic surge of the force field—which would destroy Lincoln instantly.

There might be another way to free the president. Jefferson had escaped his trap because the force field was uneven, resulting in weak spots that provided a way out. Clint could deliberately create a similar flaw in the destroyer trap, counteracting and distorting its force field to make a weak spot for Lincoln to push through.

It was the Great Emancipator's only chance.

First, Clint would need to determine the shape and intensity of the trap's force field. He accomplished this by moving his force field detector in a circle around the trap's perimeter, measuring the power of the field every ten degrees of arc.

To create the weak spot, Clint aimed a force field generator at one end of the trap, dialed it to five thousand milligauss, and switched it on.

Now it was up to Lincoln to get himself out. Clint held his eyes on the trap and waited. "C'mon, push. Come out of there," he said prayerfully, summoning the president like Lazarus from his tomb.

Ten minutes passed. Suddenly, in a split second, a figure not a half-inch tall popped out of the side of the trap. He looked around in wonder.

"Mr. Lincoln, is that you?" asked Clint in astonishment as he peered down at the tiny man in the stovepipe hat.

"Yes, it is indeed, my boy, for better or worse," Lincoln replied, sweeping his hand across his coat as if dusting himself off.

"Say, Mr. Cranberry, I seem to be standing on your table, and I'm feeling a little woozy. Could you help me down from here?"

Clint held out the palm of his hand so Lincoln could climb onto it. He set the president gently down on the floor.

"Flap your arms like a bird," said Clint. "It'll make you big again."

Lincoln did so, causing his body to expand to its normal size. He towered over Clint, who nearly fell off his chair at the sight.

The president looked around Clint's office in confusion. "The last thing I remember was...yes, that's right...I was in the Cabinet Room, and then I was...where was I? Nowhere at all, it seemed, for the longest time."

"You were inside that thing," said Clint, pointing to the trap. "You're free now."

"Free! Yes, it appears I am. Well, what do you think of that? Thank you, my boy. It was rather awful to be stuck in there, I must say." Lincoln stroked his beard pensively. "You know, I'd better find Mrs. Lincoln at once. I imagine she is frightfully worried."

The ghost doffed his hat to Clint. "Free at last," he said to himself as he walked through the wall with a smile.

CHAPTER 34

A Standard for Insanity

NIGEL PICKED HIS way through the gauntlet of reporters barraging him with questions and entered the Judiciary Committee hearing room. He glanced at the clock on the wall. The Hearings on Presidential Incapacity would start in fifteen minutes.

The place teemed with senators, lawyers, witnesses, and reporters. Nigel lowered himself into a chair alongside Patty's attorneys, who had prepared him for the barbed questions he should expect from Sartini's side.

On the advice of the attorneys, he had decided not to claim executive privilege. Doing so would say to the public that he had something to hide, they warned, and the Supreme Court would be unlikely to rule in his favor.

With growing apprehension, he studied the face of the senator who had subpoenaed him, Republican Harold Hooker of Nebraska, a slender man with small eyes set too close together. A staunch supporter of former President Diebold, the legislator was a ruthless partisan and no friend of Patty.

Hooker opened the morning's proceedings by replaying the infamous video recording of Patty talking into space, to nobody at all:

> "I don't care about your flirting with the French! I don't care about Louis the Sixteenth! I want you out of here, all of you, now!"
>
> "You know something? You're not just a ghost. You're a monster!"

The senator launched his first salvo of accusations with a sardonic smile. "As you can see from the video, President Pitypander thinks she's seeing ghosts. There's nobody else in the room. Her own Cabinet admits she's been doing that a lot—in meetings, in private conversations, even at a state dinner. It's clear she's mentally unstable. What further proof do we need that she's unable to carry out the duties of her office?"

Senator Cathy Galloway, the steely-eyed chair of the Judiciary Committee, hurried to Patty's defense. "Wait a minute! That stupid video doesn't prove she's unable to do her job. You can't kick a president out of office with such flimsy evidence as that."

"Why not, for crying out loud? She's talking to a ghost," Hooker shot back. "Can't you see she's hallucinating? Besides, as we all know, the woman's totally incompetent."

"Your personal assessment of her competence is nothing more than an expression of your twisted political views, Senator," said Galloway. "All of our presidents have had flaws, some of them pretty serious. Is she lousy at public speaking? So was Thomas Jefferson. He spoke so softly they could barely hear him at the Continental Congress. Is she handicapped? So was Franklin Roosevelt, but that didn't prevent him from fighting the Depression and World War II from a wheelchair. Should we have thrown Jefferson and FDR out of office because they had flaws?"

"Of course not," Hooker replied. "But what's your point?"

"My point is you have to prove that President Pitypander meets a high standard of incompetence—so high that it renders her unfit to serve. Without that, you have no case."

Showing that the president was incompetent enough wouldn't be easy. Galloway would make sure of that.

Sartini's team brought a constitutional law professor to the witness table and asked him what he thought the standard of incompetence ought to be.

The law professor's answer satisfied no one. "That part of the Twenty-Fifth Amendment was deliberately left vague. The actual wording says the president must be 'unable to discharge the power and duties of his office.' There is no explicit definition of what 'unable' means. That's for Congress to decide in each case."

Hooker threw his hands into the air. "We know damn well what 'unable' means! President Pitypander is a certifiable nut job, and everybody knows it. That's enough to meet my standard."

"Your standard isn't the law, Senator," replied Galloway. "And I disagree that she's a nut job. She's just eccentric. Lots of male presidents have had eccentric habits. There's some history on that topic."

Galloway motioned to an aide, who set a poster board on an easel behind her, within view of the cameras. "Did you know that John Quincy Adams used to go skinny dipping in the Potomac every morning? Yes, and Andrew Jackson had a parrot that he taught to swear. Calvin Coolidge had a pygmy hippopotamus named Billy and a raccoon named Rebecca, which he walked around the White House on a leash, like it was a dog. Franklin Roosevelt kept a one-legged rooster and a small bear. Lyndon

Johnson conducted meetings with his aides while sitting on the toilet taking a crap. How peculiar is that?"

"What the hell does that prove?" Hooker demanded.

"It proves that many of our presidents have had funny habits. So does President Pitypander. She enjoys talking to an empty room. So what? Does that make her more eccentric than those guys? I don't think so."

Sartini's supporters, sensitive to the charge that they were shameful misogynists who were treating a female president unfairly, conceded that eccentricity alone would not be enough to make their case.

If the president was to be removed from office, she needed to be much more than eccentric. She needed to be crazy. How crazy? "Bat-shit crazy," Galloway insisted. "Howling-at-the-moon crazy. The people won't accept anything less. This is the President of the United States we're talking about. She should be given more allowance for being crazy."

Did Patty Pitypander's peculiar habit of seeing ghosts rise to Galloway's high standard of insanity? Sartini's people argued that it did.

They called Nigel to the witness table.

Hooker went straight at him. "Mr. Windborne, as President Pitypander's chief of staff, have you ever seen the president behave in a way that could be described as bat-shit crazy?"

He had indeed. There was Patty's dangerous fondness for young males that had nearly cost her the election, her alarming ignorance about how the government worked, her haughty attitude, her weird addiction to romance novels, and her ditziness in general. Patty was definitely bat-shit crazy at times. But who wasn't?

"I'm not sure what bat-shit crazy means, Senator," Nigel responded.

Hooker hit him with a dozen more questions, to each of which Nigel, loyal to a fault, gave as evasive an answer as possible.

"Has the president ever seen ghosts?"

"I'm not sure what you mean by ghosts, sir."

"Come on, Mr. Windborne, don't play games with us. You know perfectly well what ghosts are—the spirits of dead people."

"I can't see through the president's eyes or read her mind, so I can't answer that question."

Hooker rolled his eyes. "All right then, Mr. Windborne, have you personally ever seen ghosts in the White House?"

Nigel hesitated. That was the question he had been dreading. He *had* seen ghosts, and there might be a video recording somewhere out there that proved it. Lying to a congressional committee was a crime punishable by five years in jail. He imagined himself behind bars, wearing an orange jumpsuit, his life in ruins. "I plead the Fifth Amendment."

A hush fell over the hearing room. The president's sober chief of staff was unwilling to deny that he had seen ghosts in the White House!

Some yelling rang out from the balcony above. Everyone craned their neck to see what was the matter. Seven little old ladies wearing pink hats had stood up in the gallery and started waving signs.

"You can't say those things about my Patty!" shouted a white-haired woman, shaking her fist. "She's not bat-shit crazy! She's just a little high-strung, that's all!"

Nigel cringed. It was Olympia. The president's mother had come to protest to Congress, and she had brought the Horizons House pickleball team with her.

"How dare you talk about my Patty that way!" Olympia screamed, pointing at Hooker. "You ought to be ashamed. You people are the crazy ones, you lying gasbags!"

The other pickleball players stood shoulder to shoulder with her, yelling in unison, "Pitypander for president! Down with Sartini!"

Armed security guards rushed toward them from both sides of the aisle.

"Wait, that's the president's mother," said one guard. "Be careful with her. We don't want a scene."

"What the hell do you think this is, Bob? We've already got a scene," replied another guard.

"Please, ma'am, come with us," a female guard pleaded gently. "We don't want to hurt you."

Olympia's jaw clenched. "No, I won't leave. I'm not going anywhere until those awful people apologize to my Patty. My Luigi wouldn't let them say those mean things about her, and neither will I."

A big, burly guard tried to grab Olympia's arm. One of the pickleball players bashed him over the head with a purse. "Let her go, you brute! She's eighty-seven. Is this how you treat your mother?"

More security guards came toward them. One of them seized Olympia, who went limp in his arms and howled, hamming it up for the cameras.

"Oh, lady," said the guard with a groan, "please don't pull that college protest stuff on me! Not here."

Olympia's black shoes could be seen scraping across the floor as two guards dragged her out.

"Pitypander for president," the old lady screamed all the way out the door. "Down with Sartini!"

CHAPTER 35

THE BOMB

CODD SETTLED INTO a green wing chair in the West Sitting Hall, his head swiveling around nervously as he ran his hand through his thinning blond hair. "I'll bet you're wondering what the hell I'm doing here."

"I sure am," said Patty.

It took a lot of nerve for the disloyal Secretary of Defense to face her after backing Sartini in the coup, so he must have something important to say. Maybe he was on a mission from Sartini to negotiate a deal.

"A while back," Codd said, "Sartini, Snoops, and I were dragged out of the Oval Office by...something—we don't know exactly what."

Patty fought the urge to throttle him. "You don't know? Well, we do! Those were the ghosts!"

Codd rolled his eyes. "Whatever they were, a little later, I received word from Strategic Air Command that these...beings... had gotten hold of the nuclear football, and SAC has been receiving launch signals from it. We have to get it back immediately."

Nigel arched an eyebrow. "If you've lost the football, why are you coming to us? Why doesn't SAC shut the thing down electronically or just ignore it?"

Codd winced. "They can't do either. For security, the nuclear football is designed to defeat any attempt to turn it off remotely so a hacker can't disable it. It's also equipped with an array of sensors to warn of a security breach. One of them is ...a so-called PPD."

"A what?"

"Paranormal phenomenon detector," Codd replied. "Sorry, working in the Pentagon, you get used to using acronyms for everything."

Nigel's eyes tightened. "Paranormal phenomenon, you say? And what would that be for, pray tell?"

"It seems this sensor was installed in case the football ever fell into the...uh...wrong hands."

"Like ghosts? Which you and Sartini claim don't exist?"

Codd scowled and shuffled his feet. "What the hell, call 'em ghosts if you like. I don't give a damn what you call 'em."

Nigel leaned forward. "If there's a ghost sensor in the nuclear football, and the Pentagon put it there, then the Pentagon has known that the White House is haunted by ghosts. Isn't that so?"

Codd coughed nervously. "I'm afraid it's not just the Pentagon. Also the CIA. They've known for many years. They were the ones who first detected an uptick in ghost activity here a few months ago."

"This is outrageous! They routinely monitor ghosts in the White House? You knew about this and said nothing to us?"

Codd looked like he wanted to crawl under the coffee table. "Hey, it's not my fault. I wasn't hiding anything from you. The Chairman of the Joint Chiefs just recently got around to telling me. Nobody thought the football would ever actually detect a ghost."

"But it did?"

"Yes, repeatedly."

"All right, so it detected a ghost. Why is that so important?" Patty asked.

"Because the PPD sent out an alert to every SAC installation in the world that something paranormal had breached the nuclear arsenal's security systems and automatically raised the Pentagon's readiness level around the world to DEFCON Boo."

"What does that mean?"

"DEFCON Boo means that our nuclear arsenal is in imminent danger of being taken over by ghosts. To protect the arsenal from them, the football has started a self-destruct countdown. Within forty-eight hours, the plastic explosives inside it will blow everything within a hundred fifty feet to smithereens—buildings, people, and ghosts. If we don't find the football and deactivate it fast, the White House will be reduced to a smoking ruin."

"Oh, my God," said Patty. "How much time have we got left?"

Codd checked his watch. "A little over an hour. A bomb disposal technician is waiting down the hall."

Nigel turned to Patty. "We have to evacuate. I'll call the Secret Service to escort you to safety immediately."

"No, you get the staff out of here," she said. "I'm going to try to save this place."

IF ANYONE COULD find the Potusgeists fast, it would be Clint. While Nigel called him to explain the situation, Patty and Codd's bomb technician raced to the Oval Office.

When they got there, Clint had his ghost radar ready to go. He examined every room in the West Wing, with Patty and the technician following behind. He didn't pick up a signal anywhere.

Where had the ghosts taken the football? Clint looked at his watch. "We have twenty minutes left."

Where were the ghosts? Patty looked out a window at the Rose Garden. "There must be someplace we are sure to find them."

Clint bit his lip. "Yes, there is. I'm not supposed to show you where it is, but under the circumstances, I'm sure they'll forgive me."

They ran to the Residence and flew down the steps to the basement. In a flash, Theodore Roosevelt, Ulysses S. Grant, and Andrew Jackson, still in uniform, leaped out of the wall to block their way.

"Halt!" Grant ordered.

The technician fell back and nearly fainted.

"Why, it's Mrs. Pitypander and that young ghost hunter," said Roosevelt. "Young fella, you know you're not supposed to bring anyone down here."

Clint explained that the so-called briefcase the ghosts took from Sartini was actually a special communications device, containing a powerful bomb set to go off in eight minutes.

"A bomb? Good God! We gave it to Jefferson. He's in there working on it now." Roosevelt threw open the door to the ghost den.

Jefferson was sitting on a crate, holding a screwdriver and studying the football, which he had placed on another crate in front of him.

He turned to greet them. "Why, hello, madam, so nice to see you. I must say, this is a most intriguing mechanism you have here. I was just about to pry off the top of it to see what makes it tick."

"No, no! Don't do that!" Clint shouted. "It's got a bomb inside!"

"A bomb?"

"Yes, it's about to go off and blow us all to kingdom come! We're here to stop it."

Jefferson jumped away from the briefcase. "Egad! I had no idea. Please take it, then!"

The technician bent over it. He took a screwdriver out of his tool bag and quickly unscrewed the cover plate, revealing a jumble of circuit boards and wires underneath.

"Easy now, Joe," he said to himself as beads of sweat formed on his forehead. "You can do this." A small gray screen was counting down, showing two minutes left.

"Oh, thank God, there's the battery!" He pointed to a small silver disc wedged tightly in a socket in the center. Stuffing his hand into his tool bag again, he felt around in it for something. "Oh, no." He looked down into the bag, and his face tensed up.

"What's wrong?" Clint asked.

The technician spun around. "I don't have the right tools to get the damn battery out!" He glanced back at the screen, and his eyes froze with terror.

Sixty seconds were left.

Jefferson calmly stepped forward, reached into his pocket, and handed the technician some tiny screwdrivers. "You may use mine, sir. I find these most useful for repairing my watch."

The technician looked at the glowing specter in amazement. "Thanks, whoever the hell you are."

Thirty seconds were left on the screen.

He jammed a couple of screwdrivers on opposite sides of the socket and pried upward. Out popped the battery.

The countdown stopped, and the screen went dark. The technician exhaled. "Success!" he yelled.

Jefferson raised his fist in triumph. "Huzzah! Well done, my good man." He looked at Clint. "Then I take it that all is well?"

Clint gave out a deep breath and put his palm to his forehead. "Yes, thank God."

Jefferson turned to Patty. "By the way, madam, if you'll pardon my asking, precisely what is that briefcase meant to do?"

Patty replied that it enabled the president to wage war at any time and place in defense of the nation, using nuclear missiles.

"Nuclear missiles? And what are they?" he asked.

She told him.

Jefferson clutched at his chest. "You possess weapons that can annihilate whole cities, which you can employ at your sole discretion? This nation has entrusted a single individual with the power to obliterate all mankind, and no one can stop you? That's monstrous!"

Patty tried to explain. "Yes, but we have no choice. We are not the only nation with this technology. Our enemies target us as well and can wipe us out in thirty minutes. This briefcase helps to keep that from happening."

"But if it did happen," said Jefferson, "think of the appalling destruction that would result from your decision! How would you justify your actions?"

Patty thought Jefferson, of all people, should understand. "Justify my actions? Well, we have to protect our freedom somehow."

He was unconvinced. "In my day, the freedom we fought for was worth something when we won it. What kind of freedom would you have if you won your war? Freedom to pick through the rubble of civilization? What will that be worth? And you people think seeing ghosts is madness. Please, madam, take away this hellish device. I wish never to lay my eyes upon it again!"

CHAPTER 36

A Surprising Testimony

A HUSH FELL OVER the Senate hearings as Secretary Codd took a seat behind the thicket of microphones at the witness table. Senator Galloway flashed a confident grin.

Codd's testimony would be a bombshell, covered by all the networks in time to make the evening news and guaranteed to have maximum effect.

Galloway banged her gavel and brought the hearings to order. She went straight for the jugular. "Secretary Codd, could you please tell the committee what DEFCON Boo is?"

Codd lifted his gaze, sweat already beading on his forehead. "DEFCON Boo is a military readiness level, like DEFCON One. It's a kind of relic, a holdover from the Cold War that nobody ever bothered to get rid of."

Galloway faked a look of surprise. "Oh? I didn't know our military indulged in keeping relics. What's DEFCON Boo for?"

Codd looked at his attorney, who whispered something into his ear.

"Will you answer my question or not, Mr. Secretary?"

"Um, it was supposed to warn of any threat to national security, any threat at all, including...including—"

"We don't have all day, Mr. Secretary," the senator snapped. "Including what?"

Codd gulped. "Including paranormal beings."

Galloway folded her arms. "What are paranormal beings? Are you talking about ghosts?"

"Yes, you could call them that."

"Ghosts? Oh, you don't say? And why would the Department of Defense be concerned about ghosts?"

"It all started in the nineteen-fifties," said Codd. "Back then, Hollywood was cranking out horror movies about UFOs and assorted scary monsters every month, and the government wanted Americans to know it was prepared for any imaginable emergency, from Godzilla to King Kong. Over the years, there had, in fact, been a few ghost sightings at the White House, some by reputable people."

"Really? Like who?"

Codd named Winston Churchill and Queen Wilhelmina as examples. "A few presidents and their wives also thought the place was haunted. The idea behind DEFCON Boo was to get the Pentagon's assets ready for battle in case of something absolutely weird, like an alien invasion or ghost uprising. But it didn't work in practice because admitting that one believes in such things proved to be a career-ender in the bureaucracy."

Galloway smiled. "If the Pentagon has a special readiness system to fight ghosts—costing billions of dollars—they must believe ghosts actually exist, correct? Surely the Pentagon doesn't waste our tax dollars preparing for non-existent threats, does it, Mr. Secretary?"

Codd conferred with his attorney again. "That would be a reasonable inference, Senator."

"And if it's okay for you, the Pentagon, and our intelligence agencies, who advise the president, to believe in ghosts, it must be acceptable for the president too, right? Or do the Defense Department and Homeland Security have some special privilege to be insane that the president does not?"

"That is above my pay grade. It's for Congress, not for me, to decide what's permissible for the president to believe."

Galloway pounded the table. "Secretary Codd, that's not an adequate answer! I submit that President Pitypander is no crazier than you and Sartini. Isn't it a fact that both of you discovered several days ago that the White House is haunted when the ghosts forcibly ejected you from the Oval Office and that you learned this truth a second time yesterday when the ghosts nearly blew up the place with the nuclear football? Yet you covered up the information and continued to pursue President Pitypander's removal under the Twenty-Fifth Amendment anyway as if you knew nothing about the ghosts."

Codd sat frozen in his chair.

"I would caution you to think carefully before answering, Secretary Codd," Galloway warned. "You are under oath, and we have witnesses—living ones—sitting right here." She pointed at Nigel.

Codd looked at his attorney, who was flashing five fingers at him. "I plead the Fifth Amendment."

Galloway scoffed at him. "The answer is that you and Sartini and the other members of his dishonest cabal knew about the ghosts, and you thought you'd get away with hiding the truth about them from the American people long enough to oust President Pitypander from office. You intended to fool Congress into replacing her. Isn't that right, Mr. Secretary?"

Codd said nothing.

"What were you going to get out of this coup, Secretary Codd?" Galloway asked.

"I don't know what you mean."

"Yes, you do," she said. "Sartini bribed you, offering to make you Secretary of State, didn't he? That was the job you always wanted, wasn't it?"

Codd pleaded the Fifth Amendment again.

Galloway turned to face the cameras. "What's happening here, ladies and gentlemen, is corruption at the highest level of our government—a travesty, an injustice to the voters, to the law, and to common sense. President Pitypander isn't crazy unless the Pentagon is too. Nor is she any crazier than Sartini, who has also seen ghosts in the White House. This effort to oust her is scandalous, treasonous, and illegal. I demand, and the people of America demand, that President Pitypander be restored to her office immediately."

THE FIRST VOTE totals registered on the television screen, alongside the video of congressmen milling around in the well of the House of Representatives. Nigel paced back and forth in the West Sitting Room like an expectant father.

Sartini would need two hundred ninety votes to get the two-thirds majority required in the House. The Senate had not yet voted.

Nigel's brows knitted together. The first numbers were bad: seventy-five for Sartini and twenty-five for Patty. The usurper was off to a strong start.

Patty gave her chief of staff a sideways glance and was unsettled by the gloom in his face. She was at least as nervous as he was, but he was usually better at keeping his cool in the face of bad news.

Finally, he lost his composure and stamped his foot on the floor. "How could anyone vote against you after hearing Codd's testimony? It blew up their entire argument that you're crazy! That alone should have ended this sordid affair."

The process had been corrupted. Sartini, backed by Speaker Underdown and financed by Benny, had purchased dozens of votes. Money and power, not the truth about the ghosts, would decide her fate.

Benny—what a louse. He had betrayed her before, but not like this, with her whole life on the line. She should have divorced him long ago, but her need for money and hunger for power had prevented that. Benny had bought her, too.

Patty resolved to redeem herself, no matter the outcome. If she survived the vote, she must forget about her own ego and rededicate herself to simply doing good deeds for the country. Maybe Thomas Jefferson would still be willing to show her how.

Even if the vote went the wrong way, all would not be lost. There was an afterlife, she now knew. She would become a Potusgeist herself one day, and on that day, the ghosts would still be here, waiting.

History was like that. It had stood by patiently for her to finally become wise enough to learn from it, understand it, and treasure its teachings. Its lessons had waited in books, monuments, battlefields, and old haunted houses like this one, as long as it took for her to discover them. The past never passed away. Time meant nothing. Salvation, for those who had grown wise enough to seek it, had no time limit.

She glanced again at the television screen. The vote was now two hundred one to eighty-nine. Sartini had a sixty-nine percent majority and falling.

Nigel's face perked up. The tide was turning strongly in Patty's favor.

Minutes later, there was no question about it. The final totals were two hundred twenty votes for Sartini, two hundred fifteen for Pitypander, leaving the usurper seventy votes short of a two-thirds majority.

Benny's money hadn't bought him enough congressmen. The Casino King had miscalculated.

"The House has just voted to keep Patty Pitypander in office," the news anchor announced. "Its members were apparently unconvinced that she is as crazy as required by the Twenty-Fifth Amendment. Reacting angrily to the news, Tony Sartini has resigned not only as Acting President but Vice President as well."

A video of Sartini storming out of the West Wing appeared on the screen. He turned toward the gaggle of reporters waiting outside and shouted, "It's a sad day for America. The White House is being run by a crackpot."

Nigel took to his feet and danced a jig, pumping his fist in the air. "We did it, Patty, we did it!"

At last, all was well.

Just then, Patty thought she heard the dulcet tones of a violin in the distance. Whether the music was Vivaldi or Corelli, she couldn't tell, but she had no doubt who was playing it. Dropping everything, she went running down the hall after him.

PATTY OPENED THE door of the Yellow Oval Room and peeked inside, expecting to see only Jefferson there.

He was there, sure enough, sitting on the settee, but he was accompanied by a roomful of ghosts.

They erupted all at once in a group cheer.

John Adams, with Abigail beside him, stepped forward and bowed. "The August and Prudential Council of White House Ghosts has voted to congratulate you, Madam President, on your splendid victory over the despicable tyrant Sartini. We thought there could be no better way to express our delight than to appear before you en masse like this. We hope our little show of support is not too overwhelming."

Patty stood in the doorway, speechless.

Teddy Roosevelt doffed his feathered hat to her. "My congratulations, Madam President. Through thick and thin, you hung in there like a real trooper, and no one can say different. Bully for you, lady!"

Dolley Madison handed Patty a vase filled with red roses.

"These are for me?"

"Yes, and at Mr. Jefferson's suggestion, we are naming them after you, Mrs. Pitypander," said Mrs. Madison. "Like you, this variety is a late bloomer, yet one of the hardiest roses in the whole garden."

Lincoln handed her a copy of the Constitution, autographed by all the Potusgeists. "You preserved this honorable house from total destruction, at the risk of your own life. We can hardly express our gratitude."

Eleanor Roosevelt hugged her like a daughter. "I knew all along you had the strength to be president, Patty. It was just waiting to come out. Always remember, dear, resolution doesn't come from a desk. It comes from the heart."

Jefferson beamed at her. "You showed yourself to be surpassingly brave, madam. Courage is the virtue we most admire because we know it is the one without which being a good president is impossible. I could teach you good policy or the principles of good government, but I could never give you the courage to overcome adversity. You brought that here with you and proved you had it all along."

He looked at James Madison. "So, what do you say now, sir? Was it not an appropriate thing that we intervened with the living on Mrs. Pitypander's behalf?"

"This time it was, sir," Madison grudgingly admitted, pausing just a moment before adding solemnly, "This time." He turned to Patty. "The Council has decided to leave you alone now, madam. The presidency is in good hands. We think you can handle things without us."

Run the country without them? But the Potusgeists knew so much. Patty wouldn't hear of it. "No, Mr. Madison, I want the Council's advice. I want to hear from all of you regularly."

As a profound silence settled over the room, they acknowledged through their signs and glances, without a word being spoken, that they realized just how close they had brought the nation they all loved to the brink of disaster. If there was to be a future for the country, they would all have to be decidedly more careful about the decisions they made going forward.

Just then, a series of explosions reverberated through the room, and the yellow walls lit up. Patty and the ghosts rushed to the windows, where they saw fireworks bursting high in the air and whistling over the Mall.

"It's the Fourth of July!" said Jefferson, his lips stretching into a wide grin.

"So it is, Thomas," Adams replied, laying his arm on Jefferson's shoulder. "The day the country was born. The day we both died and became ghosts. How could we ever forget such a fateful day?"

It was the day impossibility became possibility, in the country where nothing was impossible.

★ ★ ★

UPON ENTERING THE Oval Office the next morning, Patty looked over to her right. The celebratory portrait of Andrew Jackson in his military regalia had been brought out of storage and restored to its former spot on the wall at her request.

She walked around the room, viewing the painting from different angles, but no matter where she stood, the seventh president watched her as intensely as he had on her inauguration day.

Yet something about him had changed. His devilish eyes were not nearly so fearsome and foreboding as she remembered from back in January. There was a softness in them, a vulnerability she hadn't perceived before. Old Hickory was no longer a painting or a statue. He had become a person, a real person, who existed not just in the distant past but in the present as well. In fact, he almost seemed to smile back at her.

THANKS SO MUCH for reading *The Potusgeists*. I hope you liked it. Patty and I would love for you to leave a review (as you've seen, she's going to need all the help she can get). Your review on Amazon, Goodreads, or Barnesandnoble.com can be anonymous, and it only takes a couple of minutes.

To learn about my other books and where you can buy them, go to my website, willworsley.com.

You can also follow the latest news about me on Facebook at:

Facebook.com/willworsleyauthor.

Will Worsley

ACKNOWLEDGMENTS

I WOULD LIKE TO thank several people for giving me invaluable ideas for *The Potusgeists*, including beta readers Gary Aichele, Bob Bear, Pam Humphrey, Calvin Cutter, Natalie Freese, and Thomas Pope. Thanks also to copy editor Paula Lester of Polaris Editing, proofreader Amanda Oraha, and formatter Stephanie Anderson of Alt 19 Creative. Illustrator Ed Steckley and book designer Gareth Southwell did an outstanding job on the cover. Special thanks to my nephew, Thomas Pope, for helping me research the history of the many presidents and first ladies who have lived in the White House.

THE AUTHOR

WILL **WORSLEY GREW** up near Alexandria, Virginia, and earned degrees in English and business administration at the University of Virginia. At Time-Life Books, he wrote and edited articles on a wide variety of non-fiction topics. Later he became a money manager overseeing portfolios for several large institutions. In his retirement he has written three novels: *Investing in Vain*, *The Cougar Candidate*, and *The Potusgeists*.